Muriel had to try once more. 'Please say you'll change your mind. Once it's gone that will be the end of it. It's all the wildlife, you see, the plants and the birds and such, I've even seen wild violets growing in the shelter of that hedge. Could you think about them, please? They're all so precious.'

Mr Fitch glanced away from her pleading eyes and said, 'This might work with Ralph but not with me.' Sarcastically he added, 'After all *he* is a gentleman. You can't expect the same response from me.'

Mr Fitch's answer stung Muriel and left her with nothing more to say.

'I rather imagine from the look on your face he has pointed that out to you, so I'm amazed you should think I would be subject yet again to your particular brand of genteel persuasion.' He moved towards the door. 'You can tell everyone you meet that I am adamant that hedge is coming down. The fence will be in good taste, I assure you. Even I can manage that.'

The cold smile on his face made Muriel shudder.

Educated at a co-educational Quaker boarding school, Rebecca Shaw went on to qualify as a teacher of deaf children. After her marriage, she spent the ensuing years enjoying bringing up her family. The departure of the last of her four children to university has given her the time and opportunity to write. *A Village Feud* is the latest in the highly popular Tales from Turnham Malpas series. Visit her website at www.rebeccashaw.co.uk.

Trouble in the Village

TALES FROM TURNHAM MALPAS

Rebecca Shaw

An Orion paperback

First published in Great Britain in 2000
by Orion
This paperback edition published in 2000
by Orion Books Ltd,
Orion House, 5 Upper St Martin's Lane,
London WC2H 9EA

An Hachette Livre UK company

Reissued 2005

Copyright © Rebecca Shaw 2000

A CIP catalogue record for this book is available
from the British Library.

Printed and bound in Great Britain by
Clays Ltd, St Ives plc

The Orion Publishing Group's policy is to use papers that
are natural, renewable and recyclable products and
made from wood grown in sustainable forests. The logging
and manufacturing processes are expected to conform to
the environmental regulations of the country of origin.

www.orionbooks.co.uk

INHABITANTS OF TURNHAM MALPAS

Nick Barnes	Veterinary surgeon
Roz Barnes	Nurse
Willie Biggs	Verger at St Thomas à Becket
Sylvia Biggs	His wife and housekeeper at the Rectory
Sir Ronald Bissett	Retired Trade Union leader
Lady Sheila Bissett	His wife
James (Jimbo) Charter-Plackett	Owner of the Village Store
Harriet Charter-Plackett	His wife
Fergus, Finlay, Flick and Fran	Their children
Katherine Charter-Plackett	Jimbo's mother
Alan Crimble	Barman at the Royal Oak
Linda Crimble	Runs the post office at the Village Store
Georgie Fields	Licensee at the Royal Oak
H. Craddock Fitch	Owner of Turnham House
Jimmy Glover	Taxi driver
Mrs Jones	A village gossip
Barry Jones	Her son and estate carpenter
Kenny Jones	Barry Jones' brother
Pat Jones	Barry's wife
Terry Jones	Barry Jones' brother
Dean and Michelle	Barry and Pat's children
Revd Peter Harris MA (Oxon)	Rector of the parish
Dr Caroline Harris	His wife
Alex and Beth	Their children
Jeremy Mayer	Manager at Turnham House
Venetia Mayer	His wife
Neville Neal	Accountant and church treasurer
Liz Neal	His wife
Guy and Hugh	Their children
Tom Nicholls	Retired businessman
Evie Nicholls	His wife
Anne Parkin	Retired secretary
Kate Pascoe	Village school head teacher
Sir Ralph Templeton	Retired from the diplomatic service
Lady Muriel Templeton	His wife
Dicky Tutt	Scout leader
Bel Tutt	School caretaker and assistant in the Village Store
Don Wright	Maintenance engineer
Vera Wright	Cleaner at the nursing home in Penny Fawcett
Rhett Wright	Their grandson

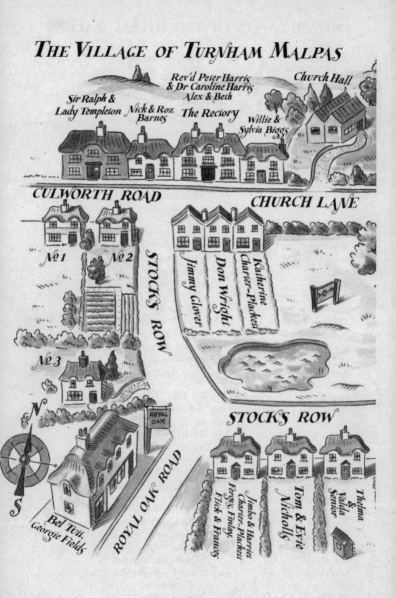

Chapter 1

Muriel glanced at the dining-room clock as she put the last of the salad on the table. Only half past three and all was ready. Would she never learn? All her life she'd been ready too early for everything and here she was still at it. But it did give her half an hour to sit quietly and contemplate life, Ralph's birthday and all these people coming to help him celebrate. How lucky they'd been to have so many happy years together. Just think, if she hadn't taken hold of life by the scruff, how much happiness and excitement she would have missed. Muriel had to confess she was an entirely different person from the one he'd married. She laughed at the memory of how precise and uptight she had been, so meticulous in all aspects of life, and tragically so afraid of it too.

She cocked an ear for Ralph and heard his light step coming down the stairs. So he was ready early as well. Dear Ralph! The sight of him could still make her heart miss a beat. The door opened and there he stood. The birthday boy. He'd decided against his sports coat then and gone for the pale blue shirt and trousers with the dark blue spotted tie she'd given him at Christmas. The shirt emphasised the sparkling whiteness of his hair and flattered his lightly tanned faced.

'My dear! You look delightful!' He came across to kiss her cheek.

'Handsome as ever, Ralph! How do you do it?'

Ralph studied her face. 'Only in your eyes, my dear. I fear others see me as a crusty, short-tempered, elderly man with a somewhat old-fashioned penchant for "doing the right thing" . . .'

Muriel protested, 'Never! Never! You're courteous and kind and understanding and a pillar of the community. And much loved, not just by me.'

Ralph bowed with a mocking grin on his face. 'You're too kind.'

'What do you think to the table? Have I forgotten anything at all?'

Ralph inspected the magnificent spread, and decided she'd forgotten nothing. 'This is wonderful. Quite wonderful. I must say, Muriel, you've really excelled yourself today. A wonderful feast. How shall we sit everyone?'

'If you look out of the window you'll see that while you were out this morning everyone brought their garden chairs and tables.'

Ralph went to the french windows to look out. He had to smile. He guessed the imposing teak set would be Jimbo and Harriet's, the green plastic would be Willie and Sylvia's because he could see those in their garden from the attic window, and the white set with the elaborate twirly pattern on the backs of the chairs and the impressively flowered seat-pads must be Ron and Sheila's or Ronald's, as Sheila called him when she remembered; she thought it common to shorten his name. The plain white with the embroidered cushions foxed him. Ah! Yes. He guessed they might be Tom and Evie's.

'Evie's coming, is she?'

Muriel answered him with a hint of apprehension in her voice. 'She is. Poor Evie. I hope she can face it.'

'Is there anyone not coming?'

'Craddock Fitch. He's in Warsaw.'

'I shan't miss him.'

'Ralph! How unkind of you! He has improved so much since he nearly killed Jeremy.'

'One can scarcely say he nearly killed him.'

'Well, he escaped death by a whisker and we all know he collapsed in the middle of their most tremendous row. It's that scathing, icy temper of his. It's quite scary.'

'He doesn't scare me!'

Muriel smiled to herself. 'Oh! I know he doesn't. You're a match for him any day.'

'Self-made men are all right if they acknowledge that they are, but he tries to pretend he's a gentleman, and one can't. One either is or one isn't.'

The bell rang and Muriel panicked. 'Oh! They're here! I should never have organised this. What a fool I am. You answer the door. Go on. Please! I feel quite dreadful.'

Muriel appeared to fade into the wallpaper so apprehensive was she, the effect heightened by her being small, pale-complexioned and fair-haired. Briefly Ralph felt concern for her but then he saw her summon up her courage and she

3

re-emerged from the wallpaper with a smile on her face. He patted her arm and hastened to the door.

They'd said four for four thirty but by ten past almost all their guests had arrived. Presents were given, drinks accepted, kisses exchanged, chairs occupied, children commended on their smart appearance, greetings given and in the midst of it Muriel was in a complete flurry. She should have accepted the help she'd been offered, she knew that now. There was Evie in the corner without a drink in her hand. Oh dear! 'Evie, what would you like to drink?'

Straining to hear Muriel had to guess she'd said, 'Orange juice, please.'

'Certainly.' In her mind and conversation Muriel always prefixed Evie's name with 'poor' because that was just how she always looked, and even more so today. Not poor in the sense of being without money but, rather, poor in spirit. Oddly dressed in a big emerald green wool jacket with beneath it a skimpy navy skirt and a black polo-necked T-shirt. Surely Tom could help her with her clothes? 'Here we are! There's plenty more. Help yourself. I'm so glad you could come.'

But Evie wasn't for answering and in any case Katherine Charter-Plackett was demanding Muriel's attention. 'Muriel! I've been away! I'm looking to you to keep me up to date with the news.'

Katherine always brought out the worst in Muriel and consequently their relationship was delicate. Muriel looked up and sighed inside. The holiday had done nothing to soothe Katherine's domineering manner and certainly nothing to diminish that jutting jawline which appeared to jut out even further when she was on the warpath. How she came to have a son as charming as Jimbo Muriel couldn't imagine.

'You must come for coffee next week and I'll bring you up to date.' Muriel immediately regretted her invitation but she couldn't stop to talk now, still less face Katherine's detailed interrogation about the smallest detail.

Katherine thanked her graciously, saying, 'I'll keep you to that.'

Muriel fled, intending to stand by Ralph's side while she recuperated, but on the way across the hall she met Caroline. 'Caroline! We're so glad you could come! Where are the twins? Have they got a drink? I've put out Coca-Cola specially, I know how much they love it.'

'You spoil them. They're in the garden with Peter.'

If anything Caroline was thinner than ever. Anyone, even someone with a turnip for a head, could feel the unhappiness emanating from her. And from Peter too. In her heart Muriel damned that actor fellow Hugo for almost persuading Caroline to run off with him. He'd gone on to magnificent triumphs at Stratford leaving this girl behind with her marriage in tatters.

'Enjoying getting back to general practice?'

Her question sparked Caroline off as Muriel knew it would.

'Indeed I am. I'd no idea how much I missed it. One feels to have such purpose in life.'

'Indeed. Purpose is so important.'

'Three days a week suits me fine. I don't feel too guilty about the children, you see.'

'It must be hard coping without Sylvia. Can she not see her way to coming back to help?'

Caroline's face shut down. Her eyes searched around to see if Sylvia was within hearing. 'Apparently not. Harriet has them until either Peter or I get back. It seems to be working quite well. Though the holidays . . .' Caroline shrugged her shoulders.

'Muriel! Have we any more ice, my dear?' She hastened off to answer Ralph's request with yet another bucket of ice cubes from her new American fridge-freezer. It was so hot. She paused a moment to pat her handkerchief to her forehead and run the cold tap over her wrists to cool her down. There! Now she had a wet patch on her skirt. No one would notice they were all too busy enjoying themselves. There was such a hubbub of conversation, always a good sign that people were relaxed and happy. That was her problem with entertaining, worrying about whether the guests were enjoying themselves. On her way into the dining room with the bucket of ice she found herself enveloped in a bear-hug by Jimbo Charter-Plackett.

'Just listen to that racket! Everyone's having a wonderful time! Congratulations, Muriel! May Ralph see many more birthdays!' Jimbo gave her a smacking kiss, which almost made her drop the ice. 'Give that to me! I'll take it. Wonderful party! We're so lucky to have you and Ralph.'

He strode off and Muriel decided to seek the shade of the garden and make sure at the same time that everyone out there was happy.

The back door from the hall was open and through it Muriel could hear loud chatter. She loved this view from the doorway. It lifted her spirits in a way no other aspect could. Framed by the door was the giant beech tree at the end of the garden under which Ralph had buried her dear,

dear poodle, Pericles; his little memorial stone only served to enhance the view. Between the beech tree and the terrace was the lawn now dotted with the tables and chairs and the bright umbrellas and, best of all, dotted about also were her dear friends, laughing and talking. The rectory twins interrupted her reverie.

'Moo! Moo!' They both rushed at her and little Beth flung her arms around her waist. 'Moo! Can Alex and I have some more Coke? Daddy says we may, if it's all right with you.' Her ash-blonde hair and those lovely rounded cheeks, what a stunning combination they were! Alex took her hand. 'Moo! May we?' So like Peter! They could be his eyes looking at her.

'Of course you may, as much as you want.' She really must stop this dreaming and enter into the hurly-burly. Muriel targeted Peter, who was standing under the beech tree alone. There was far too much of that nowadays. Peter, alone.

He gave her his lovely smile and she looked up at him and smiled back. 'I do believe, Peter, you get taller every day! Or maybe it's me who's shrinking!'

'Neither! I think it's you standing a little lower than me.'

Muriel looked down at her feet. 'So I am. How foolish of me.'

'Aren't we lucky with the weather today, though? They say the sun shines on the righteous.'

Muriel ignored his joke. 'I worry about Caroline. Is there no way we can get Sylvia back? Do you want her back? I wondered if I could –'

'Nothing would please me more, but they've had such a

fall-out, she and Caroline. I think it's something they have to sort out for themselves.'

Being warned off so abruptly Muriel stepped back to see his face more clearly and her heart trembled for him. He might be the Rector and have answers to lots of other people's problems but . . .

'I see. Your glass is empty, come and get another drink.' Muriel slipped her arm in his and drew him into the house. She subtly handed him over to Ralph and as she left the two of them she heard Ralph asking if he'd had any answers to his advertisement for a new verger. That would keep him busy.

Glancing at her watch Muriel decided it was time to eat. She checked she had the matches at the ready for lighting Ralph's candles and went into the kitchen to make the tea. She'd had kettles from the church kitchen gently simmering since before everyone had arrived and now she put the tea-bags into the giant teapot she'd borrowed and turned up the gas under the kettles.

As she filled the teapot to the brim she felt a surge of triumph. It really was going well. She'd planned and schemed to get things just right this afternoon and her hard work was being rewarded. Full of success, she bounced into the dining room with the teapot.

It was the scandalised tone of Caroline's question which gave her the first hint that all was not well. 'You have what?'

Grandmama Charter-Plackett's chin jutted but her mouth smiled. As far as the village was concerned that boded ill. 'I have agreed with him. It should be done.'

'*You* have agreed with him? What have *you* got to do with it?'

'I just happened to be having a cup of tea with him and he mentioned his intentions.'

'But it's none of your business.'

'Are you saying that village affairs are nothing to do with me?'

Caroline's eyes blazed. 'I suppose I am. You've hardly been here two minutes and you're interfering yet again, as if you haven't caused enough trouble since you came. He's getting away with this over my dead body.'

Grandmama drew herself up. 'I think you're taking this far too seriously. It's perfectly ridiculous to be making such a fuss.'

Jimbo intervened. 'Mother! I think –

'Well, then, don't. I'm quite capable of looking after myself, thank you, Jimbo.' Turning to Caroline she said, between clenched teeth, '*I'm* not digging it up, I only agreed with him that it should be done.'

Jimbo opened his mouth, intending to pour oil on troubled waters, but Caroline put a hand on his arm. 'No, Jimbo, leave this to me. This village needs dragging into the twenty-first century. There are some things I agree with, but this, however, is beyond belief. What is it, three years you've been here perhaps nearly four? Most of the families here this afternoon have lived here for *centuries*. If anyone has a right to agree or disagree it is them and not you. How dare you!'

Muriel's question, spoken in a small voice, gently cut through the bristling silence which had fallen. 'What is it we are talking about?'

Ralph quietly explained. 'Mr Fitch has decided to dig up the hedgerow behind our houses and replace it with a fence.'

Every word of Ralph's fell like a stone on Muriel's heart. Appalled she said, 'You mean Rector's Meadow hedge? Why?'

Grandmama Charter-Plackett replied, 'Because he can't find people either willing or able to maintain it, and he thinks a nice well-made wooden fence would be more economical.'

'What has economy to do with it?'

'He runs a tight ship and he can't bear for there to be waste. That's why he's rich.' She nearly added, 'And that's why he's at the Big House and your Ralph isn't any more,' but even she realised that would be a tad too far.

Muriel took a deep breath, amazed by the insensitivity on display. 'Waste? What about all the creatures who make their homes there?' Her eyes filled with tears as she thought about them.

Grandmama, genuinely surprised by the thought that anyone, four-legged or otherwise, would choose to live in a tatty overgrown hedge, almost smiled but the sight of tears in Muriel's eyes stopped herself smiling. 'They'll soon find somewhere else. It's all a storm in a teacup and I would have thought, Caroline, that you of all people would have welcomed progress. Muriel, of course, as we all know, always prefers the status quo.'

Indignant at being dismissed as a stick in the mud Muriel declared, 'I do not!' But she did about the hedge. 'But in this instance I do. There must be nearly half a mile of hedge and it belongs . . . to us.'

Caroline agreed with her. 'I shall not stand by and let that – that – hooligan ruin the village.'

Katherine ignored Caroline, preferring to answer Muriel. 'To be exact, Muriel, the hedge belongs to Mr Fitch, he bought it and he has a right to do with it whatever he wants. Considering how this village benefits from his generosity with his money, the least we can do is let him get on with it. Otherwise what has happened to liberty? It is being eroded on every side. Well, this time I think he's right.' She turned to give Jimbo her empty glass. 'Put that somewhere appropriate, if you please.'

Jimbo, white with temper, smoothed his hand over his bald head and said, 'Mother, you're spoiling the party and that's not good manners.'

'You're right, it isn't. I apologise, Ralph, even though the upset is not my fault.'

Suddenly Muriel was aware she was still holding the tea-pot and her arms were beginning to ache. She handed it to Ralph and looked at him for assistance as he took it.

Ralph placed it on the stand by the teacups and said smoothly, 'Shall we all begin to eat? Muriel has provided such a banquet for us and I can't wait to cut my cake. Come, Katherine, here's a plate for you. May I help you to salmon or do you prefer the cold chicken, or perhaps a little of the stand pie?'

Grandmama always fell victim to Ralph's accomplished charm and today was no exception. 'Why, thank you, Ralph, the salmon, I think, with just a little of the mayonnaise. No cucumber.'

Though the matter had been shelved as far as general

conversation went, it burst out in quiet outraged huddles all over the house and garden.

Jimbo and Harriet were incensed. 'Your mother! When will she learn? I should never have agreed to her coming to live here, I knew she'd cause trouble.'

'God! Wait till I get her home.'

'Caroline's right, it would be criminal to uproot that hedge. If she starts a campaign I shall support her.'

'Careful, Harriet. Think about Mother.'

Harriet looked scornfully at Jimbo. 'You would do well to remember the pledge you gave me before she came. Remember? You and I stand together.'

Jimbo raised an eyebrow. 'How much of Caroline's anger is directed at Mother rather than the hedge? Hmm? Ask yourself that.'

Thoughtfully, Harriet chewed on a stick of celery while she framed her reply. 'I agree they've had their moments, the two of them, but I genuinely believe she is also very angry about the hedge. I wondered how long old Fitch could manage without being a thorn in the flesh yet again.' She looked across at her mother-in-law, who was convers- ing with Peter as though nothing upsetting had taken place. 'I shall tread carefully. But like Caroline said over my dead body does he put up a fence.'

In the garden things were being said which were much less polite. 'That blasted woman! Here, Ron, tilt the umbrella different, I'm right in the sun and if there's anything I hate it's eating food in full sun. Pig ignorant she is. Pig ignorant, for all her airs and graces. She's really upset Caroline and it won't do.'

'She could be right, Sheila.'

Sheila glared at him, 'Right? That woman's never right. Ever. As we well know. If they get up a petition I shall sign it at every opportunity.'

Ron cleared his mouth of his pork pie and said, 'Watch it.'

'Why?'

'Mr Fitch has been very kind in the past sponsoring the Village Show and the Flower Festivals and that. You could stand to lose a lot if he takes his bat home over this. You keep out of it.'

'When principles are at stake a stand has to be taken, no matter what.' She'd read that in a book and had been storing it up for just such an occasion.

Ron shook his head in despair.

Muriel heard none of this as she was in the kitchen patiently lighting the candles on the cake and trying her best to take delight in doing so. Bracing herself she carried the cake aloft into the dining room and, as through a thick cloud, heard them all cheer at the sight of it, for it really was quite splendid. They made room for it on the table and Ralph invited the children to help him blow out the candles. Peter lifted them up on to chairs, Beth, Alex and little Fran Charter-Plackett.

Alex shouted, 'You must make a wish, Sir Ralph! Go on, make a wish.'

They all waited in silence, the children hopping up and down on the chairs. 'Right! I've done it. Are we ready? One, two, three, blow!'

Cutting up the cake with Caroline's help, Muriel whispered, 'I'm so angry, but I don't want to spoil Ralph's party. We'll have clean plates. Here they are, look.'

'So am I. That beautiful hedge! How could he? I'm working on Monday otherwise I'd go straight up there first thing.'

'He's not here, though. Oh, this slice has broken in half. Never mind, I'll have it. He's not back till Tuesday night.'

Caroline groaned. 'I work Wednesday too.'

'Don't you worry, I'll go up to the Big House myself. I've worked miracles with him before. Let's hope I can do it again. I'll take the cake round. I'll let you know how I go on.'

In the end the party was a success, despite the disagreement, and while Ralph helped Muriel to clear up he told her so several times.

'You have no need to worry, my dear, it was perfectly splendid. I have so enjoyed myself.'

Muriel kissed him. 'I'm so glad.'

'I know what you're thinking.'

'You do?'

'Yes. You're planning to tackle Fitch about the hedge.'

'Well, yes, I am. Will you help?'

'Frankly, no.'

'But, Ralph, I was relying on you.'

'All my support will achieve is his absolute determination to do exactly the opposite of what I want. He and I have crossed swords too many times for me to be of any value to you at all. Can you see that?'

Muriel thought about what he'd said and finally agreed. 'You could be right at that. You'd simply be a red rag to a bull.'

'Just like Katherine is to you.' Ralph had to laugh, and

when he caught Muriel's eye, so too did she. 'So I shall keep out of it.'

'Thank you for distracting Katherine so tactfully. We could have had a full-scale row and that would have been unforgivable. Right now I'm going down the back garden, crossing the lane and giving the hedge a pat. And I'm going to tell it it needn't worry because Caroline and I are going to save it.'

Ralph smiled indulgently. 'Off you go then. I'll finish in here, you've done enough today.'

Muriel clipped shut the gate which separated her garden from Pipe and Nook Lane, checked there were no cars coming up to the garages at the top end and went over to the hedge. It was all of three feet wide and five feet tall now, in places even taller, not having been touched since Mr Fitch had bought the house. Just where she stood a wild rose was flowering, wide single petals, of the palest of pale pink, it fluttered delicately in the evening breeze. How could he? How could he even think of destroying all this beauty?

A wren, unaware he had an audience, was hopping briskly about amongst the twigs. His pert, upstanding tail amused her and for a moment, his head on one side, the wren studied her. They looked at each other eye to eye, two living beings, in form as unlike as it was possible to be and yet . . . He flew off with a flick of his soft brown tail. As Muriel studied the hedge she spotted deep inside it an abandoned nest, a perfectly round scoop of a nest still beautifully lined with soft feathers, and wonderfully and intricately woven grass by grass, fine twig by fine twig: a miracle of construction. How could anyone think of destroying this? If only they could all see it through her eyes as she saw it now in the mellow evening light.

Trailing her fingers amongst the leaves Muriel said out loud, 'Don't worry, that monster isn't going to get rid of you. I'll see to that even if . . .' rather rashly she concluded with 'I have to throw myself in front of the diggers.' Having acknowledged she might perhaps have to do that very thing, her heart quailed at the prospect. 'But I shall. Oh, yes. I shall.'

Muriel inspected first one leaf and then another, realising that though she had lived here with Ralph all this time, apart from the wild rose she didn't know any of the other plants growing there. Shame on you, Muriel, she thought, it's time you did, and she marched inside purposefully, intent on seeking out a countryside book of Ralph's to find out exactly what it was she was being called upon to defend.

Chapter 2

That night the bar of the Royal Oak hummed with the news of the disagreement over the hedge. Those not privileged to be guests at the birthday party had had the story told them, and each and every one had an opinion to express.

Sylvia having been a guest had already told Willie she thought that Caroline and Muriel were right. 'Lovely old hedge that. Been there long before you and I saw the light of day. He's no business to be uprooting it.'

'He does own it, though.'

'I know he does, but landowners have obligations in this day and age. They can't ride roughshod over everyone just because they have bright ideas about increasing their crops.'

'Well, at least it'll give Caroline something to concentrate on.'

Sylvia fell silent. She sipped her gin and orange and wished, how she wished . . . Caroline. It had been painful seeing her. Right at that moment she deeply regretted resigning in such a temper. 'The children . . . it was lovely talking to them.'

Willie took hold of her hand. 'See here. Eat humble pie and ask for your job back. She's in a fix and she needs your help and it's what you want.'

Sylvia, glad of a chance not to answer, waved to Don who was just coming across to their table with an orange juice in his hand.

'Evening, Sylvia, Willie. Enjoy your party this afternoon then?'

'Yes, thanks. You know, it still seems funny seeing you in here without your Vera.'

Don didn't answer, he simply ran a stubby hand through his coarse grey hair.

'Have you been to see the flat she's moved into?'

'No, and I shan't.' He tapped the table with a thick forefinger. 'Nothing and nobody is moving me from my cottage. I was born in that front bedroom, in the very bed I sleep in still, and that's where I'm staying, and I'm not moving out to some poncy flat just to please her.'

Willie put his spoke in by reminding him about the dreadful condition of his cottage. 'You really can't expect any woman to put up with that dump in this day and age. I'm surprised she hasn't moved out sooner than this. You haven't done a hand's turn in years to improve it. No wonder she grabbed her chance when she could. You should have hightailed it after her to that flat if you'd had any sense. Shouldn't he, Sylvia?'

Sylvia nodded.

Don remained silent. But then they were used to Don

18

being a man of few words. Trouble was, when he did speak he was, on occasion, far too forthright.

Sylvia reached forward and encouragingly patted Don's arm where it rested on the table. 'Nice little job that nursing home offered her. It's just a pity you didn't see it that way. She had the right idea, doing up the cottage and renting it out while you both lived in the flat.'

When he didn't answer she remarked how stubborn some people could be when the right thing to do was staring them in the face.

Willie agreed. He glanced at Don. 'Another orange juice, Don?'

'No. Thanks. I'll be off. Early shift tomorrow. When you're footloose and fancy-free there's jobs to be done before yer can go to bed. But don't you fret, Don Wright 'ull survive without 'er, just you wait and see. Who needs women?' Don fixed his beady brown eyes on Sylvia and said, 'Before I go, as it seems to be a night for 'anding out advice, my advice to you, Sylvia Biggs, is to hightail it yourself, back to the Rectory, and apologise and ask for your job back because at bottom that's what you really want to do. You've never looked the same since you left and it's time to make up. Good night.' He squeezed out of the narrow gap between the settle and the table and left them alone.

Sylvia, red-faced and furious, folded her arms across her chest and said angrily, 'That Don is having a sight too much to say for himself right now. The cheeky devil, him handing out advice to *me*. What does he know about anything anyway?' Scornfully Sylvia added, 'He'll manage without Vera! Huh! And pigs might fly. I just hope that mucky cottage 'ull tumble down on top of him, and it'll serve 'im right.'

Willie gave Sylvia a sly glance. 'Seems to me he could be right about you.'

'Hmm. Thanks, anyway, for not letting on the Rector had been round to persuade me to go back.' She paused, recollecting Peter's kindness and the gentle way he'd given her the opportunity to change her mind without loss of face. 'He's hard to resist he is.'

'Then you shouldn't have resisted, you could have given in graciously to him, everybody knows how persuasive he is. You're stubborn, you are.'

Emphatically Sylvia shook her head. 'No, I'm not stubborn, I just know what's right. She came within an ace of deserting those children for that Hugo actor man,' briefly her face softened for she'd been caught up in his charisma too, just like everyone else, 'within an ace, and couldn't see where it was all leading. What I said I meant. Someone had to speak up 'cos one thing's for certain the Rector wouldn't. Seeing as you're on your feet get me another gin and orange, there's a love.'

'Will yer think about it though, to please me?'

Sylvia paused for a moment. 'I might. Then again I might not.'

Willie smiled into her large grey eyes, those eyes which had attracted him to her so powerfully those few short years ago. He bent his head to kiss her and smiled inside himself as he straightened up, certain that if he knew anything at all she'd be back at the Rectory very soon and all would be right with the world again.

While Willie waited at the bar Sylvia thought about what

he'd said. She loved those children as though they were her own grandchildren, but as for ... No, she wouldn't. Caroline would have to do the asking, not her. Willie, walking towards her now, suddenly looked older somehow. Strange that: you lived your life with someone and didn't see what was happening under your very nose. He'd been right to say he would retire.

'Thanks. Funny Tom applying for your job. Doesn't seem quite right somehow, him wanting to be verger.'

'That's what the Rector says, but he's the only applicant and to be honest I shall be glad to be shut of the job. It's all too much being at everyone's beck and call. He's coming for an interview on Monday.'

By twenty minutes to nine Tom Nicholls had his ear to one of the panels of the vestry door listening to the Rector and Willie talking. The door was too thick for him to make sense of what they said, and in any case he remembered there was no need to sneak about, not like he used to have to do. When they paused he tapped on the door.

'Come in!'

Tom snapped the door open and entered in his usual get-up-and-go style. Peter looked up at him from behind his desk. 'Good morning, Tom, take a seat.'

'Thank you, sir.' As he seated himself Tom hitched his trousers at the knee forgetting he was wearing his country scruff outfit. This consisted of a tweed hacking jacket, which had seen better days, fawn cavalry twill trousers, which had also seen better days, a tweed cap at an angle which could only be described as breezy, and well-polished brown oxfords. They were a bit out of kilter with his clothes but he couldn't abide dirty shoes. His shoulders were too narrow for his height and this made him appear much taller than he was. He had a long pale hollow-cheeked face, and when he took off his cap from his high domed head, a thick covering of larger than life gingery hair was exposed. He put up his hand to tidy his moustache, forgetting he'd shaved it off just before he came to the village. Old habits die hard, he'd have to watch himself.

'Thank you for coming, Tom. I've read your letter but I need more details than you've put in it. I must be quite frank, yours is the only application and whilst Willie here is prepared to carry on until a replacement is found I'm anxious to find someone soon, even if it's only temporary. I have to confess I'm somewhat surprised to receive an application from you. It doesn't seem quite your line of country, if you see what I mean.'

'Hit the nail on the head, Rector, but I've decided on a change of lifestyle. Spent too many years dashing here and dashing there, buying this, selling that, and it's time I gave up this entrepreneurial lark and did something more worthwhile. Something where I can get job satisfaction. So, if you'll have me, I'm giving all that up. Evie agrees "Tom," she said "I —"'

'This might sound like an impertinence when I've known you for, what is it, three years now? but I must ask, have you any references? A formality, you know.'

'I have. Indeed I have.' Out of the inside pocket of his old tweed jacket he pulled two spanking new envelopes. Handing them across the desk to Peter he said, 'You'll be well satisfied with those, I can tell you. Tom Nicholls can always find people willing to testify on his behalf.'

Peter opened the envelopes and studied what they said. He handed them to Willie, who read them with a little less belief than Peter had. Willie, having promised himself he'd leave the interview to the Rector, changed his mind and decided to speak up. 'It's unrelenting work, yer know. Locking up, unlocking, day after day. Security's very important nowadays, more's the pity. Sometimes we have bookings back to back for the hall and they all expect it to be just how they want it. Used day and night it seems, some days. Would you be prepared for that? It's very tying.'

'Evie's very amenable. If I got called away, which isn't likely, she'd stand in, very capable is Evie, she always says –'

Peter interrupted with 'If I did agree to recommend you to the Church Council they would have the last word. I can't appoint you without their approval. Why not have a look around with Willie, let him explain what has to be done, then see how you feel? We'll meet again at two, here, this afternoon and have another talk. The job is very much concerned with integrity, you know, Tom. There's things you will be privy to which must not be divulged, like people wanting to get married secretly, or a conversation you unwittingly overhear. The big plus in your favour is that you are, and always have been since you came here, a regular communicant. Nothing less would be permitted.'

Tom fidgeted self-consciously. 'Thank you, Rector. I'll be pleased to go around with Willie, have a look, get the lowdown on things. I just hope that in the future should I have any queries, which I'm sure I shall, Willie will give me the benefit of his experience. He must be a fount of knowledge. That is if I get the job.' Tom smiled at them both, that disarming smile they'd come to like. You couldn't help but like Tom: there was that something about him which drew on your sympathy: in a trice you were on his side, and you couldn't understand how it had come about. 'And I'm good with people as you know. Old and young. I've changed since I came to this village. I don't know what it is about it but it kind of gets you in its grip and makes you want to be, well, noble. Must be all that history which hits you in the face every morning the minute you open your eyes. Brings out the best in you, kind of. That's how I feel anyway.' Tom stood up. 'Shall we be off then, Willie? Let the Rector get off to Penny Fawcett like he always does on Monday mornings. There, you see? I'm getting into my stride already!'

Willie put down his cup, wiped his mouth and said, 'Question is, is he the man for the job? I can't decide. What do you think, Sylvia?'

'Oh! I like Tom. You can't help yourself, and he's always ready for a laugh. More tea?'

'Yes, please. You see, I'm a steady chap not always gallivanting off, but he's always off here, there, everywhere, whatever opportunity comes up. How he's going to settle to a rigid timetable, I'll never know. Look at Wednesdays. I'm backwards and forwards all day with one thing and another and it's eleven before I can lock up, nearer midnight sometimes. He reckons he's changed, but I don't think he's going to settle for that. I'm ready for my pud.'

'Last of the strawberries. Ice cream?'

Willie shook his head. 'It'll be nice to have more time for the garden. I've often fancied growing asparagus.'

'Then grow it you shall. I've no idea how to cook it, but

24

I can soon look it up. If he's not right for the job it won't need an Act of Parliament to oust him, will it, so don't worry yourself.' Sylvia put a dish of fat ruby red strawberries in front of him, fresh from the garden that afternoon, sprinkled with sugar more than an hour ago so it was melting and making juice in the bottom of the dish. Fit for a king, she thought. 'Get yourself outside that lot and stop fretting and leave it to the Rector.'

Not long after Willie had slipped out to unlock the church hall for an evening meeting, Sylvia heard a tap on her back door. When she opened it she found Alex and Beth standing there. A broad smile lit her face, she held wide her arms and they both ran into them and she held them close to her.

'My little darlings!' They hugged and kissed her and she hugged and kissed them, and then she stood back to admire them. 'Well, well, what a nice surprise. Does Mummy know you're here?'

There came a slight pause before they answered, but then they said confidently that, yes, Mummy knew, and could they come in?

Sylvia ushered them into the kitchen and asked, 'Either of you ready for a drink?'

'Yes, please.'

She bustled about getting them drinks and they seated themselves at the table and without speaking drank their orange. Sylvia, her heart melting with love for them, knew she'd have to go back to the Rectory, like it or not: she just couldn't miss out on their company any longer. She'd never have another chance at having substitute grandchildren and she might as well face the fact that that was what they were.

Beth wiped her mouth on the back of her hand and said, 'Sylvie! How's Willie?'

'He's very well, thank you.'

Alex asked, 'And how are you, Sylvie?'

'I'm very well too.'

'Don't you miss seeing us every day?'

'Well, Alex, yes, I do.'

Beth said, 'We miss you. Are you looking after some different children now?'

'No.'

'I'm glad, because you belong to us and other children wouldn't be the same, would they?'

'No, they wouldn't, Beth.'

Alex finished his drink and wiping his mouth on his handkerchief said, 'I expect like Mummy said now Mr Biggs is retiring you want more time to spend with him, going out and things.'

'Well, it would be nice.' She guessed what this was leading up to and felt angry that Caroline had permitted them to come to ask her back instead of asking her herself.

'I expect we shall have to learn to do without you.' Beth struggled to get her handkerchief from the pocket of her shorts. 'Mummy's a doctor again now and it being the school holidays . . . And we don't want any mouldy old person looking after us, do we, Alex? We want you!' Fat tears rolled down her sweet rounded cheeks and she brushed them away with her handkerchief, but they wouldn't stop coming. Leaping from her chair she flung her arms around Sylvia's shoulders and wept.

'There, there, Beth, don't cry, I only live next door and

26

you can come to see me as often as you like. In fact I could invite you to tea sometimes, couldn't I?'

Beth brightened up, lifted her head from Sylvia's shoulder and said, 'Really?' Then cold reason made her see sense. 'But it's not quite the same, is it? I like it when you meet us from school and we sit in the kitchen at home and talk and things. Next to our mummy you're my very best person. Except for my daddy, that is.' Beth looked at her apologetically for adding that.

Sylvia smiled and said, 'But of course, that's understood, it's only right. I'm very proud to be third best.'

Alex got up from his chair. 'Come on, Beth, it's no good. We'll go.' He tugged at Beth's arm, took her handkerchief from her and wiped her eyes. 'Come on. 'Bye, Sylvie. See you soon.'

Beth put her hand in his hand and the two of them left the kitchen by the back door, wandering slowly down to the back gate like two lost souls. Sylvia watched them, remembering how many times she'd ironed those red shorts and the red and white shirt Alex was wearing and how she'd had to mend the split in Beth's shorts because they were her favourites and she couldn't bear to throw them away. And that little T-shirt Beth was wearing was the one Willie had chosen for her when he and Sylvia had taken a holiday in Spain last year; sunny yellow with a wavy white stripe, it really suited Beth's fair colouring.

The two dear little things. It was no good. She'd have to go back: she'd accused Caroline of almost breaking their hearts and here she was doing the very same thing all because of anger and pride. First thing tomorrow she'd go next door and ask for her job back. Yes, definitely she would.

Sylvia didn't tell Willie what she intended because if they didn't want her back she'd look a right fool and she wasn't having that. But school holidays! Just how would those children cope, passed about everywhere? That mustn't be allowed to happen.

Sylvia had had a key for the front door all the time she'd worked at the Rectory but, of course, now she hadn't and she wasn't sure if knocking on the front door was quite the right thing to be doing in the circumstances: it made it all official like and one thing she didn't want was the Rector answering the door and taking her into the study. No, she preferred the kitchen and as it was Tuesday Caroline would most likely be around.

The back door was standing open when she got there so Sylvia called out, 'Helloooo! Anyone at home?'

Chang and Tonga, the two cats, came out of their basket and condescended to weave around her legs mewing. Well, at least the cats remembered her. No one was about so she called out again, 'Helloooo! It's only me.'

The door from the hall opened and there was Caroline. A short silence followed and then Caroline greeted her: 'Why, Sylvia, how nice. Do come in. I was just going to make coffee for Peter, would you like some? Do you have time?'

'That would be nice. Thank you.'

'Do sit down.' But Sylvia remained standing, uncertain and nervous.

They were silent while Caroline filled the kettle and got out the mugs. Sylvia had almost offered to make it, but thought better of it. Take things steadily, she reminded herself.

With her back to her Caroline said, 'Lovely long summer we're having, aren't we?

'Yes, we are. We could do with some rain for the garden though.'

'We could, you're right. The pleasure of watering it every evening soon palls.'

'It does. Your roses are looking wonderful.'

'I've really made an effort with them this year, pruned them back hard and fed them well. Here we are. I'll just take this to Peter, won't be a moment. Please, do sit down.'

'Where are the . . .' but Caroline had gone. Perhaps they'd manage better if the issue wasn't clouded by Alex and Beth being around. When she came back Caroline sat opposite her at the table. They sipped their coffee without speaking. Well, the silence couldn't go on for ever so Sylvia cleared her throat and said, 'Are you serious about getting Mr Fitch to change his mind? About the hedge?'

'Oh, yes. I am. It's tantamount to sacrilege to destroy such a wonderful old piece of village history.'

Sylvia hadn't seen it quite like that but she agreed it was. All went quiet again and Sylvia knew she must brace herself and come to the point. She flushed bright red and then out it all came in a rush. 'I was wondering what arrangements you had made for the school holidays. For the children, I mean.'

'Patchy at best.'

'I see.'

Caroline looked directly at her and said, 'What have you come to say? Something special?'

Sylvia shifted uneasily in her chair. 'If you can forgive me . . .'

Head down so her face was hidden Caroline didn't answer.

'If you can forgive me and have me back I would be pleased.'

Caroline still didn't answer.

'I should never have shouted at you nor deserted my job so abruptly. I can only say I'm very sorry.' Was Caroline even listening to her? She really couldn't tell. 'I was so worried, you see, about you and the children. And the Rector, come to that. I thought you were going to leave them, you see, and I couldn't bear it. We'd all been so happy.'

Caroline's head came up and Sylvia was appalled by the drained look of her face. 'We were, weren't we? If you will come back it will be such a relief to me. I just didn't know what to do about you.'

'Then I will. Three days, is it?'

Caroline nodded. 'That's right. Monday, Wednesday and Friday, all day in the holidays, of course. But schooldays perhaps you could pop home for a couple of hours in the afternoon.'

'Then you can rely on me. I shall be glad because seven days a week living hand in glove with Willie now he's retiring . . . much as I love him, absence, you know. Doesn't do to live too close, you lose the spark if you're not careful.'

Caroline stood up. 'When shall you start?'

'How about tomorrow? Eight o'clock?'

'Yes.'

Sylvia smiled, warmed and thankful that peace had been restored between them.

'Friends again then?' Caroline came round the end of the table and stood in front of her.

'Oh, yes!'

'You've no idea how pleased I am. All water under the bridge. Eh?'

'Of course.'

'I'll give you your key for the morning.'

'Thanks.' Tears came into Sylvia's eyes as her fingers closed over the key that had been hers for so long. It still had her name on it so . . . 'It's the children, you know, I have missed them. I love them dearly.'

'I know you do, and I've missed you. And thank you for coming to heal the breach between us, I'm so grateful, please believe me, I really am. It puts my mind completely at rest.'

Chapter 3

To get on to the estate land Muriel used the small gate at the back of the churchyard instead of walking all the way down Church Lane and in by the main gates. No one was supposed to take advantage of the short-cut, but this morning, somehow, it was all part of her defiance to do so. In any case Mr Fitch wouldn't know, he scarcely ever used it as his short-cut to church because he hardly ever attended.

The morning was cloudy and chill, and a stiff breeze came up once she had left the shelter of the trees which ran along the church wall. Muriel was wearing a jacket and skirt, having decided that a skirt and cardigan would categorise her as a country woman, when this morning she couldn't have felt less like one. She'd rehearsed her approach to him time and again, but knew full well that despite her preparations she would say the first thing that came into her head at the time. She'd have to tread softly: Mr Fitch was an intimidating man, and a head-on confrontation would be the last thing that would achieve her objective.

The grounds were looking particularly beautiful this morning but then so they should for Mr Fitch spent thousands on their upkeep. Thousands more than Ralph would ever have been able to find. In the distance she could hear a mower swirling about cutting grass but here where she was it was peaceful. Into view came the Big House, amazingly immaculate, almost too immaculate: it rather took away from the ancient beauty of the building.

She crossed the Tudor garden and reached the gravel laid to make a car park immediately in front of the house. How incongruous. Muriel, concentrate, she told herself. The huge ancient front door stood open, and Muriel walked straight in savouring the beauty of the door by trailing her fingers along the old weathered wood as she went.

The receptionist recognised her. 'Good morning, Lady Templeton. Mr Fitch is ready for you. I'll take you straight through.'

Muriel, though she knew which way to go, allowed the girl to lead her and inform Mr Fitch she'd arrived.

He got up from behind his desk and came round to greet her. Taking her hand in his he didn't shake it but held it between both his own, saying, 'My dear Muriel, what a pleasure. May I offer coffee? No, don't answer that. I have no other appointments this morning so I think we'll be much more comfortable upstairs in my flat. Charlotte! Ring my housekeeper and tell her coffee for two immediately.'

This morning he was dapper in the shining black shoes on his small feet, the light grey pinstripe suit, the white shirt, putting the seal on his efforts with a remarkable tie which, for some reason, reminded her of Isadora Thingummy who used to dance with scarves. He was still as lean as the day he arrived in the village though the hair was whiter than ever, and the blue eyes still as icy.

He led the way up the beautiful Tudor staircase taking each step with great precision as though he'd practised time and again to make his ascent as perfect as he could for a film. Muriel trotted after him, uneasy and tense, well aware he was doing this to intimidate her. Did he know her reason for coming?

He unlocked the door of the flat and ushered her into the sitting room. It was inclined to be a dark room and the cloudy day made it worse. He indicated a chair and then went round switching on lamps on the low tables so the room was flooded with a soft glow.

Mr Fitch sat down, placed his elbows on the arms of his chair, put his fingertips together and said, 'Well, now, Muriel. All on your own? Ralph's not ill?'

Muriel knew full well he didn't care how Ralph was, nor come to that how she fared either, but she answered him politely, assuring him that Ralph was in good health.

'I'm sorry I missed his party on Saturday. Did it go well?'

'I was sorry you missed it too, but it did go well, thank you.'

She hesitated and he filled the gap with 'So . . .?'

'I have heard something which I truly cannot believe, so I have come to ask you for the truth.'

'Am I to get a roasting?'

Muriel smiled as cheerfully as she could in the circumstances. 'Certainly not. Nothing of the kind. I'm not that kind of a person.'

'I see.'

The housekeeper came in with the coffee at this point. She offered to pour but Mr Fitch declined. 'I'll attend to that myself. Thank you.'

He busied himself with the coffee, placed a table beside Muriel's chair and put her cup on it.

'Thank you. I'll come straight to the point. Katherine Charter-Plackett says you are intending pulling up the hedge around Rector's Meadow and replacing it with a fence.' Muriel put such scorn into the word "fence" that Mr Fitch could have been in no doubt how she felt about the idea. 'I'm sure, we're all sure, she must have misunderstood.'

Mr Fitch sipped his coffee and looked at her over his cup. The icy blue eyes seemed to bore straight through Muriel.

'She's right. I am.'

'Why?'

'Because I am.'

'But you can't.'

'It is my hedge. I bought it. I do own it. Do you ask permission of me before you uproot a rose tree or dig out a lupin in your garden? No.'

'But . . .'

He held up his hand to silence her. 'No, Muriel, I won't listen to you appealing to my better nature. My mind is made up. I have bent over backwards to accommodate the wishes of the people in the village time and again, but the hedge I shall have my own way about. That is the end of the matter.' He stood up in a dismissive manner, and Muriel felt compelled to stand up too and make ready to go.

'It's such a beautiful hedge. I'm very disappointed in you, I had thought . . .'

'No matter how much money I give to one cause or another, no matter whose jobs I save, no matter who benefits from my Education Fund, no matter how I support the church I still can't get it right with you all, so I'm calling a halt, and doing as I like for once.'

Muriel had to agree with what he said: it was all true, he had done all those things. Just the same she'd try once more. 'When you come new to a village like this you have to tread carefully, so very carefully, and this is one instance when you could prove your good intentions by changing your mind. Like over the presidency of the cricket team, you stood down and it won you countless Brownie points. This is another case in point. Please say you'll change your mind. Once it's gone that will be the end of it. It's all the wildlife, you see, the plants and the birds and such, I've even seen wild violets growing in the shelter of that hedge. Could you think about them, please? They're all so precious.'

Mr Fitch glanced away from her pleading eyes and said, 'This might work with Ralph but not with me.' Sarcastically he added, 'After all *he* is a gentleman. You can't expect the same response from me.'

Mr Fitch's answer stung Muriel and left her with nothing more to say.

'I rather imagine from the look on your face he has pointed that out to you, so I'm amazed you should think I would be subject yet again to your particular brand of genteel persuasion.' He moved towards the door. 'You can tell everyone you meet that I am adamant that hedge is coming down. The fence will be in good taste, I assure you. Even I can manage that.'

The cold smile on his face made Muriel shudder. She

picked up her handbag and left, finding her own way to the front door, having declined his offer to escort her. She wouldn't let the receptionist see her tears, but as soon as she was in the Tudor garden they did come, mostly brought on by the thought of that little wren losing his stamping ground and the wild rose being pulled up by its roots.

Well, he wasn't the only one who could be determined. Oh, no! She'd see Caroline tonight and report to her. By the time Muriel had reached the little gate in the church wall she had pulled herself together, stiffened her shoulders and determined she wouldn't tell Ralph what Mr Fitch had said about being a gentleman – well, about not being a gentleman. Which he wasn't, and couldn't be, but it needn't stop him from behaving well, now, need it?

'Well, my dear, how did you get on? Worked your charm on him as usual?'

'No. Nothing worked.' Muriel told Ralph everything they'd said except that bit about . . . 'I can't help feeling that he is very hurt somehow. He's blaming it on people never being grateful, and he's right, they'd die first before admitting to being in his debt for what he does for the village, but I don't think that's the real reason. There's something else. However, I shall ask Caroline round tonight and we'll discuss tactics.'

Ralph smiled ruefully at her. 'I did tell you he wasn't a gentleman.'

Muriel blushed.

'He wasn't rude to you, was he?'

'No, of course not. No, he wasn't.'

Muriel went round to the Rectory that night to discuss

strategy. When Caroline had rung to invite her she'd been told that Peter was out and could Muriel come to the Rectory. So she did.

They sat comfortably in the sitting room, with a bottle of wine between them.

'This seems awfully naughty for a business meeting, sharing a bottle of wine. I mustn't have more than two glasses or I shall not manage to get home. It tastes wonderful.'

'Why not? It might get the brain cells working.'

'Well, mine certainly need some stimulus. One gets very rusty if one is not careful. *University Challenge* defeats me completely nowadays.'

Caroline had to laugh. 'Really, Muriel! Come along then, tell me what happened.'

So Muriel did, and included the bit about him saying he wasn't a gentleman. 'I tried my hardest but had no success and am completely stumped about what to do next.'

'So am I.'

'I had thought Peter might have some ideas. He is on our side, isn't he?'

'Of course. More wine?'

'That will be sufficient for me. Thank you. Have you had a chance to discuss it with him?'

'No, I haven't. The only thing I can suggest is contacting the environment people. They'd advise, wouldn't they?'

Muriel clapped her hands. 'Oh, Caroline, of course. How sensible you are. Peter always admires your common sense and here it is again.'

'Neville Neal, now he's a councillor, isn't he on the environment committee?'

'I do believe he is. Of course. Yes. The very man. It doesn't affect his house but he's got to see things done right, hasn't he? Even if he isn't on that committee he could perhaps point us in the right direction.'

Caroline didn't appear to be paying attention. She was fiddling with her wine-glass, turning it round and round and round in an abstracted fashion.

'My dear, you seem . . . not well.'

'Worried. You know.'

'Would it help to talk to me? I'm very discreet.'

Caroline half smiled at her. 'I know you are. It's Peter. He's gone.'

Muriel, appalled at her news, tried in vain to keep the shock from her face. 'For a little holiday, you mean.'

'Kind of. Just needed to get away.'

'I see.'

'It's me you see. Can't quite cope. Not since I made such a mess of things.'

'But you need him more than ever, then, surely?'

'He's been under a lot of strain.'

Muriel went to sit beside her on the sofa and put a tender hand on hers. 'Of course. Of course. He'll be back, my dear, believe me.'

'He has to come back because of the church, but . . . I don't know . . . Enough of my troubles. Will you see Neville or shall I?'

'I will. You've enough on your plate without all this.'

'I need to keep my mind occupied.'

Muriel stood up. 'I'll see him at the weekend then, and let you know. If you come up with any more bright ideas share them with me.'

'There's the conservation people too, of course.' Caroline made a fist and thumped it into her other hand with gusto. 'He's got to be stopped. I can't think what's got into him, he must have gone mad.'

'There's certainly something the matter, I know that.'

'I thought we'd do a leaflet and put it through people's doors, and posters for the trees and the noticeboards in the church hall and in the Store, in the Royal Oak and such. What do you think?'

'Oh, excellent! Of course. We make a good team, don't we?'

'We've got to move smartly. Knowing Mr Fitch he'll have the diggers in before we have a chance to protest.'

'I hadn't thought of that. He could, couldn't he?'

Caroline nodded. 'He will, without doubt.'

'Ralph knows someone who does posters. I'll get him on to it straight away.'

'We'll have to hold a protest meeting. I'll see Tom about that.'

'Of course.' Muriel put her hands to her temples and groaned. 'My head's in a whirl.'

Caroline laughed. 'I'm determined we'll win.'

'So am I.' Heading for the door Muriel turned back to say, 'You've got Sylvia on track again, I hear? That must be a help.'

'I have. Thank goodness. She's saved my life.'

'Good. Things will work out, I'm sure. He'll be back, you wait and see. Good night, my dear. God bless.' Muriel leaned forward and kissed Caroline's cheek.

As Muriel walked between the Rectory and her house she chanced to meet Neville Neal walking home with Liz.

'Hi, there, Lady Templeton! How are you?'

'Very troubled, Neville, and it's lucky that I've met you. Good evening, Liz. Have you heard about Mr Fitch insisting upon digging up the hedge round Rector's Meadow?'

'I heard a rumour.'

'Well, Caroline and I are organising some opposition and we thought, well, Caroline did, that as a councillor you might be able to point us in the right direction for mobilising some official support.' Muriel put her head on one side and smiled sweetly at him. In the fading light she thought she saw a momentary glimpse of guilt in his face but then he was saying, 'I'm afraid there's nothing we can do, Lady Templeton. Quite out of our hands. It is his hedge, you see.'

'Oh, I know that, but I would have thought . . .'

'He is putting up a fence which will be very sympathetic to the environment, not some ghastly white plastic picket fence so . . .'

'Oh I see. You know his plans then.'

Caught on the hop by this innocent-looking member of the aristocracy – and one mustn't forget that was exactly what she was and had Sir Ralph influence? By Jove, he had – Neville stuttered a little, and then said, 'Well, I did happen to meet him in the Conservative Club the other week and we were discussing it.'

'Ah! I see. I'm very sorry you can't help our campaign.'

'Campaign?' Neville appeared to shuffle a little uneasily.

'Oh, yes! Caroline and I are determined he shan't do this to our village. Whatever his reasons. We shall fight him every step of the way, and believe me, we mean it, so if you

41

see him ... by chance ... in the Conservative Club you can tell him just that. I'll say goodnight then. Good night, Liz.'

'Good night!'

Muriel reported her evening's activities to Ralph, not forgetting to mention the look of guilt on Neville's face.

Ralph muttered with disgust, 'Our esteemed councillor is, to put it bluntly, a slimy toad.'

'Ralph!'

'I beg your pardon, my dear, but he is. There's something else behind this fence business which has yet to be revealed.'

'I shall bypass Neville and go straight to the fountain head.'

'Who is that?'

'I don't know but I shall soon find out and I shall unashamedly use my title to gain access to whichever pompous, self-satisfied council official can do the trick.'

'My word, Muriel Templeton on the warpath is someone to be reckoned with.'

'I hope you're not laughing at me, Ralph, because I am willing to do anything to stop that man from committing this terrible deed.'

'Anything?'

Muriel nodded and answered, with a firm nod of her head, 'Anything.' After a moment's pause she added, 'Within reason.'

Chapter 4

On the first Monday morning that Tom and Willie were working together Willie made sure he got to the church five minutes early. But even that was not early enough, for Tom was already there sitting on the old wooden bench outside the boiler house drawing eagerly on a cigarette. He had on what looked like a new pair of overalls, bright orange with the words Constable Construction Company printed up each leg and in larger letters across the middle of the back. On his feet were a pair of steel-capped boots, in pristine condition. His unnaturally red hair was covered by a baseball cap, also bright orange with a logo of three capital Cs intertwined above the peak.

'Morning, Tom! I like punctuality! Like the outfit, pity about the cigarette. No smoking whatsoever anywhere on the premises. Church, church hall, churchyard. Nowhere at all. Insurance, yer know.'

'As you say, boss.' He heeled the butt into the soft ground at his feet and stood up. 'Nervous, you know. Sorry.'

'That's OK. So long as you remember. On Mondays I

always get the logbook out and see what's what for the week. What bookings we've got, what grave to dig if need be, what gardening jobs there are an' that. It's the verger's Bible, as yer might say. That plastic box.' Willie pointed to the smart box lying on the bench.

Tom smiled and bent to pick it up. 'That's my lunch. Evie's out today so she made it up for me. My Evie always says –'

'Bring it with you into the vestry and leave it there. We'll have a brew up while we study what needs to be done this week. In the winter, with no grass to cut and no gardening to do, life gets a bit easier, but in the height of summer like now it's one body's work keeping everywhere looking smart.'

He unlocked the side door of the church and switched on the lights. 'And don't think for one minute that because the Rector's a gentleman he won't speak out if needs be. Right shaming he can be, if things aren't as they should be. Likes the churchyard looking neat, between every grave, all the paths, all the land not used yet, no weeds growing at the foot of the walls, no overturned urns or vases, no sunken gravestones. Well, that is except the very old ones, he doesn't mind those, says they've a right to topple a bit but anything less than two hundred years 'as to be straight, like soldiers on parade. He likes the bedding plants by the lych-gate to be well weeded and colourful in the summer. I can help out with that 'cos I always have plenty growing on in my greenhouse so don't be spending church money in garden centres . . .'

Tom raised a hand to silence him. 'No need to worry about that. I grow plenty myself, and I've a good source for bulbs too. Don't you fret.' He tapped the side of his nose knowingly. 'Tom Nicholls knows a thing or two.' He laughed confidingly. 'I take two sugars in tea. Thanks.'

'Here you are then.' Willie handed him a mug of tea and pushed the sugar bowl across the table. He looked round the vestry for a moment, took a sip of his scalding hot tea and said, 'Every inch of the church has to be dead clean, every statue dusted – I'll show you the long-handled feather duster I 'ave for 'em – every inch of floor swept, every brass cleaned down each aisle, every tomb, every surface, the altar, the pulpit. You name it, you clean it or else he'll know.'

'The Rector or the Almighty?' Tom laughed, till he noticed Willie's disapproving face. 'Sorry. Didn't mean that.'

'It's not funny – well, to me it isn't. I've watched over this church for sixteen years and I shall be on the look-out every Sunday and any other time for lapses. And don't think I shan't notice 'cos I shall. It may not pay well but it's still to be done right and if you don't want to do it right, say so, and we'll put an end to it. I might be getting older but I'm not going blind and I'm not going daft either.'

'I know that. I'm just surprised you're taking early retirement. Fifty-five's no age for retiring, not for a man with plenty of go in him.'

'You know full well I'm a lot more than fifty-five so save your flattery for them as appreciates it.' He turned to point to a padlocked cupboard. 'That's where we keep the cleaning materials. Brushes, cloths, disinfectants, polish. I polish all the woodwork once every two months. Between polishing yer dust. Carefully. When yer need more supplies the Rector has the petty cash and he needs receipts for everything. Everything, mind.'

'Of course, I wouldn't have it any other way. Show me some of the keys then.'

Willie pushed a heavy bunch of keys across the table. 'Each one's named. No problem there.'

Tom took it up and began to examine the keys. He queried some of Willie's shorthand on the varying tags and then asked what the heavy ornate key with no name was for.

'Ah! That's for the music cupboard. It's a spare just in case Gilbert Johns comes without his. I haven't named it 'cos I never use it.'

'Funny chap for a choir-master. Never seen him wear a coat even in the depth of winter, always looks half starved. Thin as a rail.'

'Thin he may be, but he's well looked after and he's a first-rate choir-master.'

'Never said he wasn't.'

'You don't touch that cupboard, he knows exactly what's in there and exactly where it is so don't go reorganising it for 'im.'

'I shan't. This one? What's it for?'

'That's the key to the safe.'

'Safe?'

'Don't kid on yer didn't know we had a safe. Everybody knows that. Rector bought it after we had the church silver stolen.'

'Stolen! Who the blazes would steal from a church?'

'A teenage girl, daughter of the licensee of the Royal Oak before Georgie. Poor girl. She met a grisly end, believe me.'

'Before my time, that. What happened to her then?'

'Stabbed straight through her innards with a carving knife trying to escape the police. A holy retribution.' Willie pointed skywards and nodded knowingly.

Tom shuddered theatrically and hastily put down the key. 'I shall need to know the combination, though.'

'There's two keys and they're both needed to open it. The Rector has the other. So both of yer have to be there.'

'Seems a big fuss for a few bits of silver.'

'Bits of silver! Few bits of silver! Don't let anyone hear you say that. The whole village got together to stop it all being sold. It's a long story but, believe me, that silver's precious to us all and you're not a true villager if you don't subscribe to that either. So watch your step.'

'Sorry! Sorry! I didn't realise.'

'It's not just its sale value it's its value to the village as a whole. We're very proud of it. Most churches have had to sell their silver to keep going but we have benefactors who make sure we don't need to. Like Mr Fitch at the Big House, and Sir Ralph too.'

'Of course. A real gentleman he is, is Sir Ralph. Got the common touch.'

'Indeed. Real aristocracy. Finished?' Tom nodded and Willie picked up his cup, opened the vestry door and threw the dregs out on to the grass. 'Not much on this week, it being almost August. We'll take a good look at the logbook and study it properly another day when I'll show you how to manoeuvre things to get the best out of the bookings. For now we'll go to the shed and get the gardening stuff out and get a move on while the weather holds.'

Almost too casually Willie thought, Tom asked him, 'The Rector's wife? Does she have much say in things?'

Willie looked at Tom and wondered what was behind the question. Somehow there seemed to be a reason he couldn't fathom behind everything Tom asked. 'The Rector's wife keeps a low profile. You've no need to worry about her.'

'Oh, I'm not worrying. Just wondering. Tales going about. Wish I'd been at the party after the play when old Don spilled the beans.'

Willie couldn't help but chuckle. 'I was and, believe me, it wasn't pretty. Never seen him drunk before. Teetotal all his life and then that exhibition. Yer could have laughed if it hadn't been so awful.'

'There was some truth in it, then? Her and that actor fella? It wasn't just the beer talking?'

'You know as much as me. Let's get on.'

'My Evie says . . .'

'With all due respect I don't give a damn what your Evie says, I'm being paid to work, so let's get on.'

Tom followed him out into the sun and meekly mowed and weeded all morning. Willie couldn't fault his application and he took orders and started the mower first time even though it was temperamental and sometimes took ten or more goes before it started, and altogether proved a willing pupil. When it got to lunchtime Tom sat on the bench ouside the boiler house and opened up Evie's tempting packed lunch saying a bright 'See yer later,' to Willie as he left for home.

Half-way through his lunch Willie heard the latch lift on

the front door and Ralph calling out, 'With Peter being away, thought I'd call to see how things went today.'

'I'm in the sitting room.'

'Sorry to interrupt your lunch, I won't be a moment. I've seen Tom, had a word and he seems quite happy. Very appreciative of your help and advice.'

'He's quick to learn, I'll say that for 'im, and he's got the hang of the mower in no time at all. If he can keep his trap shut I think he'll do very nicely.'

'Keep his trap shut? He's got to ask questions.'

Wryly Willie answered that, yes, he had, that was quite true.

'You think he'll be satisfactory then?'

'Well, we've no choice, have we? But, yes, I think he will. I 'aven't had an opportunity to go through the book work with him, though.' Willie nodded at the window. 'Got to take my chance with this good weather and get the outside work done first. Bookings for the hall could be a different matter. Money an' that.'

'He's been in business for a long while, he should be *au fait* with accounts.'

'Yes, I expect he should.'

'Altogether then seven out of ten so far.'

Willie grinned. 'Hit the nail on the head as Tom would say.'

Ralph stood up to go. 'We could do with having a review of what we charge for letting the church hall. Whilst we don't want to appear greedy, we mustn't be running at a loss. Perhaps Tom would have some input about it.'

'I'm sure he will. We'll have to get the signwriter out to

49

alter the board outside. Verger: Thomas Nicholls, Orchid House,' Willie sniffed derisively, 'Stocks Row, and his telephone number.'

'It'll be strange not having the name Biggs on the board. How long was your father verger?'

'Forty years almost to the day, I believe. So it's fifty-six years there's been a Biggs on that board. If I'd had a son he wouldn't have wanted a job like mine, he'd have been off into Culworth or London even. The young don't settle for jobs like mine nowadays.'

'But do they lead happier lives?'

'Ah!'

'I'll be off.'

The signwriter's arrival two weeks later was cause for comment in the bar that same night.

As he waited for his orange juice Don said, 'I see Willie Biggs has got his marching orders. Where is he by the way, Georgie?'

'On holiday in Torquay. That'll be eighty pence. Thanks, Don.'

Jimmy called out, 'Come over and sit with me, Don, I'm lonely without Willie and Sylvia and I never see hide nor hair of your Vera nowadays. How is she by the way?'

Don slid his plump backside on to the settle opposite Jimmy and took a drink of his orange like a man reaching an oasis after a long hard slog across a desert. 'It just fits the bill does this, sitting 'ere with an old friend in pleasant surroundings, drinking my favourite tipple. Six shifts a week I'm doing now – this is me only day off this week.'

'Yer should be taking it easier not working harder at your age.'

'Less of the "your age". A man's as young as he feels. But I have to say that night work is stopping soon once they've finished this big order. They're going to be cutting right back, so I shall be working eight till five, five days a week. Shan't know meself! I see the signwriter's made it official. Lord Tom's been installed.'

'Official. I can't fathom out why he wants it, 'im with his import-export lark, settling down to a two-bit job like verger.'

With a dead-pan face Don answered, 'Don't let Willie hear you say that. According to him the verger at St Thomas's is a mainstay of the Church of England I have heard said the Archbishop consults him on theological matters from time to time.'

Jimmy looked at Don in surprise. 'Come on, Don, be careful, yer nearly made a joke. It does my blood pressure no good at all.'

'Did I? Perhaps I did. Grand chap is Tom. You can't 'elp but take to him. Right laugh when you get him going. He can't half tell some tales about the East End when he was a boy. Like another world.'

'That's just it, he doesn't fit just right, does he? What's the son of an East End barrow boy doing being verger in Turnham Malpas?'

'Come to that, what's Jimmy Glover Esquire, late poacher and ne'er-do-well, doing owning a taxi, eh? Jimmy?'

'Yer right.'

Gloomily Don reflected on his life. 'Come to think of it,

what am I doing shifting for myself with no Vera? I wouldn't want you to think I'm missing her 'cos I'm not, I'm as happy as a sand-boy, and I don't want her back, not if she begged me. No arguing, no nagging, only one mouth to feed . . . I tell you, there's a lot to be said for the single life.'

Jimmy stared into the distance. 'Not much from where I'm sitting, but then you've only been on your own a matter of weeks. Tell you what, you've lost weight and look better for it.'

Don looked down at the gap between his big stomach and the edge of the table. 'You could be right. By the way, they tell me Tom's put up the charges something ridiculous for the church hall. The Flower Club are, as Sheila Bissett put it, "outraged". Doubled, she says, but pay early and you get a discount.'

'Who says?'

'Tom. He's warning people before the notices go out.'

'Speak of the devil. He's just come in.'

Tom took off his tweed cap as he entered and waved it in general at whoever cared to acknowledge him. 'Evening, Jimmy, evening, Tom.' Jimmy, looking forward to a bit of sport at Tom's expense, called out, 'Come and sit with us, Tom. Two lonely bachelors, we're in need of cheering up.'

Tom chatted up Georgie while she got his order and then came across to them carrying a tray with his own lager and a drink each for Don and Jimmy.

'Here we are then, lads. Drinks all round. One thing, you don't cost much, Don. Orange juice!'

Don nodded his thanks. 'Evie not with yer?'

Tom took a sip of his lager after he'd toasted the two of

them, placed his glass neatly on the beer mat in front of him and said, 'Evie doesn't take to life in a bar. She always says –'

'Nice woman, your Evie, you're lucky to have her.'

'I am. What about you then, Don? Not got Vera back yet?'

'There's no yet about it, she won't be back, and as I'm not going to live in that tarty flat of hers, that's how matters stand. Married all these years and she's marched off without so much as a backward glance. Women!'

'Nothing quite like a woman to cuddle up to on a cold night though. Evie always –'

'What's this about putting up the charges for hiring the church hall. Whose idea was it?' Jimmy asked, before Tom could tell them what Evie always did or said.

'The Rector's.'

'The Rector's! Doubling 'em! It doesn't sound like the Rector.'

Tom leaned across the table and tapped a thin finger on it several times. 'Do you know when the prices last went up? Five years ago. Time they were increased, with costs as they are.'

'But double!'

'Double. But discount for cash and early payment.'

'That doesn't sound like the Rector either.'

Tom had the grace to blush. 'No, that's Tom Nicholls bringing the church into the twenty-first century.'

Don sniggered. 'It's hardly into the twentieth century, never mind the twenty-first. Doesn't seem right somehow.'

Jimmy looked straight into Tom's eyes and said, 'Don't look now but Sheila Bissett's just come in with Ron. From the looks of her she's got the light of battle in her eyes. Too

53

late, she's spotted yer. She's ordered Ron to get the drinks. 'Ope you've got some good reasons 'andy . . . Yer going to need 'em.'

Tom stood up, the only one of the three to do so. 'Good evening, Sheila. Let me get you a chair.' He went to another table and asked permission to remove their spare chair. 'Here you are. I'll put it on this end where there's more room. Ron won't mind the settle, will he? Move up, young Don, make room for Ron. I'm a poet and didn't know it!' He beamed at Sheila, patted her shoulder and seated himself again.

She wagged her finger at him. 'I'm glad you're in here tonight, it gives me a chance to put my case. Don't think playing the gentleman will undo the harm you have done, because it won't.'

Tom looked shocked. '*Playing* the gentleman. I *am* a gentleman.'

Sheila snorted. 'You might appear to be one but how can you be when the moment you take charge the price of booking the hall doubles? I shall have to put up our membership fee for the Flower Club and it's going to be hard for some of them to find the money.'

'It isn't my responsibility, putting it up. The Rector came up with the idea and he's waiting for confirmation from the committee.'

Taken aback Sheila said, 'Oh, I see. The Rector.'

'So I'm not to blame. I'm only the poor geezer in the firing line.'

'Yes, but I bet it was you who sowed the seed. Yes, I can just see it, all comfy over a cuppa and . . . Thank you, Ron.'

Ron placed her drink in front of her and eased himself on to the settle beside Don. 'Evening, everyone.'

Jimmy greeted him with 'Your Sheila's getting stuck in about the charges for the hall.'

'I've told her it's only reasonable but she won't listen.'

'I do listen, Ron, I do, but I don't have to agree with you, do I?'

Tom said vehemently, 'The church can't afford to subsidise everybody.'

'No, but I bet you've had a hike in salary. I bet my bottom dollar you're getting more than Willie did.'

'Now, Sheila . . .'

'"Now, Sheila" nothing, Ron, I bet he is. Go on, deny it.'

Tom spilt his drink and made a bother of wiping his jacket and the pool of lager on the table. 'Just look at that. What a mess. Evie will have something to say about this. "Just back from the cleaners," she'll say. I'll get a cloth from Georgie.' He got up and went to the bar, leaving Jimmy and Don laughing quietly.

Ron said, 'You nearly nailed 'im there, Sheila, but he's too quick even for you.'

'I'm right, though, aren't I? Otherwise he'd have denied it.'

Tom came back and made a fuss of wiping up the lager. 'How clumsy of me, what a mess! Evie says I'm –'

'Never mind, don't make such a fuss. I jogged yer elbow, didn't I?' Jimmy said slyly.

'You didn't do it on purpose, though, did you?'

'Oh, no.'

'Well, then.' Tom took the cloth back to Georgie and stopped for a chat. 'Where's Dicky tonight?'

'Everyone knows and so should you. It's Scout night.'

'Of course! Grand job he does, you know. A grand job. The two of you no nearer being able to marry?'

'No. We still haven't tracked down that husband of mine. He's probably dancing the night away under some southern sun with that disgusting Electra clinging to him. If only he knew the heartache he's causing.'

Tom placed a sympathetic hand on hers as it rested on the bar. 'Never mind, one day he'll turn up and you'll be able to get him sorted out. Dicky's the sort of chap who's worth waiting for. And wait he will, with you as his prize.'

Georgie blushed. 'Now, Tom!'

'In fact if I wasn't well and truly married I'd be elbowing him out!'

'Would you indeed!'

'I would! You're a gorgeous woman, Georgie. A fitting tribute to womanhood!'

'Get away!'

Tom laughed and went back to his table. While he'd been away the others had been silent.

On Tom's return Jimmy said, 'Now Willie Biggs isn't verger I'm hoping for some inside information from you. Never uttered a word about any secrets he learned as verger, played his cards too close to his chest for my liking. People, including himself, got married on the quiet and he never let slip a word. At funerals, and we all know the bother they can cause, all sorts 'appened and he never let on.'

'What can happen at a funeral, for goodness' sake?' Tom asked.

'Well, there was a funeral once and the deceased's bit on the side turned up looking really dramatic, in black, with a black veil over her face and shoulders, and there was a terrible row and almost a fight at the graveside when she tried to take her turn throwing soil on the coffin like yer do. Willie never let on, never told us a word. Another time someone stood at the graveside and fell in as the Rector was praying, sprawled dead drunk on top of the coffin he was. You should have heard the screams. He went spark out and they had to hold everything up till they'd managed to haul him out. 'Nother time the wrong person got buried in the wrong grave. Right dust-up that was. They'ad to dig 'em up and rebury 'em. That was before this rector's time too. All that 'appening and Willie never let on.'

'Sounds as if I shall be having an interesting time.'

'We shall gather here on a night waiting for any snippets of gossip.' Jimmy winked at Don who, keeping a poker face and quite unable to see what was funny in Jimmy's stories, said, 'Remember that time when the Rector, this one, that is, was conducting a wedding? Great big do it was with a carriage and horses for the bride and groom and the church full and a big reception at the George in Culworth. Top 'at and tails. Church bells ringing. You name it, money no object, and when the Rector got to the bit about any just impediment why these two should not be joined in matrimony someone stood up at the back and shouted, "I'm the impediment, me and my four kids," and she turned out to be the bridegroom's first wife and they weren't divorced. She marched the kids down the aisle and presented 'em to the hopeful bride. "Now", she said, "what are you going to do about this lot?" The father caught the bride just as she fainted. They'ad to call an ambulance for the bride's mother. Had a heart-attack she did, right there in the front pew. 'Bout six months ago it was, maybe a year.'

Jimmy drew a little closer to Tom and whispered, 'For a start what do you know about the Rector?'

'Being on holiday, you mean?'

Jimmy scoffed at Tom's comment. 'Holiday! Holiday! That's a laugh. You see? You've started being secretive already and you've not been in the job scarcely a month.'

'Honestly! God's truth, that's all I know.'

'Is it indeed! You know and I know and we all know he's left home.'

'Never! No, no, he's not. He's taking a break.'

'Well, keep your ears and eyes open and let us know. He's our rector and we've a right to know what's going on, and we can't ask Sylvia 'cos she'd die first before tell us.'

'He went unexpected, I can say that.'

'Exactly! Usually he has it all planned out, meetings postponed, clergy from Culworth to take the services, and that, but not this time. So don't you keep your mouth buttoned like Willie did. *We want to know.*'

'I have promised not to divulge —'

'Well, I 'ope yer 'ad your fingers crossed behind your back.' Jimmy looked him straight in the eye. 'Nothing, and I repeat *nothing*, goes on in this village without someone finding out. Eventually. That includes any tales about you, Tom Nicholls, and any tales about anyone at all, so you might as well tell all as not. Got the message?'

Chapter 5

Muriel Templeton had come to the conclusion that cleaning the church brass on alternate weeks was therapeutic not only for Muriel herself but for whoever happened to be in the church at the time. It so often happened that as she polished she met someone in there who needed to talk. She'd counselled Louise Bissett when she'd had that dreadful time falling in love with the Rector, she'd talked with Venetia when she'd been unfaithful to Jeremy. Though as it turned out they weren't even married so could one be unfaithful if one wasn't, and should one be living as though married in the first place when one was not? Morals nowadays had become so confusing: perhaps they were best left to the people themselves to square it with their own consciences, if they had any, that is.

From the understairs cupboard she got out her neat wooden box, which Ralph had made especially for her; she loved the old dark wood he'd made it from and best of all the curved handle to hold it by. Before leaving the house she checked she had all she needed. Spotlessly clean yellow dusters, her pieces of old towel cut into neat squares for putting on the polish, the old toothbrush for the wiggly corners the duster couldn't reach into, her household gloves to protect her hands, yes, they were all there.

As Muriel was about to shut the front door she remembered. The brass polish! How silly could she get? The new tin stood on the kitchen worktop. She went back in, picked it up and put it in her box, but not before she'd taken a glance around her kitchen and admired it for the umpteenth time. Despite Ralph's opposition she'd been right to insist on this deep gold colour for the walls above the tiling. It gave that added warmth and provided a good background for those icon things she'd bought at the craft fair. Artistically they deserved only four out of ten but she loved them. Muriel paused to recollect where Ralph was. Good heavens, he was in the study and she hadn't told him she was going out.

Muriel opened the door and said, 'I'm going now, Ralph dear, back for lunch. Don't work too hard.'

Ralph looked up from the post he was opening. Muriel's heart flipped. He was so good-looking. How did he manage to keep his looks? Those frank, intelligent dark brown eyes, that proud forehead, the snow-white well-barbered hair, and that aristocratic nose! She wondered sometimes if that was the real reason she'd married him: her attraction to his arrestingly handsome nose combined as it was with his well-tanned fresh complexion.

'Enjoy!'

It was his voice too. So deep but not rumblingly deep, and his top-drawer accent, now that really could set her heart-strings vibrating and no mistake. Muriel rushed across the study carpet on winged feet and planted a kiss on his cheek.

Ralph laid his hand on hers as she rested it on his desk. 'My dear!'

'I love you so. So very much!' She gave him another kiss on the top of his head and fled. Having slammed the front door behind her she found she'd left the brass-cleaning box on the hall chair and had to go back in to pick it up. After such a disastrous start would she ever get the brass cleaned?

This morning she decided she would begin with the cross on the altar. She spread a clean duster on an altar chair and stood on it so she could reach. Now which hymn should she hum while she polished? 'Jesus Wants Me for a Sunbeam'? The rhythm fitted just right. As she hummed she paused to wonder how long the cross had been standing on the altar. One of her favourite phrases was 'time immemorial' but she didn't think that applied to the cross, not like it did to the tombs, especially the Templeton tomb at the back of the church, or the stone flags of the church floor or the old uncomfortable pews. No, she rather felt it was much younger than that.

Having brought the cross to a fine high glow Muriel stepped down from the chair and stood back to judge if she was satisfied. Yes, she was. Now for the lectern. She replaced the chair, removing the duster from its tapestry seat and carried the box to the lectern. This eagle holding the Bible she had never really liked, she watched birds-of-prey programmes on the television and tried hard to like eagles but she couldn't. Nevertheless it had to be cleaned. The eagle's beak was slightly open and she had to be careful not to leave brass polish in it. Muriel turned to pick up the toothbrush and heard a sound. It wasn't the sound of the heavy outside door opening nor the sound of a footstep, just the old building creaking. She expected she'd creak too if she was as old. The wind under the tiles perhaps. Or Willie in the vestry. Oh! but it wasn't Willie now, was it? It was Tom. At the thought of his name Muriel smiled. He really was a delightful man. Rough diamond, true, but always so polite and considerate and very amusing.

Just as she had grudgingly polished the eagle's outspread wings and attended to his feet Muriel heard the noise again. A rustling kind of noise. Not mice. Oh, no! Not that! She stopped to listen. There it was again. 'Tom! Is that you? Tom!' But there was no reply. The sound stopped. Muriel gave herself a talking-to. 'Get on with the job, Muriel, and don't be so pathetic. If Ralph had been here you wouldn't even have noticed there was a sound.'

Now for the brass plates on the altar: one depicting the risen Christ, the other His ascension into heaven. She noticed that there was old brass polish in the folds and creases of the moulding of the plates. Oh dear! Sheila Bissett had slipped up last week. Working away, absorbed in thought, Muriel missed the second spate of creaking and rustling but not the third: this time they were so loud they made her jump. She dropped the tin of brass polish and a great splash of it ran down the side of the altar. It trickled steadily down the oak wood like a great putty-coloured tear. Quickly Muriel grabbed a duster and rubbed it away. Concerned about staining the wood she rubbed furiously and didn't notice until she'd finished that it was her polishing cloth she was using and not the putting-on cloth.

'Oh, no. Now, what a mess I've made! My lovely yellow duster all smeared and horrid. What a nuisance.'

There came a creak and muffled rustlings and all thoughts of the ruined duster went from Muriel's mind. 'Now, see here! Who is it? Is it you, Tom? Tom!'

But the only reply was the familiar deep silence of the church.

I really must pull myself together. I'll finish the polishing then straight away I'll find Tom and tell him. It must be mice. Those scamps of angelic choir-boys will have left crisps and things in some corner and a mouse has crept in and decided to make a home in here. That'll be it. If I get Tom to put out traps, by the time it's my turn again to polish they should be caught and the traps gone, then I shan't come across them by mistake.

Muriel put 'risen' and 'ascension' back on the altar and then she went to the rear of the church to polish the brass decoration on the font. She loved the stone bits of the font and the two angels which decorated it, but the Victorian addition of the brass with its pompous inscription rather annoyed her, but who was she to . . . there was that noise again but this time much closer. Then there came a loud bang, as though something had been dropped. From the Templeton tomb not three yards from where she stood.

Her flesh crept, goose pimples rose on her skin, her scalp prickled and her knees went to jelly.

The church was ice cold and so too was she.

Her hands chilled to the marrow. And trembling.

Her mouth bone dry.

The silence now was almost worse than the noise.

Who moved and then didn't?

Who wouldn't reply to her calls?

Was it haunted like Willie had always said?

But one of Ralph's ancestors? Surely not.

Her ears caught a slight scratching sound.

Dear God!

Muriel lifted the heavy handle of the main door and escaped out into the sunshine, running, running for the safety of Ralph and his sane no-nonsense world.

She croaked, 'Ralph! Oh, Ralph!' as she shut her front door behind her.

Startled, Ralph stood up and went out into the hall to find Muriel sitting on the chair, breathless, speechless and shaking.

'My dear! Whatever is it?'

Muriel tried to speak but couldn't.

Ralph put his arms about her, and hugged her. 'You're safe now, my dear, but whatever's happened? Tell me!'

Muriel pointed to her mouth.

'Glass of water?'

She nodded.

She drank half the water and then gave a great shudder.

'Tell me, Muriel. *Please*!'

'Oh, Ralph! I've been so frightened.'

'By whom?'

Muriel shook her head. 'By mice. It must be. But they couldn't make a big bang, could they?'

'You're not making sense.'

She explained what had happened, ending with 'And I've left all my polishing stuff there and I've got to go back to get it and I daren't.'

Ralph said, 'We'll both go. The two of us. If it's mice, well, Tom will have to do something about it.'

'If it's not?'

'Well, if it's not . . . it could be a tramp gone in there for the night out of the rain. Or . . . Muriel's vivid imagination?' He looked gently into her face and she felt both foolish and indignant.

'I'm not in my dotage, Ralph. I heard those noises. I'll finish this water and then we'll go and we'll sit quietly in a pew by the tomb and we'll listen together. If you'll hold my hand that is and I put my feet up on a hassock just in case.'

'Gladly.'

Ralph pushed open the heavy door and there was Tom in his bright orange overalls busy dusting round the heads of the statues with Willie's special long-handled feather duster. Everything so ordinary and commonplace it was alarming in itself.

'Good morning, Sir Ralph, Lady Templeton! Lovely morning. If you're wanting a quiet moment I can come back later.'

Tom's cheerful greeting flinging her pell-mell back into normality somehow worsened Muriel's fear. Ralph, clasping her hand firmly in his, found she'd started trembling again. 'That's all right, Tom, you carry on. We've come for Muriel's brass-polishing box. She thinks she left it by the font.'

'She did. I've put everything back in it, Lady Templeton. You'd dropped it.' Tom sounded slightly puzzled but was too polite to ask why she'd obviously run away in haste. He went up to the font, picked up her box and took it across to her. 'There we are. If you feel it's getting more than you can fit in I'll gladly take over and do the polishing myself.' Tom's smile was so kind, Muriel felt quite restored.

'That's very kind of you, Tom, but I do enjoy my polishing. There's not much I can do for the church but this is something within my capabilities and I should hate to give it up. Thank you all the same.'

'That's fine.'

'Have you been in here all the morning?'

'No, I came in about five minutes ago. Before that I was clearing the weeds away from the old gate at the back that leads to the Big House.' He went to the main door and opened it for them.

Ralph carried the box in one hand and held Muriel's hand with the other. She was gripping his fingers so tightly he had no circulation in them.

When they were safely out on the path she whispered, 'I wish he wouldn't wear those orange overalls. They make him look like some kind of malevolent insect, made huge by a mad scientist in a laboratory somewhere and released to take over the world. Do you think there are more of them?'

'Muriel!'

'It's true, they do. But you see I *was* in there by myself and I did hear those noises, but we couldn't very well sit there to listen for them with Tom working, could we?'

'No. Are you sure you heard noises?'

'You have never doubted my word before, Ralph, so why do you doubt it now?'

'I'm sorry, my dear. I'll go back and ask Tom to put down some traps just in case. We have had mice in before, some years ago, so you could be right.'

'Thank you. I'll go home and get the lunch.'

Muriel went into the Village Store after lunch to collect the video of *Shakespeare in Love* which Jimbo had ordered especially for her.

'Jimbo rang me yesterday and said it was in, Bel.'

'Right, Lady Templeton. I expect he's put it in the back office. I won't be a moment.' Bel trotted away into the back, leaving Muriel with Linda behind the Post Office grille doing her accounts and Sheila Bissett occupied with choosing a birthday card.

'Good afternoon, Sheila.'

'Good afternoon, Muriel. I was hoping to see you, Is it possible you could do my brass cleaning next week and I'll do the next two weeks instead? Ron-ald is going up to London for a few days to some union meetings and I'd love to go with him, shopping and things, you know.'

Somewhat disconcerted, Muriel hesitated before she replied. Sheila, who easily took offence, said, 'If it's not convenient . . .'

'It's not that. I've been polishing today and I was sure I heard mice in the church moving about, you know, and I hate mice or . . . rats and such and I've not really got over it.' She trembled again at the thought. 'But I'll get Ralph to sit with me and read or something just in case. Tom's going to put traps down and I hate them too, but there's no other way is there?'

Sheila drew her confidentially to one side. 'I don't think he's doing all that good a job, actually.'

'You don't?'

'Night before last the lights were left on in the church. I

67

got up to make a cup of camomile tea because I couldn't sleep and while I waited for the kettle to boil I looked out of the window and the lights were on. Some of them, not all. And if we've got mice in then . . .' She shook her head as though despairing of Tom. 'I can see straight across the green down Jacks Lane between the school and the old oak and there was no doubt about it. Lights had been left on. And obviously, if there's mice, he's not cleaning properly, is he?'

Muriel, hating to agree with her for really she liked Tom, replied, 'I wouldn't go as far as to say that . . .'

'Willie was much more conscientious. However, if you are able I would be grateful.'

'You can rely on me.'

Muriel realised that Bel was patiently waiting for her, 'Oh, thank you. I paid when I ordered it.'

'That's right, that's what it says. Is it good then?'

'Oh, yes. We missed it when it went the rounds of the cinemas and I did want to see it.'

Sheila joined in with 'You've missed the last two Flower Club meetings too. We need all the people we can get now the hire charge for the room is going up.'

'I know, we just seem to have been so very busy lately, but I will make an effort.'

'It's that Tom. It's all his fault the charges going up. Bring back Willie, I say.'

'I understand it was the Rector who broached the idea first.'

'Spurred on by Tom, I've no doubt, and he's got more salary than Willie got.'

Somewhat primly Muriel said, 'We don't know that.'

'I do.'

'Well, then, Sheila, I'll do next week and you can do the next two weeks and then we shall be straight again. That right?'

'Fine. Everywhere I look there's posters about the protest meeting. Very stylishly done and very eyecatching. Who's made them for you?'

'A friend of Ralph's. Will you be there? We're very keen to get everyone on our side. Almost everyone I speak to is sympathetic to our campaign, except for . . .'

'I know, except for Grandmama Charter-Plackett. I think she's the only one on his side. But I'll do my best to drum up support wherever I go. I'm so glad Caroline is at the forefront of it all. She carries such weight with her opinions. Do her good too. She's never looked the same since . . .'

Muriel hastily diverted Sheila from saying any more. The Village Store was not the place to air one's views about anything, least of all about the upset at the Rectory.

'Thank you, Sheila, I shall be glad of your support, and Sir Ronald's if he can see his way.'

'He won't dare to do any other than support you once I've had a word with him,' she patted Muriel's arm, 'and don't worry about the mice, I'm sure they'll have been caught by next week.'

Muriel debated about taking Ralph with her the following week when she went to clean the brass. In fact she even thought about not going at all. Was it perhaps a little excessive to clean it every week? Perhaps every other week would be sufficient? But Muriel recognised the coward in herself and brushed her weakness aside. The Christian martyrs had had far worse things to face than a few mice and she, Muriel Euphemia Templeton, was not one for weakness. No, she'd go all by herself and face the music.

There was a chance Tom had already caught the little horrors. She'd find him and casually introduce the subject. What she didn't want to happen was to come across a decapitated mouse still in a trap awaiting Tom's ministrations. Maybe even with the cheese still in its mouth. Or did the trap smack shut before it had actually – No, she wouldn't think about that.

Tom was getting rid of the cobwebs on the underside of the lych-gate. 'Good morning, Lady Templeton, overcast today, isn't it? I've never seen so many cobwebs as this in my life. It must be a real good summer for spiders.' He stood in her way energetically brushing with a soft, long-handled brush. 'They're sticky, you know.'

Muriel kept well out of the way of any spiders running from Tom's murderous intentions. 'Tom. Talking of spiders, have you caught any mice?'

Tom, hands behind his back, crossed his fingers. 'Two the first night. None since, so I reckon we've got the all-clear.'

Muriel put a hand to her heart and said, 'Oh, I'm so relieved. I was dreading . . . I know you'll think I'm silly but . . .'

'Not at all. I see you've got your brass box with you. I wouldn't go in just yet, I've been spraying in the church for spiders too. Best let the air get clear a bit first. Not good for the lungs.' He held up a spray can with evil pictures of spiders and ants on it. 'Brilliant stuff this, if you have any problems, but very potent for the breathing. Stand clear, I'm using it on here now.'

Muriel stood away and watched him squirting the spray on the old beams. He stood on the seat at one side and sprayed right into the corners, and then stood on the opposite seat and did the same. Tom appeared to Muriel to over-egg the pudding a little but she supposed there was no point in doing it at all if one didn't do it well. A waft of the spray reached her and she waved it away. It was certainly potent. She'd better not go in the church for a while.

'I'll sit on the seat by the old oak and wait ten minutes.' Muriel planted her box beside her and set herself to wait. She checked her watch because she was never any good at guessing the passing of time. Twenty minutes to eleven. Right! Seated there Muriel looked like an elderly lady taking a nap, but she didn't feel elderly and she most certainly wasn't taking a nap. She was admiring the old church and thinking how lucky they all were to have one kept so beautifully. Tom had gone round to the side door, and out of it, through half-closed eyes, she saw Kenny Jones emerge.

The sight was so startling! She couldn't believe what she saw. Kenny Jones coming out of church! It was such a shock to her, but it didn't appear to be a shock to Tom for they were talking quite amicably. Tom took his cap off and scratched his red hair, Kenny wagged a finger at him and then waved goodbye and came down the side of the church, wearing his old navy anorak, which Muriel knew would tell a rare old tale if it could speak. Wearing an anorak on such a humid day.

If Muriel wasn't mistaken he glanced round as he came

out into the open as though looking for someone, or was he checking no one was watching? Well, that was understandable: considering how many years it was since he'd been in there he'd surely be embarrassed for anyone to see him. Muriel guessed that the last time Kenny had visited the church was when he was at the village school, and that must be at least twenty years ago.

Kenny marched briskly down the church path. Muriel pretended to be asleep. As she heard the lych-gate creak shut she opened her eyes just a slit and through the veil of her eyelashes glimpsed him marching towards Jacks Lane to go past the school, down Shepherds Hill and home.

When her ten minutes were up Muriel wended her way up the path and into church. It was only when she was applying the brass polish to the wings of the lectern eagle that it occurred to her that Kenny Jones hadn't given a thought to his lungs being affected by Tom's spider spray. She hoped he'd be all right.

Chapter 6

'You there, Mum?' Kenny pushed open the house door, shutting it at the same time as hanging his anorak behind it, all in one swift practised movement.

She was sitting in her chair, head down, crying.

'What's up?'

Mrs Jones endeavoured to make herself look as though crying was the last thing on her agenda but she wasn't successful.

'What yer crying for?'

'Yer dad's just rung. He's lost his job. Finishes end of the week.' She sniffed loudly and wiped her eyes again.

'Aw! Mum! How's that come about?'

'Council put the road-maintenance work out to tender, company from the other side of Culworth has won it and they don't want him. Too old, they say. He can shovel with the rest of 'em, it isn't fair. I don't know whatever we're going to do. He'll never get another job at his age. Oh, Kenny.'

Kenny lay down on the sofa, not knowing how to cope

with a mother he'd never ever in all his life seen crying. 'Something 'ull turn up.'

Mrs Jones snapped out in her distress, 'Don't be bloody daft, nothing will. All we'll have coming in will be my money from the Store. We can't manage.'

'There's our Terry's wages.'

'And how much do I see of that? Tell me. Go on. Tell me.'

'Nothing.'

'Exactly. Well, things will have to change.'

'They will?'

Mrs Jones' head came up and she looked him straight in the eye. 'For a start . . .'

'Any tea going? And I wouldn't mind a sandwich.'

'No, Kenny. You're collecting the social every week and what does your mother see of that? Zilch! It's supposed to be for you to live on. So by my reckoning that means paying for your food and laundry and the roof over your head. I'm keeping you no longer. In fact, I can't no more, neither you nor our Terry.'

'Just as you like, but when I come into money —'

'You come into money! And pigs might fly! You'll have to move out. Get your own pad.'

Kenny pretended to be shocked. 'Mum! How can you say that to your little boy? Your little boy who's —'

'Who's been a pain in the whatsit since the day he was born.'

'Mum!'

'I mean it, Kenny. Why should your dad and me keep you, a grown man? Just get a real job, please! Either that or you're out. Full stop! The estate's always wanting help of

74

one sort and another. Our Barry 'ud put in a good word. Ask him.'

Kenny lifted his feet from the sofa arm and sat himself up. His keen brown eyes looked at his mother's back. 'Don't, and I mean don't ever suggest again that I should work for that old faggot Fitch. Our Barry can kow-tow to 'im if he wants, but not me. I'm made of different stuff.'

'You're right, very different. He's got a nice wife and family, a nice house, a steady job, money coming in regular, you name it.'

Kenny sneered at the prospect. 'Who wants a life like his? Boring. Boring. Boring. Coming home covered in sawdust and smelling of glue with thick fingers and swollen hands from working outside. Not even the kids are his own.'

'Only because they both felt they were too old to start another family, that's all. Families cost money and with Pat having two already . . .'

'There's one thing, though. I know for a fact I'm firing on all cylinders don't I? He doesn't.'

'Don't bring that up. Two children you don't own up to, and I can't acknowledge. Not a single real Jones grandchild. It's not right.'

'There's always our Terry.'

'Fat chance.'

'You're hard, you are. Not long since you'd have given me your last ha'penny.'

'I've seen the light.'

Mrs Jones turned to switch on the iron and while it heated up she looked at him. Her three boys had been the joy of her life for years, she'd defended them against all the odds, no matter what they did, and sometimes done it against her better judgement for their sakes, but she'd finally run out of steam. She didn't know who was worst, their Terry or him laid on the sofa, idle as they come. If it wasn't for her job doing the mail order at the Store they'd all have been in the cart. Vince had always done his best, but labouring on the roads wasn't exactly the sort of job that brought the money rolling in.

'If you had some money you and Terry could rent from Sir Ralph. One of his houses is coming up empty. That would be nice.'

Kenny ignored her remark. He knew better than to latch on to an idea like that: before he knew it she'd have him and their Terry installed and then where would they be? No meals cooked, no shopping done, no shirts ironed, no clean sheets, and if there was one thing he approved of it was clean sheets on a regular basis. There was nothing quite like sliding into bed with the sheets all fresh and smelling nice and feeling smooth and sexy. In fact it could be said it was one of Kenny Jones' passions. The word passions brought on a daydream about the barmaid at the Jug and Bottle in Penny Fawcett, and his mother's next words simply fell on deaf ears.

'However, from now on, no money, no food. Two weeks of that and if there's still no sign of money you're out. Lock, stock and barrel. Including your air-guns and all that exercise paraphernalia you bought last time you were in the money. I've dusted round it for two whole years and now that's it, it's going, and you with it, and our Terry. I've finally reached the end of my tether after all these years. You've been conspicuous by your absence this morning, where've you been?'

76

Kenny didn't answer; he'd just remembered the feeling of getting the barmaid up against the counter in the empty lounge bar and was about to kiss her luscious tempting lips to see if she was as good as their Terry had claimed. You don't answer daft questions like that from your mother when you're occupied like that.

His mother pursued her theme. 'I'll ask about it tomorrow.'

'Ask what?'

'Ask Lady Templeton about the house coming up. See what the rent is.'

Kenny's daydream was replaced by the picture of Muriel sitting nodding on the new seat the parish council had had constructed round the foot of the oak on the Green. Daft old thing she was. None dafter.

A big stumbling block to the scheme sprang into his mind. 'We've no furniture for it.'

'Oh, God! Yes. Ah! but I've just had a thought. They're having a right turn-out at the nursing home where Vera works. I could have a word. Good stuff being thrown out, I understand. I'll ask.'

Kenny cackled. 'Your friend Vera! After what you did to her she'd be more likely to choke yer than give yer furniture. No, sorry, Mum, that little scheme isn't going to come off.' He lay back on the sofa smiling a self-satisfied smile as only Kenny could.

His mother, enraged at the memory of how close Vera had come to going to prison over the stolen paving stones because of her and more so at his disregard of her terrible dilemma, suddenly retaliated. She clenched her fists and began beating him about the head and shoulders. He put up his arms to protect his head as the blows rained down on him. His mother's face so close and so venomous turned him into a child again and he feared her. 'Hey! Mum! Don't! Don't! Please don't!'

'I'll give you don't! Get a job! Go on! Get a job! I'm sick to death of yer. Sick to death!' Her energy drained, she flopped on to the sofa Kenny had vacated and wept again.

Restored to adulthood now she'd stopped beating him, Kenny turned away from her so she couldn't see what he was doing and extricated a thick wad of notes from his back pocket. Peeling off five twenty-pound notes he rammed the rest back into his pocket and turned to give her the hundred pounds.

'All right, Mum. Stop the yelping. Here, take this towards the housekeeping.'

Mrs Jones, silenced by the shock of what he'd said, looked at the money in astonishment. 'Why, Kenny! How much is that?'

'Hundred pounds. Now can I have a sandwich?'

Alerted by his nonchalance Mrs Jones asked, 'Just where did you get that from?'

Kenny tapped the end of his nose. 'Ask no questions . . .'

'Well, thanks very much. It's not left you short, has it?'

He used up another of his guises and played the part of the martyr. 'Don't you worry about me, I can manage, I don't need much to live on.'

'But where did you get it?'

'Business deal, with a chap in the market in Culworth. Owed me a favour.'

'Oh! Right. It's not illegal, is it, Kenny? I wouldn't want you to get into trouble just because we're desperate.'

'As if I'd be so daft. Come on, Mum. Use your brains. Kenny Jones in trouble? Huh! I'm not stupid. Not a word to our Terry that you're flush.'

'No, of course not.' She tucked the money into the pocket of her apron and went into the kitchen to make him a sandwich. Kenny lay on the sofa again, berating himself for allowing her to dominate him like she'd done when he was a kid. There'd be no end to her demands now she knew he had money. Might be better if he did move out. In fact after his sandwich he'd get the car started and go see the Templetons himself about the house.

After half an hour messing about with jump leads and with the help of their Terrry's old banger, Kenny eventually got the car started and drove off up Shepherds Hill into the village.

Yes, Sir Ralph was at home and, yes, of course he could see him, do come in. He followed Lady Templeton into their sitting room and there sat Sir Ralph in an imposing winged armchair, *The Times* open on his knee, his gold-rimmed reading glasses in his hand, wearing a smart checked suit, gleaming brown shoes and a welcoming smile on his face.

'Come in do, Kenny. Long time since I saw you. What are you getting up to nowadays?'

'This and that, Sir Ralph, this and that.'

'Me too. This and that. What can I do for you?'

'I've heard you've a cottage in Hipkin Gardens coming free. I wondered if I could, well, me and our Terry, could rent it from you?'

'Have I? I didn't know.'

Kenny, surprised that a property owner was so disinterested in money as not to know, patiently explained. 'Yes, it's the Nightingale's cowman at number seven, he's been dismissed and he's got a job somewhere in Devon so he's off. Next week. So Mum says anyway.'

'He didn't tell me. If it's true, which I expect it is, I have to say I am very particular about my tenants. I won't have unreliable people. I won't tolerate tenants who neglect or abuse the cottages and the lease is for six months in the first instance and if I'm not satisfied then it's out. I mean that, Kenny. I'll ring my agent, if you'll excuse me, and ask him what he knows.'

While Sir Ralph went to his study to use the telephone Kenny looked around the room. This was just the sort of décor he'd like in his house. Mellow, friendly, welcoming, quality. Yes, that was it. The key was quality. Not a thing in poor taste. He quickly leaped to his feet and tried out Sir Ralph's chair. The suppleness of the leather upholstery was stunning. Your hands wanted to stroke it, to enjoy the lovely expensive pliable stuff, to caress it almost. Oh, yes! This fitted the bill all right! Kenny sat back enjoying the comfort and the sensation of importance the chair gave him. This was what he lacked, possessions which gave him prestige. No wonder Sir Ralph could be the sort of person he was: sitting in this chair would without doubt bolster his feeling of authority. Kenny felt envy trickling along his veins. One day! One day! A chair like this could be his. He leaped up at the sound of the study door opening and was seated back in his original chair before Sir Ralph had set foot in the sitting room.

'You're right, Kenny. He is going and the agent hasn't

got a tenant in view as yet.' He seated himself back in his chair. 'But what about money? I don't usually have anyone who can't provide references from their employer. Why should I make an exception for you?'

'I'm self-employed, Sir Ralph, sir.' A bit of deference never did anyone any harm and what's more it cost nothing. 'I can give three months' rent in advance if you prefer.'

'Self-employed doing what, might I ask?'

'Like we both said, this and that. But I'm on to a good thing at the moment and there's no likelihood of the market drying up. In fact I'm well pleased with how things are going.' He delved into his back pocket and hauled out the thick wad of notes, which looked not at all depleted by his gift of one hundred pounds to his mother. He loved the action of peeling notes off a wad with his thumb. So he did it rather slowly and dramatically but with a carelessness meant to signify it was all nothing to him. He'd reached the fifty-pound notes now, peeled off twelve of them and swaggered across to give them to Sir Ralph.

He shook his head. 'I haven't said yes yet and I don't touch the money. That's for my agent to deal with.'

Kenny could have kicked himself. Of course, Sir Ralph wouldn't be touching *money*, not he. The first he knew about it would be when it arrived in his bank statement. That was what being a gentleman was, if indeed he ever bothered to look at his bank statements. Kenny put his money away in his pocket and found himself apologising.

'Please don't apologise. Your gesture has reassured me that you do have money, for now. So, seeing as you're a village person born and bred, I'll let you rent it for six months. After that if you wish to stay longer, then you can, subject to how you have behaved yourself in the meantime. Is that agreeable?'

Kenny nodded.

'Nothing is confirmed until you've seen the agent, paid the first two months' rent, or more if you wish, and you've signed the contract.'

Remembering his new status as a businessman Kenny asked, 'If I pay for six months all at once do I get a discount?' The moment the words were out of his mouth he knew he shouldn't have asked. He realised by the look of disapproval on Sir Ralph's face that they had very nearly undone the whole arrangement.

Sir Ralph rose to his feet and said rather coldly, 'It is not negotiable. If you wish to proceed, then see the agent and get it signed and sealed. If not, someone else will. Rented accommodation hereabouts is hard to find.'

Kenny held out his hand. 'Thank you for approving of me. I shan't let you down. I was thinking . . .'

Sir Ralph shook his hand saying, 'Good afternoon, Kenny. My kindest regards to your mother.'

It was a dismissal, kindly done, but it was there. Kenny hurtled into Culworth and got it all signed and sealed, using a telephone call to Sir Ralph as his reference. He rushed home to his mother to tell her and to tell their Terry, who nearly collapsed when he heard. Terry's comment to Kenny was 'You shouldn't have.'

Ralph's comment to Muriel was 'I can't help feeling I've made the kind of decision I shall live to regret.'

'I saw him coming out of church this morning, so perhaps he's turned over a new leaf. You have to give him the benefit of the doubt.'

Kenny and Terry kept out of the Royal Oak that night to avoid any questions, for they knew, the village being what it was, that everyone would know by now and if they didn't they would before the night was out. But seated in their usual places were Jimmy, Sylvia, Willie and, unusually for her, Vera.

'Is this Kenny Jones we're talking about? The idle good-for-nothing womaniser we all know and love?' Sylvia asked.

'The very one, Sylvia.'

'Well, I never. Where's he suddenly got money from?'

'That's the question, isn't it? Where has he got it from?'

Vera chuckled. 'Maybe he's done someone a good turn and they've left him it in their will.'

'Good turn! He wouldn't know what a good turn was if it jumped up and bit 'im!'

The four of them roared with laughter.

Jimmy related a story he'd heard about Kenny and so too did Willie, and before long they'd agreed he'd paid his way into the cottage with dirty money but from what source they'd no idea.

Sylvia, having dried her eyes and pulled herself together, said, 'I'm amazed at Sir Ralph! Letting Kenny have a cottage. We all know his mother's waited on him hand and foot all his life and that he won't know where to start with anything domestic. The cottage will be a tip from day one. I reckon Sir Ralph's made a big mistake.'

'So do I. So do I.' Willie nodded his head in agreement. 'But yer never know, maybe it could be a turning-point for him. Out from under his mother's wing, fending for himself, it might do him good. It's not often Ralph makes a bad judgement where character's concerned.'

'They say their Terry's moving in too.'

Vera spluttered into her vodka. 'Terry! A right den of iniquity that'll be then. But with Vince having got the push, I expect they'll be glad to see the back of those two boys.'

'Either that or they can't take any more of her bossiness.'

Sylvia, seated alongside Vera on the settle, said, 'You know, Vera, this is nice having a drink with you, quite like old times. It seems ages since I saw you.'

'Is it? I've been so busy settling in I haven't had time to think.'

'You like it then?'

'Like it! I should say so. What a pleasure it is to go upstairs into that flat after work, all bright and airy!'

Willie asked her how many times she had to get up in the night to give a hand.

'I suppose it's about two nights a week on average. So it's not that bad. They've two nursing staff on, you see, so they only want me if they've several crises all at once. I change sheets, make tea, ring for the doctor, sit with the old dears when they've had a fright, go looking for them when they've gone missing, that kind of thing. Nothing medical, thank God!'

'So it's been worth it?' Jimmy wanted to reassure himself that she didn't regret it.

Vera nodded. 'Definitely.' She took a sip of her vodka and tonic and, almost casually, asked how was Don, had they seen him at all?

'Don't you worry about him, he's as happy as a sand-boy. He says. Don't quite believe it meself but there you are. He mentions you a lot, yer see.' Jimmy smiled at her.

'Don't grin at me.'

84

'I wasn't.'

'You were! It isn't funny. I never thought I'd finish up a single woman after all these years.'

Sylvia reminded her it was she who'd left him.

'I know that, but I thought he'd follow meek as a lamb and he didn't. Right called my bluff he did. But I was determined. I couldn't take any more of that house. The trouble is he can't see what I mean. He thinks it's lovely.'

Willie nodded wisely. 'It's a tip. Even I can see that. Mine was till I met Sylvia and I realised I couldn't ask her to visit me like it was, so I did it up.'

'Did you? Just for me?' Sylvia's face lit up at the thought of what he'd done for her sake. Her lovely grey eyes, which unbeknown to her were what had attracted Willie in the first place, brimmed with tears.

Willie squeezed her arm. 'Just for you.'

Sylvia stood up and leaned across the table to kiss his cheek. 'Thank you. I'd no idea.'

Vera watched this private moment between Sylvia and Willie and her heart almost burst. It was Don more than the house that she was sickened of. More loving consideration had passed between Willie and Sylvia in that moment than she'd experienced in years from Don, and she was envious. She looked up to see Don at the bar and his arrival at a moment when she had been made so vividly aware of his shortcomings put her in a steaming temper.

'Oh, no! Just look! The fool's come in. What does he want to come in for right now, spoiling everything when I'm enjoying myself?'

'Comes in a lot nowadays. He must be lonely.' Jimmy's wry grin did nothing to assuage Vera's temper.

Don spotted Jimmy's back view and, picking up his orange juice, drifted across. He stopped abruptly when he saw that the smartly dressed woman opposite Jimmy was Vera. In her new jacket and skirt he hadn't recognised her. And she'd had her hair cut shorter and made curly and she looked altogether more . . . well, sort of different, and she made him feel shabby. He hadn't changed his shirt all week because he couldn't be bothered to iron the ones he'd washed and he remembered he hadn't had a bath since . . . How could she put him in such a fix? Without any warning she turns up and . . .

Jimmy leaned over and pulled a chair across from the next table. 'Sit down, Don.'

'In the circumstances, I won't bother. Thanks.' He turned his back and, because all the other tables were occupied, went to perch uncomfortably on a bar stool, drank his juice as fast as he decently could, said good night and left.

Vera watched him depart and very briefly felt sorry for him, then remembered that pigsty of a kitchen; the only shining thing about it was the fridge-freezer which she'd got from the nursing home when they were throwing it out, and even that was speckled with pinpoints of rust. As for the rest, if they needed a kitchen for a museum it would qualify hands down. Victorian most likely, or even earlier. But worse she remembered his unattractiveness, his neglect of her, his disinterest, the boring life his inertia forced her to lead. No. She'd struck out for a better life and if he didn't want it, well, it was bad luck, Don. She was better off where she was and so long as she closed her mind to what she would do when they retired her, things were pretty good.

Chapter 7

Tom helped Kenny and Terry move. Not that there was a great deal apart from the exercise equipment Kenny had bought and never used. It took three car loads and a lot of heaving and pushing to achieve it, though. The beds came from a second-hand furniture store in Culworth, and their mother gave them two easy chairs she was glad to see the back of, and the dining table and chairs she'd appropriated via Vera from the nursing home.

Just before he went to bed that first night Kenny stood in the little kitchen drinking his nightly tot from a mug and thought, this is only the beginning. From now on Kenny Jones is on the up. He'd had nothing to buy in the kitchen because it came fully fitted and looked really good. He wandered into the sitting room and his heart sank. There was no two ways about it, he'd have to graft to get this looking anything right. He recollected the feel of Sir Ralph's leather armchair and yearned for it. His envy set him on a path from which he determined there would be no turning back until he'd achieved his objectives.

Being new to housekeeping he went round securing windows, locking doors with almost religious fervour and then meandered up to bed. Pity about his dad losing his job; at least with the two of them out of the way they'd manage better, and he'd see them right, his mum had no need to worry, even if he gave them money just to show how successfully his new business career was progressing. They'd be proud of him from now on. He'd no idea where their Terry was at the moment, but he guessed it was the barmaid at the Jug and Bottle who'd enticed him away tonight. From now on Kenny Jones was aiming higher than her. She no longer suited his lifestyle. Quality was his watchword from now on: there'd be no more scuttling about in the gutters with tarts and fleabags, oh, no!

Tom, climbing into bed beside Evie that night, said, 'They've no furniture to speak of and no stuff like pans and dishes and such. Just a mug and a cereal bowl each they've borrowed from their mother.' He put an arm round Evie's thin waist. 'Like it here, do you, Evie? I do. Like as if I've come home, and this job as verger, it's given us respectability. Lovely that. We've been accepted. Haven't you noticed people's attitude is different now? We've arrived as you might say. They do say it takes fifty years to become a true villager here but, well, I reckon as far as Tom and Evie are concerned we've reduced that to three!'

He gave her a squeeze. 'All those years of worry, all finished with.' He nuzzled her with his chin. 'Orchid House. I'm glad we chose that name. Better than Lilac Cottage or Chez Nous. Orchid House. Has a ring to it. And we do, grow orchids I mean. So it's genuine. Honeysuckle growing round the door. Like a picture book. Always dreamed of a house with honeysuckle round the door. There isn't a house in Turnham Malpas with such style as ours. Long may it remain so. Buying all Sadie Beauchamp's furniture did the trick. We'd never have made it like this, would we, buying the stuff ourselves? We don't come from the right background, you see, you and me, to know what to buy. It takes class to furnish a place like this is furnished.'

He took his arm from Evie's waist and lay on his back. In the light of the full moon creeping round the edges of the curtains he surveyed the bedroom and remembered other rooms he'd slept in, and he decided that here in Turnham Malpas, in this room in his dream home, he felt the safest, most secure and happiest he'd ever been for many a year. Yes. Here was pure heaven.

'Shall we start doing a bit of entertaining? Ask people round, casual-like for a meal. Let's see. I know, we can start with Sheila and Ronald. What about it? Eh? What do you say? They're our kind. Cut our teeth a bit with someone we feel happy with. Ask them for Friday night, Evie. Just knock and ask. If they say, "No," well, OK, it's not the end of the world. Who else could we ask? I know: Vince Jones and his missus. They're our kind. But we'll start with Sheila and Ron. Sir Ronald and Lady Bissett, oh, yes! I'll look forward to that. Something special to eat. Yes, that's what we'll do. You do the food, I'll see to the drinks. We'll show 'em!'

Tom rolled on his side and put his arm round Evie again, kissed her earlobe, pulled the duvet up around her shoulders seeing as the night was chilly, and fell asleep. But in the small hours of the night he woke sweating and fearful. Kenny! Oh, God! Kenny. Kenny was his only threat.

★

'Come in, come in! Let me take your jacket, Sheila. You don't mind if I call you Sheila, do you? Good evening, Ron.' They shook hands even though they'd seen each other only that morning, because Tom couldn't kiss Ron's cheek as he had Sheila's and other than that he was at a loss to know how to greet him.

Ron handed over a bottle of wine. 'Thought it might be useful. I know a little man in London, you see, and he always makes sure I buy only the best.'

'London! My word! We are privileged! Do come in. Evie's busy in the kitchen, she won't be a moment. Come in, sit yourselves down.'

Sheila took a brisk look around the sitting room. Just as she'd thought, they'd bought Sadie's furniture and pictures and done nothing at all to imprint their own taste on the house since they'd moved in. Oh, well! She would have liked the odd little touch which said, 'This is mine and this is how I like it.' She seated herself carefully, hoping not to crease her skirt. This suit was an absolute pest for creasing. She'd worn it to a dinner with Ron and when she got home she'd realised she must have looked a perfect ragbag all evening. Ron was looking quite handsome tonight. His dark lounge suit, with that tie with the hot air balloons on it that added just the right touch of colour, made him look debonair. She looked at Tom and decided he'd gone a bit over the top with his smart country suit like Sir Ralph wore sometimes but not a quarter the quality of his, oh, no! You couldn't fool Sheila Bissett where clothes were concerned.

'Thank you, Tom.' The sherry was just how she liked it. Sweet and cloying and restorative. What she was waiting for was a sight of Evie. Evie the silent. Evie the elusive. Evie the shadow.

'Can I give Evie a hand in the kitchen at all?'

'That's very kind but she's happier coping on her own.'

'I had hoped Evie would join the village Flower Club. Is she a flower person?' Privately Sheila thought Evie wasn't a person at all.

'No, not really. Embroidery, yes. But not flowers.'

'Embroidery! Oh, my word. I wonder if we could start an embroidery class. Culworth is such a long way to go for things like that. A class here in the village would be excellent. I'll ask her.'

'I don't think . . .'

At this moment Evie came in carrying two dishes of nibbles. Sheila often categorised people by naming the animal most akin to their personality. Evie was definitely a little dormouse. Or could it be she was more like a shrew? No, a dormouse: she hadn't got it in her to be a shrew.

At a signal from Sheila, Ron, reminded of his manners, stood up to greet her. He'd intended giving her a kiss like Tom had Sheila but Evie shrank away and he ended up with empty arms, kissing the air.

Evie placed the two dishes of nibbles on the coffee table beside Sheila, then with a nod at Tom, she scuttled out. He apologised and darted after her.

They were left to themselves for such a long time that Sheila began to wonder if she should alert the rescue services. She and Ron tried to make conversation but it was difficult as all Sheila wanted to talk about was their hosts and to question whether or not Evie would ever be heard to speak. She'd known right from the start when Tom first knocked on their door to invite them that they should have trumped up an excuse, but taken unawares they hadn't thought fast enough.

Tom reappeared. 'Right, we're ready. Do come through.'

Sheila noted that the dinner service was a popular line in Boots kitchen departments, but even her sharp tongue couldn't fault the laying of the table, nor the presentation of the starter: pâté with small green bits of salad, a thin quarter of tomato on top and tiny triangular pieces of toast. Very tasteful.

Tom and Ron talked trade-union affairs almost continuously and left Evie and Sheila to make the best of it. Sheila began by saying she'd heard Evie was an embroiderer. Evie nodded.

'I was wondering if you might be able to start an embroidery class in the village? Although we're all busy people a class like that would create a lot of interest.'

Evie looked up startled, as though confronted by a large and threatening cat. After a pause she answered, 'I could.' Sheila was surprised by Evie's voice. For such a small, quiet person it was amazingly deep and strong.

'Really? Would you? That would be wonderful! Have you got some embroidery I could see? Just to look at.'

'Yes.'

'After we've eaten then?'

Evie nodded.

When Evie took her into the study which had been converted into a workroom Sheila was astounded. She'd been expecting only mediocre talent or even none at all and perhaps having desperately to wriggle out of her idea about the embroidery class. But no such thing. The walls were hung almost from floor to ceiling with embroidery. Well, was it embroidery? Sheila asked herself. Evie had used lots of fabrics to make the pictures, sewn it down with embroidery stitches and in some places padded it for extra effect. Some framed, some used as simple wall hangings but each and every one an outstanding example of the craft. The colours she'd used almost made Sheila's head spin. They were strong and vibrant but so subtly chosen that they didn't clash at all.

'Why, Evie, they're wonderful! Such skill. You're an artist. This one, and this one, and *this one*! They're wonderful. Quite wonderful! Did you design them all?'

Evie shook her head. 'That's a copy, and so's that.' She pointed to two wall hangings, which appeared to Sheila to be medieval originals. 'The rest are my design.' She stood hands clasped in front of her with no emotion showing on her face.

Sheila, stunned by the sheer beauty of the work, said, 'Why have you never let on about all this?'

Evie shrugged her shoulders.

There was a large, square, floor-standing antique embroidery frame to one side with a white cotton cover over it. Sheila pointed to it and said, 'May I?'

Evie nodded. Two-thirds finished, it was a religious collage depicting the Nativity. The glorious choice of fabrics, glowing and almost sparkling in the intensity of their colour, was stunning. The robes of the Three Kings were superb, their crowns and their gifts padded underneath to make them stand out, and with gold thread embellishing them. Yet the rough simplicity of the manger and the animals, and the dryness of the spiky hay so cleverly depicted and the tiny mouse going about its own affairs were captured quite beautifully. And Mary, so cool, so still, dressed in a soft pale blue gown, which might have been overshadowed by the richness of the colours about her, but which actually drew the eye as much and more as the vivid colours did. Joseph, still to be finished, was already looking homespun and earthy.

'What's this for?'

'Church.'

'Our church?'

Evie nodded.

'When the Rector sees this he'll be amazed. Absolutely amazed. Such talent, Evie.' Sheila patted Evie's arm. 'Talk about hiding your light under a bushel. I've never seen anything so beautiful. How do you do it?'

Evie simply smiled, pulled the cover over the frame and invited Sheila to return to the sitting room, to join the two men.

She'd enthused to Ron and Tom before they'd decided to started to play a game of cards but that was nothing to her enthusiasm when they got home.

'How can such a mousy person produce work like that? If it was in an exhibition up in London it wouldn't go amiss. It is sensational! I wish you'd seen it, Ron, I was speechless with admiration. All that from a . . . well, let's face it, she's as mad as a hatter, isn't she? Hardly a word for the cat. Not exactly someone you'd choose as a dinner guest. I wonder if she'd do something for me? I've that space in the hall between the kitchen door and the cloaks, wouldn't have to be too big or it wouldn't fit, and the colours would have to be just right, I wouldn't want it to clash. I'll ask her. But what a triumph for us if I can persuade her to do a class.'

Riffling through her handbag looking for her reading glasses, Sheila clicked her tongue in annoyance. 'Drat it, I've left my reading glasses in the chair where I sat. It's too late to go knocking now! I'll go back tomorrow to get them and make it a chance to thank them again for a nice evening. And such good card players too!' The doorbell rang. 'Oh, that must be Tom bringing them for me, how kind of him. Such a very nice man, so thoughtful. You go answer the door while I put the kettle on.'

From the kitchen she listened to Ron answering the door, and hoped he'd demonstrate real gratitude to Tom; sometimes he could be so off-hand. She heard the door bang shut, then heard Ron grunt, and after that a thud as though something heavy had crashed to the carpet, breaking by the sound of it her entire collection of delicate glass ornaments that had taken so long to get together.

'What on earth –!'

But by then two men, with black balaclavas over their faces and evil menacing eyes peering through the slits, were in the kitchen wielding their coshes on her and she went down, the kettle bouncing across the rush matting, spewing its contents as it went. Before she fell unconscious under their repeated blows Sheila squinted a floor-level view of black trainers and, mysteriously, drops of blood spraying across the floor close to her eyes.

Well, there was one thing for certain, Muriel declared to herself after a whole hour of tortuous struggling, she was going across to ask Sheila Bissett to give her a hand: if anyone could put things right it would be Sheila. She pushed back her hair from her face, pulled out her handkerchief from her skirt pocket and dabbed her forehead and top lip. It really was all too much and she'd never ever attempt this again.

All this angst had come about because Muriel had volunteered to arrange the church flowers for the weekend. A series of unusual coincidences had brought the situation about and here she was deputising for an official flower arranger and wishing to heaven she wasn't. The greenery was limp and wouldn't hang right, the oasis kept crumbling, and the tape holding it in place was not doing a proper job of it at all. Now she couldn't push in the stems of the flowers, and whoever had chosen roses that had no intention of standing straight? Muriel stood back to assess her arrangement and could have wept. A child of seven could have done better.

Leaving everything as it was Muriel stepped as quickly as she could across the Green towards Sheila's house, hoping against hope that though it was Saturday they would be in, and she'd get Sheila to help her. Muriel never got on very well with Sheila, but give her her due, where flowers were concerned . . . She knocked lightly on the door. Rather apologetically she knocked again and then to her surprise found that the door appeared to be knocking back at her. How odd! Low down, there it was again. How peculiar. Maybe it was Sheila's new cat playing games. But then she thought she heard a quiet groan.

Muriel lifted the latch and tried the door; she could open it a few inches but then no more. Cautiously putting her arm at shoulder level through the gap she had made she could feel nothing, so she went lower still waving her hand about in the hope of coming into contact with something. Then, low down close to the floor, she did. Exploring but not able to see what she explored, she felt around and came to the conclusion she was actually feeling someone's knee. Embarrassed, she stopped, retrieved her arm and knelt there wondering what on earth to do next.

She stood up, dusted off her knees and gave the door a heave. Something gave way and it opened a few more inches. Muriel, being slim, pressed her way through the enlarged gap. There at her feet lay Ronald Bissett, curled up like a baby. Muriel stuffed her knuckles into her mouth to stop herself screaming. He looked horrific. His head and face were bloody, swollen and so badly bruised he was barely recognisable, and his suit and shirt looked as though someone had stood on him in dirty shoes. Great splashes of blood had sprayed across his shirt front in a wild psychedelic pattern. Beside him his glasses had been ground into the carpet, and his bloody hands were in a claw-like grip grasping the fringe of the hall rug.

Ron groaned.

'Oh, Ron! Whatever's happened? Where's Sheila?'

But she got no reply. Fearing what she might find, Muriel tiptoed around the ground floor in search of Sheila. She tried the sitting room first, then the dining room and all that was left was the kitchen so she pushed open the door and found her. Surely no one could take a beating like that and not be dead? She must be. There was blood all over the place, up the cupboard doors, on the dishwasher, even as high up as the worktops. In fear and trepidation, for she'd never before touched a person she thought might be dead,

Muriel stepped over the kettle to put her hand to Sheila's ghastly bruised and battered neck and found, she thought, a slight pulse. Oh, Sheila! Oh, Sheila! An ambulance! With hands scarcely able to hold the receiver she tremblingly dialled nine nine nine on the kitchen telephone, but there was no life in it at all. Glancing at her hand still furiously tapping the number nine button Muriel saw it was red with blood. Sheila's blood, thick and dark and congealed. Oh, God! Oh! God!

Ralph! No, he wasn't at home.

Peter! Neither was he.

Jimbo! Of course!

The door stood wide open so Muriel was in the centre of the Store without any warning at all, distraught, hands and dress streaked with blood shouting as loud as she could, 'Police! Quick! Ambulance! Dear God!'

Silence fell. Everyone there was transfixed at the sight of this terrible apparition. What on earth was she talking about? What on earth had she done?

The first to gather his wits was Jimbo. 'Muriel! Muriel!' He put an arm around her shoulders and asked, 'Who for? Who do you want the ambulance for?'

'Sheila and Ron.' Bel just managed to get a chair under her as she collapsed.

'Nine, nine, nine, Linda. Quick.'

Bel grabbed a bag of frozen peas she'd just sold to a customer and put it to Muriel's forehead, hoping it might calm her down and stop her fainting.

Tom raced out and headed for Orchard House as fast as he could.

Linda said,' 'Are they murdered, do you think?' and promptly fainted.

The two Senior sisters began chanting like a pair of demented nuns. 'Oh, God! Oh, God! Oh, God!'

The two Charter-Plackett boys, Fergus and Finlay, having been commandeered for shelf-filling that morning, ran out after Tom. Within seconds they were back ashen-faced and Finlay had to rush back out again to be furiously sick in the grating outside.

'Dad! You should see. It's terrible,' Fergus shouted. 'Just terrible. I don't think they'll live.'

At this the remainder of Jimbo's customers squeezed out of the door and ran round to Orchard House, leaving Bel to get a glass of water for Muriel and one for Linda. Jimbo, still holding Muriel, muttered dark threats about coming to the village for peace and security for the children and then this happening, but he reproved himself when he recollected that Ron and Sheila were probably at death's door.

It was on the regional TV news that night and in the papers the following morning. Trade-union leaders, eager for the exposure the media would give them, spoke grimly of this atrocious crime, of in what high esteem this elder of their movement was held, how shocking and apparently motive-less it was. Potted histories of Ron's career appeared, hastily pulled together by journalists taken by surprise.

In the village the reaction to it was more sincere. For those who'd lived alongside them these last years this wasn't just a ten-day wonder to fill the newsreels and the papers in the dying days of a newsless August. In the Store Jimbo did a brisk trade in newspapers, having to double his order of some to satisfy demand. In the Royal Oak Georgie, Dicky and Alan worked like slaves to keep up with the meals and drinks all the journalists and sightseers demanded. At night the village was as quiet as the grave. The nonchalant attitude most of its inhabitants had had about locking their doors was tossed to the wind and every door and window was locked and checked both day and night.

But for heaven's sake why? Sheila and Ron had never done anything to deserve such a vicious attack. Mild, innocent lives they'd led. Mind you, Sheila couldn't half be provoking and verging on abandoned with her outspoken comments, as most of them knew to their cost, but to deserve such a beating? No. This was some outside job, but what was the motive?

Louise had searched through the house but found nothing of her parents' possessions missing, so far as she could tell. Agreed there'd been a bit of vague throwing about of drawer contents to make it look like a burglary but it was obvious that murder had been the intention or at the very least a serious warning.

Sheila was the first to speak. Muriel and Ralph were visiting the two of them in the hospital and talking to her about the village. 'So you see, Sheila,' Muriel said, 'we're having the meeting tonight to mobilise everyone. We can't let Mr Fitch ride roughshod over us all, can we? I'm just sorry you can't be there. But I'll let you know what goes on. We have to move quickly, you know, or else. You've not to worry about anything though, just you get well. All the things you are responsible for are being attended to. All you've got to do is get better. Grandmama Charter-Plackett has taken over the Flower Club,' at this Sheila stirred, 'just temporarily, of course, and she's going to oversee the Harvest Festival for you, so there's no need to worry about that. She's . . .'

Sheila's mouth opened and she whispered hoarsely and almost unintelligibly, 'She'd better not 'ave.' Her false teeth having been removed Sheila appeared to Muriel to be extraordinarily vulnerable, and she felt more moved by the intimate glimpse she'd had of her helplessness than she was by her injuries. Ralph had to chuckle: apparently just the mention of her old adversary taking over had penetrated her unconscious mind and stirred her into a reaction.

Chapter 8

Muriel and Caroline had been tempted to book the small committee room for their protest meeting but as an act of faith had chosen to book the hall. 'We shall look foolish, Muriel, if there's only a handful there – they'll be lost in the big hall – but we've got to think big. Tom's putting out twenty chairs and having the others ready as and when. Shall you want to speak?'

Muriel shook her head. 'Only a small speech in support of you. I get so nervous.'

'Very well. We'll have coffee afterwards then you and I can circulate. I've rung up quite a few people and they've promised to come.'

'Caroline, are we doing the right thing, do you think?'

Caroline looked surprised. 'Of course we are. Are you getting cold feet?'

'I always do. It is his hedge, you see, just like our garden is ours. It's just that his is bigger.'

'I know, but he has responsibilities to the land. After all, it is his in trust during his lifetime, in the end the land belongs to itself. He's simply privileged to look after it for a while.'

'I hadn't seen it like that, but of course you're right.'

'See you tonight then. Sylvia's sitting in for me and she's coming round at seven so I'll be there in good time.'

'Peter not back yet?'

'No.' Caroline turned away saying, 'See you tonight,' and leaving before Muriel could ask another question.

When Muriel walked into the hall at five minutes past seven she was surprised to find it a hive of activity. Posters were up round the walls, a leaflet on every chair, and six of the chairs were already occupied.

They all turned to look at her. Arthur and Celia Prior were there, two of the weekenders, Miss Pascoe from the school, and Georgie from the Royal Oak.

'Good evening! So good of you all to come.'

Arthur, Ralph's so-called cousin, stood up. 'Good evening, Muriel. Celia and me, we've come to give you our full support. Someone's got to put a stop to him and I for one am willing to stand up and be counted.'

'Thank you, Arthur, Celia. I do appreciate that.'

Georgie patted the chair beside her, 'Do sit with me, Lady Templeton.'

'I'm supposed to be sitting at the front with Caroline, thank you, Georgie. I've a speech to make.'

One of the weekenders called out, 'We're right behind you. The man's a monster. We can't let him get away with it.' He clenched his fist and raised it in the air. 'Down with Fitch, I say!'

Gently Muriel reminded him, 'It's not Mr Fitch himself but rather what he's doing that we're protesting about.'

'Same thing in my book. We haven't bought a house here in this lovely village to have it spoiled by a man with no understanding of what the countryside is all about. I and my wife have taken time off work to stay on specially to attend this meeting and, please, count us in with any protest you intend to make.'

'There are people who think he should be allowed to dig it up, you know.'

'Are there indeed! Just show them to me and I'll give them a piece of my mind!' He laughed loudly and nudged his wife, who almost toppled off her chair. 'Sorry, pet, but I'm so incensed.'

At this point Grandmama Charter-Plackett came in. Muriel thought she heard a slight booing sound but sincerely hoped she hadn't.

Grandmama went to sit on the front row, ignoring the murmur of protest, calmly placed her bag beside her and folded her arms. 'Good evening, Muriel!'

'Good evening, Katherine.'

'Is Mr Fitch coming?'

'He has had a leaflet but not a personal invitation.'

'And what about the council? Anyone from there daring to face the flack?'

'Those concerned have been invited but they have not replied.'

'I shall be the only one then?'

'Only one?'

'The only one on Mr Fitch's side.'

Muriel's heart quailed at the prospect of answering her, but that dear little wren needed her support. 'We'll have to wait and see.'

'Hmmmph.'

The hall was beginning to fill and Tom had to find more chairs. Caroline was already there, standing behind the table on which she had placed her notes. Muriel, whilst highly delighted at the interest their meeting had attracted, shook with nerves as she took her place beside Caroline. Why on earth had she said she would spearhead a protest they hadn't a hope of winning? Ralph smiled at her from his seat at the back and she gathered courage. There must be forty people at least already and there were bound to be latecomers. At seven thirty prompt Caroline tapped the end of her pen on the table and brought the meeting to order.

'Good evening, everyone. First I should like to say how pleased and impressed Muriel and I are to see so much interest in this protest of ours. Obviously it isn't just Muriel and I who have taken this threat to our village to heart, apparently you all have too. I shall begin by . . .'

Muriel listened to Caroline's well-reasoned argument and felt proud to be associated with her. Observing the reactions of the crowd she noticed that most kept nodding their heads in agreement and at one stage some shouted, 'Hear, hear!' or clapped their hands in approval.

Then suddenly it was her turn and Muriel, knees knocking, stood up as the applause for Caroline faded.

'I'm a country woman at heart though not a very knowledgeable one. But what I do know is that we have to fight to preserve our countryside. It simply will not do for us to stand by and bow to the destruction of it. I have been to the county records office and I have seen with my own eyes ancient maps and there, as large as life, is that hedgerow, already well established by the seventeenth century. Living in that hedgerow are dozens of wild creatures and wild flowers and plants which must not be left homeless.'

Muriel picked up her notes. 'There are holly, yew, hazel, wild rose, dogwood, blackthorn and ash as well as flowers such as wild violets, to say nothing of birds and small mammals which rely upon it for food and for bringing up their young. So determined am I to stop the destruction of this hedgerow that I am prepared to stand in front of any tractor, any digger, any tree-destroying equipment, at the risk of my *life*, to stop this happening. If it comes to it, how many of you will join me?'

Her challenge was greeted by cheers and the noisy weekender stood up and called out, 'Me for one! I'll be right beside you, shoulder to shoulder!' He faced the crowd eyeball to eyeball. 'Well?'

'And me!'

'And me!'

In the midst of the excitement the door opened and in came Mr Fitch. The proverbial pin could have been dropped and everyone would have heard it. The whole room froze into silence.

Mr Fitch paused for a moment and then marched between the chairs towards the table. He stopped in front of it and faced the meeting. 'Permission to speak, Madam Chairman.'

Muriel couldn't answer him, but Caroline could. 'Of course, it's a public meeting.'

He glared at each and every one sitting in front of him. 'In all the years I have lived in this village I have bowed to your wishes. Because of your opposition I have stood down from being chairman of the cricket club whose pavilion and equipment *I* financed, I have paid for the church bells to be rehung, I have paid for the church central heating, I have set up an educational trust to help talented children and young people, I have underwritten the Village Show, the like of which has never been seen in this county before, and I have hosted the Bonfire Night party. I employ nineteen workers of one kind and another from this village and the surrounding ones, and I am always a soft touch when it comes to donating to charitable causes. Now this time I want my own way. A simple thing, the replacing of a hedge by a stout wooden fence. That is all. I have come simply to inform you of my intentions. I *will* remove the hedge and I *will*, despite your opposition, erect a fence.'

Mr Fitch turned on his heel and left the hall.

The silence, which had fallen when he arrived, was nothing compared to the deep silence he left behind him. Muriel felt ashamed. Caroline questioned her own motives. Grandmama Charter-Plackett smiled smugly. Ralph looked grim and an awful lot of them were embarrassed.

'He is right, he has done a lot for us. We'd miss him in more ways than one if he sold up.'

'He's paid half our Lynn's ballet-school fees. We'd never have been able to let her go if he hadn't.'

'Look at that time when he . . .'

'And when he paid . . .'

'We owe him a lot.'

'Perhaps we shouldn't oppose him. After all it is his hedge, isn't it?'

Muriel, realising that in another minute her cause would be totally lost, was about to stand up to implore them to back her and Caroline, when the door opened again. Who was it this time? Not Mr Fitch come back?

Heads turned to see. 'Why! It's the Rector!'

'Hello, sir, glad you're back.'

'Just the person we need.'

'The man for the moment.'

Muriel sneaked a look at Caroline. Her eyes were fixed on Peter. He was wearing that royal blue pullover which picked up the colour of his eyes and emphasised his blond good looks in a way no other colour could. His jeans hung on him a little, but otherwise he looked the same except that the peace and joy which normally emanated from him was missing. Finally, after a long stare, Caroline smiled at him and he smiled at her.

Muriel said quietly, 'Glad you've come. We do need your help.'

Ralph stood up and gave Peter a brief résumé of what had taken place. 'So we have stalemate. We're all well aware of what he has done for this village but at the same time . . .'

'One thing we have to be careful of is to be sure we're not objecting simply because it's Mr Fitch being high-handed again. There must be some legal way of stopping him. Have we investigated that?' He put the question to Caroline directly.

Taken so completely off-guard by his sudden appearance Caroline stammered, 'W-w-we've been advised that the – council can't stop him.'

'Officially?'

'Not in writing.'

'That's what we need then. Cannot Neville Neal advise us?'

Muriel told him of her conversation with him. 'So we assumed we'd drawn a blank.'

'I think there must be something somewhere we can use. But first I shall go visit Mr Fitch myself. Tomorrow. First thing. If I might suggest, seeing as you are all obviously very much concerned about this matter, that you leave your names and addresses before you go so that you can be contacted and told of future developments?'

Muriel clapped her hands when she realised that the fight might not be ended. 'What a good idea! Of course. How splendid.'

Hastily she found clean pages in her notebook and laid it out on the table alongside her pen. 'Here we are! Here we are!'

Grandmama, who'd felt herself to be on the winning side for a moment, forbore to add her name to the list and strode towards the door, distinctly put out by the turn of events.

Peter went to sit down at the back of the hall and wait for the meeting to close. By the time Caroline had had a word with people, collected her papers, thanked Tom for getting the hall ready for them and for locking up, and coped with her emotions at Peter's unexpected reappearance, she was exhausted.

It was Peter's key in the lock, Peter who thanked Sylvia for babysitting, Peter who made a hot drink for them both and Peter who carried it into the sitting room. He placed the tray on the coffee table and handed Caroline her mug.

'Thank you. You're back then?' She looked up at him as she spoke, not knowing whether she should be glad or not.

'I am. This problem of the hedge. I certainly don't want it

uprooting. It's a delightful sight and precious too. I'm glad you've decided to do something about it.'

'I was incensed when I found out.' She explained about Ralph's party and how furious Grandmama Charter-Plackett had made her.

Peter, having listened attentively to her explanation, said, 'As one of his tenants she has a lot to lose if she opposes him and so have a lot of other people in this village – Jimbo with his catering contract, which I understand is a sizeable percentage of his turnover, and all Mr Fitch's employees. It will be very difficult for them to come out in protest, especially workers like Barry Jones and Greenwood Stubbs so soon after their last scare about losing their jobs.'

'I hadn't quite seen it like that. Harriet didn't come and I thought perhaps she might.'

'Like I said, many will have divided loyalties. That's why I think it might be best to approach it from the legal direction. I'm amazed –'

'Peter! Have done!'

He put down his mug and looked at her. 'Have done?'

'Have done! Where have you been? I daren't tell anyone that you'd disappeared off the face of the earth. If they asked where you were I said you were taking a holiday. You appear without warning and wonder why I'm ... *hurting* like I am. I need an explanation.'

'I've been walking in the Dales and I've come back because the Bishop will shortly be making enquiries as to my whereabouts and so ...' he looked down at his hands '... but I needed to be back anyway. Couldn't manage, you see, without seeing you.' He looked up and smiled apologetically.

Caroline got up, walked across to him and knelt in front of him, a hand on his knee. 'I have wept bitter tears for what I've done to you. Bitter tears. A thousand years of saying sorry won't be enough.'

'Darling!'

'Hush! Let me finish. I know now that given a little more time the old Caroline you once knew will be back. Can you wait for her?

'I can. I'm sorry to have left you like I did, but I couldn't cope any longer.'

'You'd every right, I behaved abominably. I must have been out of my head. In fact today I am positively cringing about what happened. When I went to church the morning Hugo left and I saw the love and the compassion you were offering me in front of everyone . . .' Caroline shook her head. 'It was only because I had died inside that I couldn't accept it, and it's only everyone else's love for you which has saved my bacon over this.'

'They love you too.'

'Only because I stand in your shadow.'

'Leaving you was selfish, I thought only of myself and my own pain.'

'Not before time. Everyone needs to put themselves first some time or other in their lives.'

Very tentatively he stretched out his hand to touch her hair. He fingered the soft dark curls above her forehead, trailed the back of his finger along her jawline, traced the outline of her mouth; his finger excessively gentle.

'Whatever happens, you are the great love of my life and always will be. I've read somewhere the line "you are the beat of my heart" and you are, just that. I've pined for your touch.'

Caroline pushed his knees wider so she could kneel between them and get closer to him. 'Pine no more.'

They put their arms around each other and held each other close, not speaking. The simple humane gesture of hugging each other made them both feel cherished, and it comforted and nourished each of them more than words could ever have done.

After a time Caroline said, 'It'll be a while before things are as they were before, but we'll get there, I know that now, given time.' She sat back on her heels and asked, 'You love me still despite everything?'

'Of course.'

'And you're on my side about this hedge business?'

'Of course.'

'God bless you then. Welcome home. Had the children gone to bed when you got back?'

'No. I saw them both.'

Caroline placed a hand on his cheek. 'They have missed you.'

'Have you?'

'Now you're here I realise I have. But, like I said, it's going to be a while before I get my life with you completely sorted out, you understand what I'm saying?' Very tenderly Caroline saluted him by kissing his mouth, then in a business-like tone said, 'However, first things first. This campaign . . .'

First thing the next morning Peter went up to the Big House and insisted upon seeing Mr Fitch. He held up his hand when the receptionist said he was too busy saying, 'I insist. It's important.'

'Very well, Rector. I'll go plead your case.' Succumbing as always to his masculinity she twinkled her fingers at him and disappeared into Mr Fitch's study returning in a moment saying, 'He'll see you now.'

Peter towered above Mr Fitch but in no way at all did it intimidate the man. They shook hands and Peter seated himself in a chair.

'Good morning, Rector, nice to have you back with us again. Had a good holiday? Good. Good. What can I do for you?'

'I came home last night to find Caroline was at a protest meeting. I understand you had left just before I arrived so you don't need me to tell you what it was about.'

Mr Fitch nodded. 'I know. So they've sent you to persuade me otherwise, have they?'

'No one sends me anywhere I don't want to go.' Peter left a silence.

Mr Fitch tolerated it with an amused smile on his face until eventually it was he who gave in. 'One of your well-known silences won't trick me into giving in. I'm not one of your parishioners.'

'Oh, but you are, Craddock. You live here and if you never darken the door of my church you are still in my care. Like it or not you are.'

Mr Fitch shuffled in his chair and settled himself more comfortably. 'So?'

'As it is obviously a commercial decision, what is there in it for you pulling down this hedge?'

Peter knew instantly from the momentary startled look in Mr Fitch's eyes that he'd hit the nail on the head.

'What possible commercial benefit could I get from pulling down a hedge which is good to neither man nor beast and for which I can't find anyone with the skill to attend to it as it should be attended to? It's fast becoming an eyesore and it needs dealing with.'

'You tell me.' Peter waited and so too did Mr Fitch.

Eventually Mr Fitch said, 'All at my expense, please note. I did intend putting the fence a little further into Rector's Meadow so that your access to the garages would be wider and it would make life easier. Of course, the fact that I am losing two or three feet of my own land is nothing in anyone's eyes I expect.'

'We like it as it is. That end of Pipe and Nook is perfectly adequate for our needs. We enjoy the cut and thrust of squeezing our cars past if someone else is in the lane.'

Mr Fitch shrugged his shoulders. 'Stuff and nonsense.'

'So, I can't change your mind. Not even if I find someone who could tackle the hedge and put it to rights?'

'No. I'm sticking to my guns on this one.' But he couldn't meet Peter's eye and Peter guessed he was getting too close for comfort to Mr Fitch's real reasons.

A wider lane, better access, what did that add up to? For the moment he couldn't answer his own question so Peter decided to fire his broadside and leave. He stood up and leaned his hands on the desk. 'Please think again. There are more things in life than money; qualities like love and affection and admiration and loyalty. The village is intensely loyal as I have found in the past, isn't that worth something to you? It is to me. Ask yourself what your relationship with them really is right now.' He didn't get an answer. 'I can tell you if you don't know. They will take with both hands anything you offer, they'll thank you and then go home and mock at your generosity, simply because they don't care a fig for the man who is doing the giving. Wouldn't it be immensely worthwhile to have their enduring affection and admiration?'

Peter shut the door behind him as quietly as he could.

Chapter 9

Since the attack on Ron and Sheila the whole village had appeared to be swarming with police officers, some in uniform, most in plain clothes. Men in white overalls had trawled through Orchid House testing for this, and testing for that, and an interested group of spectators appeared to have taken root around the front door curious to find out what on earth they could be doing all this time.

'Them in white overalls 'ave been through it three times now. I reckon they suspect something serious.'

'Couldn't be more serious, could it, with Sheila and Ron nearly killed?'

'One thing for certain they won't find any dust. Sheila, bless 'er, might have her faults, but dust isn't one of 'em.'

'All right you saying "bless 'er", that wasn't what you said that time when she put the flower arrangement you'd done for the festival right at the back and no one couldn't see it.'

'Well, I know, but she 'ad a cheek, 'adn't she?'

'Comes to mind you called 'er something disgusting.'

'You would have to bring that up right now, wouldn't

you? Just show some respect.' A large car pulled up and out of it stepped the well-dressed man who'd been interviewing everyone since the first day.

To the assembled crowd he said, 'Excuse me! There's nothing to see, I think it might be best to move on.' He went into the house without waiting to see if they did what he asked.

'That's Detective Superintendent Proctor from Culworth CID. Our Kev says . . .'

Someone raised their eyes to the sky and said scathingly, 'As if we didn't know. He's practically lived here since the attack.'

'That's 'im what came when the Baxter sister kidnapped poor little Flick, isn't it? Remember? 'Ccpt hc was Inspector then. I don't think he's got anyone left he could interview. Course, he could always start questioning Sheila's cat if he's short of clues. Just think what Topsy could tell if she could talk.'

'Where is her cat, by the way?'

'At the Rectory. Dr Harris took her in. They aren't half taking it seriously, yer know. After all, it was only a burglary that went wrong, not like it was a gangland revenge for something. I mean, Sheila and Ron aren't those kind of people, are they? Come on.'

'I 'ave 'eard a rumour that they're thinking of opening up the police house and us 'aving our own constable again.'

'Really? Well, not before time. That Kenny Jones and their Terry need a policeman all of their own.' She nudged her companion and winked significantly.

They drew closer together. 'What d'yer mean?'

'You know my Amanda? Well, she goes clubbing up in

town – them in Culworth think they've got brilliant clubs but she says they're nothing to the ones she goes to – and she's seen the two of 'em these last few weeks hanging about, two and three o'clock in the morning.'

'No! That's where . . .' She thrust out her chest and, hand on hip, imitated a provocative walk. 'Isn't it?'

'Exactly, and they have had a lot of money just lately, haven't they? Renting the cottage and that and buying furniture. So are they pimps or what?'

'A bit of stealing's all well and good, but pimping! 'Ow low can yer sink?'

'Might as well be off, there's nothing going on 'ere. We've run out of Ovaltine and our Amanda loves a cup before she goes to bed. Coming?'

'Might as well. Pimping though. I bet their mother doesn't know.'

'And if Mrs Jones did know, what could she do about it?'

They both wandered into the Store, one to the shelf where the Ovaltine was kept and the other to look around to see what kind of a treat she could buy for her lunch, both of them relaying their conclusions about Kenny Jones and their Terry to anyone who would listen. It was their misfortune that Mrs Jones had come through from her mail-order office to collect a jar of apricot preserve. 'I've run out, Mr Charter-Plackett, so is it all right if I take one from the shelves in the Store?'

'Of course. I thought you'd rung the woman who makes it and told her we were running short?'

'I have, last week, but it's not arrived.'

Jimbo's lips tightened. 'It won't do. That's the second time she's let us down.'

Mrs Jones slipped past the post office counter with a nod at Linda through the grille and headed past the soups to the preserves. As she reached up to pick out the jar of jam she was looking for she caught the tail end of a sentence. '. . . so what other conclusion can you draw but that Kenny and their Terry are pimps?' Swinging round in fury Mrs Jones spotted the customers nodding their heads in agreement.

The listener nearest to her burst into hysterical laughter, which Mrs Jones immediately choked at source by bringing her arm back and smacking her hard across her face. What had been a bustling cheery morning, busy with customers from Little Derehams and Penny Fawcett as well as Turnham Malpas, turned instantly to chaos. Tins flew from shelves, packets cascaded to the floor, customers clutched the freezer cabinets as they tried to prevent themselves from being knocked down by Mrs Jones' flailing arms. Her intended victim scuttled between the shelves desperately trying to avoid being caught by this friendly neighbour turned raving lunatic. Linda, safe though she was behind her grille, took to screaming; at the till Bel made for cover as the customer she was serving took a lunge at Mrs Jones, who was hurtling by in pursuit of the woman who had maligned her boys. 'How dare you! How dare you! My boys aren't pimps! I know they're not.'

The attack continued right the way around the Store: hardly a shelf or a display escaped destruction. Finally by the stationery Mrs Jones caught hold of the front of the woman's cardigan with both hands and shook her violently. 'That's disgusting that is. Disgusting! You foul-mouthed old *bitch*!' Bursting into tears, Mrs Jones fled from the chaos she'd created into her office at the back, and left behind her a stunned and shattered collection of shoppers.

For a moment there was complete silence and then uproar ensued. The customer on the receiving end of her wrath cried, heartbroken, on Bel's shoulder. 'I wouldn't mind, I never said a word! Not a word!' The two who'd started the ball rolling by accusing the Jones boys of being pimps crept quietly out, while others began picking up the tins and packets which had flown from the shelves and the rest pulled themselves together and tried to continue collecting their shopping.

Jimbo stood arms akimbo, for once lost for words. His straw boater askew, his moustache bristling with temper, he viewed the ruin of his beautiful Store and vowed Mrs Jones would have to go. He went to go in to the back to tell her so before he changed his mind.

The Store was a shambles. Linda came out from the post-office section and began putting the stationery back on the shelves, Bel went to start tidying the fruit and vegetables: apples and oranges and pears had rolled all over the floor to say nothing of the grapes, which had been stamped on and flattened and therefore posed a danger. Anyone coming in at that moment would have thought the fight of the century had just taken place.

'Go out through the back. I don't want to see you on these premises again. Never!' Jimbo's loud voice boomed round the mail-order office and Mrs Jones cowered. 'Never, do you hear? A brilliant career in mail order has just ended. I will not have my business ruined in this manner. I shall send what I owe you at the end of the month. After that your name will be *expunged* from my records, never to be seen again. You understand? You're not even to shop here.' He turned on his heel and left her perched on her beloved stool, quivering with the shock of what her temper had brought about. The humiliation! Mrs Jones fingered the marking pen she was so fond of, the address book she loved with the glorious roses in full bloom on the cover, the fancy sticky labels with the pattern of summer fruits around the edge which she'd introduced, and the stapler, red and business-like, which had always given her such pleasure when she used it.

She picked up her cardigan and bag, looked round her well-stocked shelves and remembered Jimbo always lodging his boater on top of the jars of chutney while the two of them had a policy meeting, and her eyes filled with tears again. Such an understanding man, but where his business was concerned . . . All this lost because she'd sprung into action, as usual, in defence of her boys. What mother wouldn't? But suggesting they were pimps!

She marched round to Hipkin Gardens and shouted through the letterbox of number six, 'It's your mother. Come on, open up, I know you're in!' While she waited for one of the boys to open the door she had a good squint at the inside. She could see they'd had carpet laid and that looked like a new table to the right of the door.

Peering through the letterbox at the same time as hammering on the door she eventually saw Kenny's stockinged feet coming down the stairs.

'About time!'

She did him the courtesy of waiting until the front door was safely shut before she began her tirade rounding it off with 'So now because of you I've lost my job. Them saying

121

something like that about my boys! I was wild.' Kenny
shook his head. 'Saying you and our Terry were pimps! As if
my boys would be involved in such a filthy business. Pimps!
I almost died of shame. What your father will have to say I
don't know.'

'Well, he's never said anything all my life so I don't
expect he'll start now.' Kenny leaned forward and with his
eyes only inches from hers he said, 'We are not pimps!
Right! So you can go and put those nosy old besoms right
on that score. See?'

'That's what I said. I said you weren't. But I've lost my
job for ever. He meant what he said. Nicest job I've ever
done. I'm not allowed in there even to shop, let alone to
work.'

Kenny rubbed his eyes and then his face to wake himself
up. 'Coffee, Mum?'

'Oh, yes, please.' She went to sit in their living room and
her jaw dropped when she saw the latest addition; a huge
leather armchair with wings. Mrs Jones sniffed it. Yes, it
was, it was leather, none of your imitation. The real thing.
This had cost a packet and not half. She gently lowered
herself into it and practised resting her head against the
right-hand wing. My! This was comfortable.

'Kenny! What did you pay for this new chair?'

'Too much!'

'All right then, don't tell me if you don't want to. But I
bet it wasn't a penny under a thousand pounds. You are
doing well. Wait till your dad sees it, he will be proud. I
'ope you're making our Terry pay his way.'

Coming in with the coffee Kenny replied, 'Don't you
fret, our Terry's doing well for himself too.'

'Him too? Brilliant. I'm that proud. Getting this house has changed you both round. Time you were making your way in the world.'

'I've forgotten the sugar.' Kenny went back to the kitchen and when he returned not only did he have the sugar in his hand but two fifty-pound notes. 'Here, add this to your housekeeping. Say nothing to no one. Right? It's a thank-you for defending me.'

'What we'll do now I'm out of work as well as your dad I don't know. It won't be any good me crawling back and apologising, 'cos he's that blazing mad with me. Thank you for this. Thank you very much, it won't half 'elp. I'm that grateful.'

'Shut up, Mum. Take it and say nothing.'

'Well, thanks. Thanks very much.'

When she was leaving she turned back to say, 'You're not doing anything wrong, are yer, Kenny? Yer know.'

'Course not.' But he didn't look her in the eye as he said it.

With Sheila in hospital it fell to Muriel to polish the brass every week. She'd got over her fright about the mice, with Tom reassuring her he'd caught two, and went off happily to do her polishing thinking she would say a prayer for Sheila and Ron while she was there. Ralph she left studying the *Financial Times*, with a pot of coffee beside him and a small fire lit as autumn was creeping in and the mornings could be cold.

Tom had been hosing down the path leading up to the main door of the church so when Muriel got inside she made a point of wiping her feet well on the doormat before she walked down the aisle. She heard a sound and stopped. But to her relief it was only the Superintendent. He was standing looking at the Templeton tomb.

'Why, good morning, Lady Templeton. You look as though you're going to be busy.'

'I clean the brass alternate weeks with Lady Bissett, but I'm doing her turn for her.'

'Of course. I've been to see her this morning and been able to speak to her.'

Muriel's pale face lit up. 'Oh, how lovely! How was she? Could she tell you anything? We'd be so glad to get it cleared up. It has been such a worry, Sir Ralph has been most concerned. So unlike our village to have anything quite so ghastly happening. The odd argument, the occasional bit of bad feeling, but this! Of course, there was poor Sharon McDonald and Toria Clark. Now that was dreadful! But it's all been so peaceful since. I expect it's an everyday occurrence for you, Superintendent, but for us, well, it's so puzzling. I've racked my brains for an answer to it and the only thing I can come up with . . .'

'Yes?' Mr Proctor, his stern world-weary face grey with fatigue, stood looking down at her waiting, hoping, for some dynamic clue.

'Mistaken identity. They were beaten up in mistake for someone else. But then who else? Oh dear. Maybe that's not grammatically correct but you understand me, don't you? If they were not deserving of a beating up, then who was? Who in this village is less than well behaved? Kenny and Terry Jones spring to mind but that's just petty thieving and car crime . . .'

'For which we've only once managed to catch them. Very fly young gentlemen, Kenny and their Terry.'

'Exactly, but . . . they live down Shepherds Hill, or they did, there is no way their house could be mistaken for Sheila and Ron's. So whose house could be mistaken? Anyone around the Green. They're all thatched and they're all white with black timbers, most have roses around the door, except for Glebe Cottages and Glebe House. So I went round the Green in my head the other night and there isn't a single person who could possibly be in need of a beating.'

Muriel picked up her polishing box from where she'd rested it on the flat bit of the tomb. 'While I polish I'll have another think.' She turned back to say, 'You see, our houses are not numbered. The Post Office wanted to number us all a few years back but we all said we wouldn't use them if they did. I can tell you there was quite a row about it and an official came down, but we stuck to our guns. One must, you know, about such things. The same with the street lighting. They said it would help to cut crime. Crime? we said. What crime? Now I am beginning to wonder. If there'd been lights perhaps Sheila and Ron would . . .'

'I'll say good morning, Lady Templeton, pleasure talking to you.'

'I've just thought, what did Sheila have to say?'

'While you polish think of all the people around here who wear trainers. Black trainers.'

Muriel's eyes opened wide. 'She saw them then?'

'Only the trainers.'

'I see. Were you wanting time for prayer? I could come back later.'

The Superintendent smiled. 'Not much in my line of country, but maybe I might solve crimes quicker if I did.'

Muriel patted his arm and smiled. 'Maybe you would, maybe you would.'

Being such an ancient church it was much visited by enthusiasts for church architecture so she was accustomed to strangers wandering about while she worked. But this morning no one was around and she hummed and polished in solitude. Muriel was in the corner by the font, working on the brass decoration. It was the Victorian brass addition to the font she'd taken exception to. She heard the main door open. She couldn't see who had come in and she was hidden by the wall anyway so she worked away ignoring them. Then, standing back to inspect her handiwork, Muriel missed her footing and slipped down the shallow step which separated the font area from the main aisle.

'Oooh!' She saved herself from falling by grabbing the staff of a saint in the niche by the font. 'Oh dear!' Muriel rubbed her ankle and hopped about for a moment till it felt better. She packed up her cleaning box and went to walk towards the main door.

Standing by the Templeton tomb was Kenny Jones. His tatty anorak had been replaced by a black leather jacket, his grubby T-shirt by a royal blue shirt and a tie with a dazzling design on it, his old jeans by black twill trousers and on his feet were smart leather brogues. And always before he'd worn . . . Oh! No! Black trainers!

Kenny was so surprised to see her you could have thought he'd imagined she'd simply materialised from behind the tomb.

'Oh!' He recovered himself and said, 'Good morning, Lady Templeton. Nice morning. Been busy, I see.'

'Yes, that's right. I always take my turn to polish the brass, and now I'm doing Sheila Bissett's turn too. How are you, Kenny?'

'Very well, thank you. Nasty that. Beating 'em up.'

'Sheila's come round. That nice Mr Proctor told me. He's been talking to her. I'm glad to see you coming to church. There's nothing quite like a sit-down in here for sorting yourself out. Worries, you know. Problems and such.'

'Not my cup of tea really, but yes, I thought I'd come in.'

'Of course. There's nothing like it for calming the soul. Such a solace.'

'Indeed. Wouldn't know much about that, but it's worth a try. How's Sir Ralph? Keeping well, I hope?'

'Oh, yes, very well. Are you settled into your house? I hear tales of you making it very habitable.' She looked at him with a teasing grin on her face, though that was the last thing she really wanted to do. Black trainers? Surely not.

'Doing our best. We're glad of the chance, all thanks to Sir Ralph 'aving faith in us. Our Terry and me, we know what everyone thinks of us, and it doesn't help you to pull yourself up out of the mud, and that's what I'm doing by hook or by crook. I'm sick of being at the bottom of the pile.' He looked round the church. 'All this history. Wonderful old place. We're always so busy-busy, aren't we? But here it's so calm.'

'Exactly.' Muriel was surprised by his thoughtfulness; there was more to him than she had realised. 'I'll leave you to it then. Bye-bye.'

'Be seeing yer. Take care.'

Kenny opened the door for her and watched her going down the path. If she knew, he thought, if she just knew. Gracious old bat, though, but so, what's the word? That's it, naïve.

Muriel, having seen such a nice side to him, decided not to mention about the black trainers, for he couldn't really be the kind of person who would attack Sheila and Ron, not when he was so thoughtful. What's more, it wouldn't do to throw suspicion on him because there must be dozens of men wearing black trainers besides Kenny. She wouldn't even tell Ralph.

Chapter 10

The bar and dining room of the Royal Oak were always first-rate places for learning what was going on in Turnham Malpas, as well as all the happenings in Little Derehams and Penny Fawcett. By nine o'clock on the Saturday night the dining room was full, and the bar was filling up nicely. Dicky and Georgie, with Alan's help, were busy supplying the drinkers and Bel was standing in for the dining-room manager who had flu. Most of her diners were from outside the village, a lovely mellow autumn evening having tempted them out from Culworth and some from as far away as the other side of the motorway.

In the bar it was mainly the local people who filled the chairs. There was a full house at the table which had the settle down one side of it. Jimmy was there with, under the table, his dog Sykes, who knew he wasn't supposed to be in there and who kept quiet because past experience had taught him that if he did keep quiet he would be rewarded with a long drink from Jimmy's beer before the end of the evening. Sitting with Jimmy were Sylvia and Willie and also Vera, making one of her rare appearances.

Vera, feeling flush with the bonus she'd received, said, 'Next round's on me. Busy tonight, ain't it? Any more news about the hedge? 'As that dratted old Fitch decided to climb down?'

Sylvia shook her head. 'The Rector's has been up to see him as well as Lady Templeton, and neither of them have budged him an inch. So they're planning a petition and I shall be the first to sign it.'

Vera placed her glass neatly in the middle of the beer mat and said knowingly, 'I reckon this hedge business is only the first step in a bigger scheme.'

Scornfully Willie asked, 'What bigger scheme?'

'I reckon he's wanting to build houses on Rector's Meadow and thinks if he gets the hedge question out of the way there'll be nothing to stop him. I have heard that he's widening the lane when he does it, so the council can't put a stop to it because of access.'

'Vera! Sometimes . . .'

Sylvia stepped in with her support. 'She could have a point. He's a devious one you know, and he's never done anything with that field, has he? Never planted it, never had the cows in it from Home Farm, never nothing. I think Vera could be right.'

Willie and Jimmy laughed. 'You two, you get worse.'

Vera tapped the table with her finger. 'Mark my words. He's coming round to it step by step. You can laugh, I shall remind you about this when it all comes to pass. Any news about poor Sheila and Ron? Have they got anybody yet?'

'No. The police are baffled, as they say.'

'Glad enough to take a fat rise, but not so enthusiastic about getting crimes solved. Our Rhett thinks it's a gangland revenge.'

Jimmy laughed. 'Aw! Come on, Vera! What on earth have Ron and Sheila to do with gangs?'

'He reckons someone's after silencing Ron. He did make that speech, didn't he, about workers' rights and the right to strike not being taken from them? He got a lot of publicity in the papers an' that.'

'Yes, but –'

'Yes, but nothing. You never know. Them in high places don't want unions getting up on their hind legs and making a fuss. They're all earning big, big money nowadays and they're committed to big mortgages and that and high living and they don't like the idea of doing without, so they sink to beatin' people up.'

Willie looked sceptically at Vera. 'I reckon those old dears you look after are addling your brains.'

Sylvia, shocked by his remark, nudged him. 'Willie!'

Vera looked hurt. 'I may not have much up top, Willie Biggs, but I'm not daft. Those people who've come up from the bottom rung are enjoying a lifestyle they never thought possible in their wildest dreams and they've no intention of losing it all. They'll stick at nothing. Lying in their teeth, cheating, fraud, anything.'

Jimmy tried pouring oil on troubled waters. 'I'm ready for a refill.' He pushed his glass towards Vera.

She stood up saying, 'Rightio. Same again, everybody?' They all nodded.

Sylvia watched her walk towards the bar. 'You shouldn't

pour scorn on her, it's not right. She's doing her best to improve things for her . . . self . . . Well, I never!'

Jimmy and Willie, their backs to the door, turned round to see what or who had caught Sylvia's attention.

Together they both said, 'Blimey!'

'It's Don, isn't it?'

He'd used too much hair dye and the result was an over-exaggerated head of jet black hair, but the barber had given him a very good cut, well tapered into his neck, parted and thinned, and it had taken years off his age. He'd been shaved immaculately: even the tufts of hair he always kept missing around the cleft in his chin had been banished. His skin, instead of being muddy and looking suspiciously as though it hadn't been washed properly in weeks, was positively glowing. He was wearing a smart checked sports jacket with dark trousers, a sober tie and matching shirt. Conversation came to a standstill as the entire bar gazed in amazement at this unbelievable spectacle.

Vera hadn't seen him, with her back being to the door, and he hadn't seen Vera and he went straight across to their usual table.

'Can I get anyone a drink?'

Sylvia was the first to answer. 'Well, my word. I have to say it. You do look so smart, I am impressed.'

He tried to pass off her remark by shrugging his shoulders and showing them a ten-pound note. 'Well?'

Willie found his tongue. 'You've lost weight too. By Jove, Don! I could nearly think you were courting.'

Sylvia nudged Willie again. 'Take no notice, Don. We're all right for drinks, thanks, Vera's just getting us a refill.'

Don glanced across to the bar. 'Didn't realise she was

'ere.' They watched him pinch the knot of his tie to make sure it was just right and as he marched across to Vera their eyes followed him.

Jimmy whispered, 'I swear I can smell aftershave.'

Willie agreed. 'So can I. This could be interesting.'

'I've never seen him in that outfit before, have you?' Sylvia asked, with her hand over her mouth so he couldn't possibly hear her. 'Let's hope he isn't meeting someone in here tonight.'

Jimmy finished the last drops of his beer and said, 'No, I reckon it's Vera he's courting. We could have some fun.'

Sylvia tapped Willie's arm. 'And just you watch your tongue. We don't want to upset things, not when he's making an effort.'

At the bar Don took hold of the tray. 'I'll pay for these, Vera. Add an orange juice, would you, Alan, please?'

'Certainly, Mr Wright.'

Vera hadn't seen him yet, but she'd smelt the pungent aftershave. She wondered how it could be Don's voice she heard, but not the old musty smell of the Don she remembered. At the sound of his voice she hesitated and then very slowly turned to face him. Conversation fell away. Everyone in the bar knew the state of affairs between Vera and Don and most agreed Vera had been justified in leaving him in that pit he called home. They watched quite openly to see her reaction.

But there was none. She looked at him in complete silence, her face composed and giving nothing away. No surprise. No amazement. No pleasure. No consternation. Without a word she walked back to the table and sat down. Jimmy got up and pulled a chair across for Don. There was a quiet hum of conversation while everyone waited to see what would happen next. Vera sat mute. Don handed round the drinks, returned the tray to the bar and came back to sit at the end of the table, his knees almost touching Vera's where she sat at his right hand on the settle.

Don asked her, 'Gin and tonic now, is it?'

'Any objections?'

'No, no, none at all. Bit different from your usual port and lemon, that's all.'

'It is. But then I've moved on, you see.'

'Of course. Job working out all right?'

'Yes, thanks.'

'Rhett liking the flat, is he?'

'He couldn't but. Nice room overlooking the gardens. He's well set up.'

'He hasn't called to see me.'

'Not surprising, is it? You've not been to see him.'

'I am still his grandad.'

'Are you now?'

'What do you mean by that remark?'

'Nothing.'

'Have you stopped him coming?'

'No. He does as he likes, like I do.'

'I can see that.' Don looked her up and down, noting the flattering dress she wore and her smart hairstyle. 'You look nice. How do you manage to get your hair done in that dead-alive hole?'

'The hairdresser who comes to do the patients' hair does mine in exchange for a nice meal and a sit-down in my flat before she leaves.'

'Got it all organised, haven't you?'

'Oh, yes! My life's got style now. I'm off on holiday in a fortnight. Torquay. I've always wanted to go. 'As just that air of distinction which I quite fancy nowadays.' She stood up. 'I'll be off now, the company doesn't suit.'

Don stood up. 'Can I give you a lift?'

His suggestion put the torch to her temper. 'Lift? You? Give me a lift? I wouldn't accept a lift from you if I had a hundred miles to walk. A lift? In that stinking uncomfortable sidecar I've put up with all our married life? Why I've stuck with you I'll never know. But at last, thank Gawd, I've come to my senses.' She gestured at his new clothes. 'Another thing whilst we're on the subject, you've no need to think you're making an impression on me with this lot, because you're not. Underneath you're still the same old Don. Selfish! Inconsiderate! Dull! Boring! Hidebound! Yes, hidebound. You'd no more think of going to Torquay than – than . . .'

Vera picked up her bag and pushed him full in the chest so she had room to get out from the settle. His chair fell over but he managed to remain upright. 'See! Stolid from head to toe. Immovable! That's you! Immovable. You haven't that much spark in you, not that much!' She held her finger and thumb a centimetre apart close up to his face. 'Good night to you!'

Don bent to pick up his chair and he sat down in it, his head lowered, giving the remains of his orange juice close scrutiny. Jimmy, to cover his embarrassment, put his glass under the table for his dog Sykes to finish.

After a few moments Sylvia shuffled along the settle and sympathetically laid a hand on his arm. 'She's just a bit upset, you see.'

In a very subdued voice Don replied, 'What about?'

'That's just it, Don. It's like she says. You don't *think*.'

'About what?'

'About *her*.'

'But this is for her.' He gestured towards his jacket. 'I thought she'd be pleased.'

'She is. But she won't let on because it's like she says, nothing's changed. You've made a good start, but it's only skin deep, you see.'

'Tell me then, Sylvia, what can I do?'

Needing to get the position absolutely clear Sylvia asked him, 'About what?'

'About getting her back.'

Willie intervened: 'It all depends on how much you want her back.'

Don looked up at him. 'Well, I do. It was all right at first, the novelty yer know, but now, well, I miss 'er and it's not just the cooking an' that. I miss 'er. I want things like they used to be.'

'Nay, Don.' Jimmy sighed. 'Nay, Don. Yer haven't listened to a word what Sylvia said. Vera doesn't want things like they used to be, that's what she's rebelling against.'

'But look at me, I've tried. What more can a fella do?'

Sylvia took hold of his hand. 'How could you expect her in all conscience to want to have a lift in that rackety old sidecar, dressed like she is and with her hair newly done? Answer me that.'

'But it's a classic! Worth a lot.'

Scornfully Jimmy muttered, 'Then sell the damn thing.'

Don reacted violently to Jimmy's suggestion. 'Sell it? It's my pride and joy.'

'But,' said Jimmy, 'it doesn't make your meals, or iron yer shirts, or keep yer company, or keep yer warm in bed, does it? So make up yer mind.'

Sylvia gave him an ultimatum. 'It's Vera or the bike, Don.'

'It's make-yer-mind-up time.' Jimmy stood up. 'I've to be off. They'll all be wanting taxis soon and outside Culworth Station is where I've to be pronto, pronto.' He popped a mint in his mouth from a packet he kept in his pocket, called a cheerful goodnight to everyone and left with Sykes slinking along beside him, licking froth from his lips and trying to look as if he didn't exist.

'Night, Jimmy.' Don turned to look at Sylvia. 'I'm going to have to do better, aren't I?'

'Yes, you are. After all, she's only wanting you to live at the nursing home while ever she has a job there. She'll go back to the cottage when she retires. It's not for ever, is it?'

'That's it though, she won't. That's the problem, my cottage.'

'Well, that's for you to decide, because you're the one who'll have to change things.'

Don looked up at Sylvia and gave her one of his very rare smiles. 'She did look nice tonight, didn't she?'

'Yes, she did, very nice. Come on, Willie, that programme'll be starting in a minute and if we don't see the beginning you'll be asking me who's who and what's what all night. Good night, Don. Think on what we've talked about.'

Don sat a while longer contemplating his orange juice. He'd never been a sociable man so no one bothered to come over to keep him company. After a while if they'd been watching him they'd have seen him almost visibly come to a decision. He got up, drank his orange juice right to the bottom, banged down the glass and marched out, leaving the swing door crashing back and forth behind him.

It must have been close to eleven o'clock, because the last of the Royal Oak customers were leaving for home, when the village became aware of loud noises coming from Don's cottage. There were horrendous hammerings, vicious bangings and huge thunderings as though someone was taking a fourteen-pound hammer to the entire contents of his cottage.

Grandmama Charter-Plackett, sitting up in bed in her silk nightgown and matching bed-jacket enjoying her nightcap of whisky and water, leaped out of bed with alarm, convinced that very soon, if not sooner, Don would be appearing through a hole in her bedroom wall. She put on her fluffy mules and her winter dressing-gown and marched down the stairs preparing for war.

When she saw the crowd gathered outside she tightened her belt and joined them. 'Someone,' she said, 'must go in there and do something. The man has gone mad.'

There were murmurs from the crowd but no one stepped forward. It was as well they didn't because the front door flew open and Don came out of it backwards dragging large pieces of wood, which jammed in the doorway and brought him to a halt. Willie, who'd been on his way upstairs to bed and had just come out to tear a strip off the person about to disturb his sleep, offered his help.

''Ere, let me give you a hand.' Between them they freed the wood and got it out in the road. 'Now, what's all this?

You can't be a-doing of this now. It's eleven o'clock. We're all off to bed.'

Don simply climbed over the wood and back into the house where the banging began all over again.

Grandmama asked, 'Is the Rector in?'

Willie shook his head. 'Gone to a meeting in Gloucester. Should be back any time, though.'

'Then who's going to put a stop to it? He's gone mad. Quite mad.' She looked imperiously around the crowd to find several of them avoiding her eyes and others looking very sheepishly at her. Windows were opening, voices calling out asking what was going on and could they keep quiet. Two weekenders came out to see which of the local yokels had finally gone mad, and were obviously looking forward to some good entertainment.

'In that case, then, I shall have to go in. Though what you men are made of I cannot begin to imagine.'

Sylvia protested. 'Mrs Charter-Plackett, I don't think it's fit for you to . . .'

But she was already climbing over the wood.

The front door led straight into the sitting room, a sitting room stacked on every surface with the contents of the kitchen cupboards. Don was in the kitchen at the back. Inside the house the noise was ear-bending. She couldn't actually get into the kitchen because pieces of wood were flying off his hammer in her direction as he attacked the dresser right by the door, but she recognised the terrible desperation which had triggered his lunatic attack: telling him to stop would only increase the frenzy. Sweat was rolling down his face, a puce-coloured face which caused her extreme anxiety about whether or not he would see the night through without having a heart-attack. Telling him off would be like putting a match to a very short fuse. When he paused to get his breath she shouted, 'Mr Wright! It's me from next door. I've just called to see if everything's all right?' Looking into the kitchen she added, 'My word, you have been busy. What a good idea. Just what it needed. Shall I give you a hand getting it all out? Here, you get the other end of this piece and between us we'll take it out, then you'll have more room to work.'

When the banging stopped those outside had smirked at each other, imagining the dressing-down Don would be receiving, but when Grandmama appeared backwards out of the door heaving another large piece of wood out on to the road they couldn't believe their eyes. She threw it on to the pile and marched back in without a word.

Taking their cue from her there followed a glorious united effort from everyone to rid Don and Vera's kitchen of every single last inch of shelving and cupboard: the sink and the cooker and the fridge-freezer were all dragged out too. Under Grandmama's instruction some marched in and out removing the results of Don's manic attack, others stayed outside stacking the remnants of the kitchen as they were brought out, while Don continued to swing the hammer. Finally the entire kitchen was outside on the road.

'Well,' said someone under their breath, 'that lot's what I call rubbish and no mistake. That cooker isn't even good enough for Culworth Museum. As for the cupboards! And that table and chairs! Every leg ready to fall off any minute, and not a decent lick of paint left on 'em!'

'Wait till Vera hears!'

To their final astonishment they heard Grandmama

inviting Don round for breakfast. 'You can't even boil a kettle in there now, so, I breakfast at eight thirty prompt on Sundays and you'll be more than welcome.'

For the first time since the whole episode had begun Don spoke. 'Thank you, Missus, eight thirty it is. Goodnight.'

It had always been recognised that they broke the mould after Mrs Charter-Plackett was born, but to their total amazement as the church bells rang out for the ten o'clock service on Sunday morning and everyone was making their way to church, she topped even her Saturday night performance. They were stunned to see Grandmama Charter-Plackett, a scarf tied over her summer going-to-church hat to secure it against the wind, graciously waving to them from Don's sidecar and the two of them steaming down the Culworth Road as though the hounds of hell were after them. And, yes, it was true then, they had cleared Don and Vera's kitchen out, right to the bare walls, because there was the evidence for all to see, still stacked outside the door.

Chapter 11

Kenny Jones walked into the Store on the Monday morning. It was too early for Bel to have finished her caretaking duties at the school so it was Linda behind her post-office grille to whom he spoke.

'Boss in?'

'If you mean Mr Charter-Plackett, yes, he is.'

'Can I have a word?'

She looked him up and down. 'Heck! What's happened to you? Surprise, surprise! Quite the country gent, aren't we?'

'Cut the sarcasm, Linda. You should have married me instead of that creep you call husband, then you'd have been sharing in my good fortune.'

Linda flushed. She'd always known people thought of her Alan as a present day Uriah Heep but to have it said outright, on a Monday morning too, was a bit much. 'Nasty sod! I'd a lot rather be married to him than a no-good like you.'

'Watch your tongue, you. I might need a stamp or two and I'm not having a cheeky bitch serving me.'

'Didn't know you could write.'

'Eh! Watch it.'

'There's no law that says I'm compelled to serve you.'

'No? We'll see about that.' Being securely locked in her post-office section, according to regulations, he'd no means of getting to her other than unlocking her door. He slotted his fingers through the wire triangles around the door lock as though intending to gain entry. His furious rattling alarmed her and she pressed her panic button.

Jimbo, busy in the mail-order office in the absence of Mrs Jones, sprang into action picking up as he ran the rounders bat he kept for the purpose. When he saw Kenny collapsed with laughter propped against the stationery shelves Jimbo felt disappointed. He was just in the mood for confrontation.

'What the blazes, Linda? It's only Kenny.'

'Only Kenny! He was rattling the door trying to get in here.'

'Were you?'

'Only kidding, just to get her going.'

'It's not funny, Kenny, not funny at all.'

'Sorry. But she was impudent to me. Refused to serve me.'

'I didn't, you didn't ask.'

'I said I might.'

'Well, there is no law that says I must.'

Jimbo interrupted, 'There's the law according to Jimbo. That says you must.'

'Does it indeed? Insulting he was to my Alan. Real insulting, and I won't stand for it.'

Aware that another row with Linda was looming, which might end with him sacking her yet again, Jimbo turned his attention to Kenny. 'What's the reason for your appearance at this early hour?'

Kenny nodded his head in the direction of the back office. 'Can I have a private word?'

'If it's about your mother getting her job back, no, you can't. She isn't. Full stop.'

'But –'

'Sorry, but no. I've put a notice in the window advertising her job and the first suitable applicant to walk through that door gets it.'

'But she's done a good job here. I know she has.'

'Agreed. But she isn't coming back.'

'You can't sack people like that nowadays.'

'I have done.'

'We'll take you to a tribunal.'

'You will? Try me. Behaviour prejudicial to the good conduct of my business.'

'Sod off! You think 'cos you've got money you can throw your weight around, well, just you wait and see. Next it'll be Kenny Jones with money and then I'll get my own back on you.'

'That's likely. What money I have I've got through sheer hard graft and that's something you know nothing about.'

'Then you're daft. There's ways!' He tapped the side of his nose. 'Anyway, you'll regret sacking my mother, just you wait and see.' He prodded the air with his index finger and stepped closer to Jimbo.

Jimbo raised the rounders bat. 'Are you threatening me?'

'Me? No! Threatening you? Certainly not.' He laughed, made a rude two-finger gesture to Linda and slammed the door behind him.

'Oh, Mr Charter-Plackett, you are brave. The no-good disgusting slob that he is. Wait till my Alan hears about this!'

144

'I should advise your Alan to steer clear. He isn't a match for someone like Kenny Jones.'

The slight on her Alan's capacity for standing up to that loathsome slob upset Linda and she burst into tears. 'Let me out! Let me out!'

'You've got the keys.'

'Oh, yes!' She unlocked herself and fled into the back. Jimbo threw his hands up in despair.

'God! What have I done to deserve this? Linda! Linda!' He locked the post-office door and, taking the keys with him, followed her through and put the kettle on. A cup of tea always did the trick with Linda.

Kenny, angry because he'd hadn't succeeded in getting his mother's job back for her, realised he'd gone about it in totally the wrong way. Men like Jimbo appreciated good manners and civility and he should have remembered that, like he had done when he asked Sir Ralph to let him rent the house. He really would have to curb his tongue. No good wearing the smart new clothes if the man inside didn't fit them.

He wandered across to the church. Pushing open the main door he recalled his conversation with Muriel. That had been pleasant and he'd managed it very well. Given her such a good account of himself that he'd made her feel better about him. Almost sympathetic she'd been.

He went to sit in the church to wait for Tom.

Tom had a big rubbish bag in his hand and was going round the churchyard collecting up the dead flowers from the graves, and generally casting his eye about for any imperfections which might offend the Rector. He hadn't had a chance to speak to him yet but no doubt he'd be in later this morning to see what was what. Of course he'd have been in for his early prayers before most people had opened their eyes and then off for his morning run. Such discipline. Such dedication.

He leaned against a headstone and thought. Thought about how much he loved this place. Never imagined in all his life he'd come to such a position. Verger of St Thomas à Becket! Men he'd worked with in the past would have reeled about laughing at the thought. Let 'em. He had the last laugh. He had the peace, the comfort. The trees waving in the breeze, the flowers flowering, the grass growing, the pulse of life at his fingertips. Yes! He wouldn't swap it for all the money in the world. There'd felt to be something so right about buying the house in this sleepy village. He likened himself and Evie to a ship crossing the stormy oceans, plunging through wild waves as high as mountains and finally coming into a safe haven at last. He liked that idea and ruminated on it for a while.

The only fly in the ointment was Kenny. A blast from the past. He shook his head and decided not to dwell on him.

Straightening himself up he went off to the very back of the churchyard to try out the gate which led to the grounds of the Big House. It swung easily on its hinges now he'd used WD40 on it, useful stuff. Satisfying that. He stroked the old timbers of the gate. Nobody used it now, but it was nice to keep such a lovely old gate in good fettle. Better get on. According to Willie's schedule, it was the day for polishing the pews. With the rain just beginning to come down it seemed an appropriate time for doing it, and he was looking forward to it.

The huge tin of furniture polish awaited him in the cleaning cupboard, with the cloths beside it. The label on it showed a dear old chap wearing a green apron, lovingly polishing a shining table; there was an aspidistra on a stand close by and old paintings on the wall. He smiled to himself. He hadn't got the green apron but he did have his orange overalls. He felt a twinge of conscience when he remembered where he'd pinched them from. All in a good cause though.

He went through into the church, faced the altar and bowed his head as part of his ritual for keeping Lady Luck on his side. He prised the lid off the tin and dipped a cloth into the polish. Must take care to rub it all off, otherwise they'd all be complaining about polish on their clothes. Absorbed in his task he whistled a hymn tune and looked forward to a rewarding morning's work. The church clock struck quarter past ten. Nice that. Glad they'd got it mended. He pondered what Evie might have put in his lunchbox. If it was one of her good days it would be appetising, if not he wouldn't fancy anything she'd put in and he'd have to tip it in the bin and say nothing . . . He smelt smoke. Cigar smoke. He looked up and there was Kenny, sitting at the back, his feet propped on the pew in front.

'Morning.'

'Have some respect, Kenny, if you please.'

After a pause Kenny very slowly removed his feet from the pew and sat up, taking another drag on his cigar as he did so.

'And the cigar. You know we're not allowed to smoke in here.'

'I haven't finished it yet.'

'Well, stub it out.'

'On the pew?'

'For God's sake, don't be so stupid. Here, stub it out on this lid.' Tom walked up the aisle and offered the lid of the polish tin to him. He sat down on the pew in front of Kenny and said, 'Well?'

'Well?'

'What's up?'

'What's up? You tell me.'

'I've nothing to say.'

Kenny leaned an elbow on the top of the pew in front of him to get closer to Tom. 'What the blazes *are* you doing here?'

'Making a real life for myself. All I want is leaving alone.'

'You call this a real life? God! Tom, you must have lost your marbles.'

'No, I haven't. It's what Evie and I want. We've never been happier.'

Kenny shrugged his shoulders. 'Each to his own.'

'Exactly. Now buzz off and let me get on.'

Kenny leered. 'Pity about Ron and Sheila.'

When Tom looked closely into Kenny's eyes he found they were giving nothing away. 'Surprising how you can get beaten up and you've done nothing at all to deserve it. Not fair, is it?'

'No.'

'Could have been killed.'

'Yes. They could.'

'Good morning, Tom.' Kenny got to his feet, picked up the parcel beside him on the seat and left.

Tom eased the collar of his overalls away from his throat, and felt the sweat trickling down his neck. Picking up the lid of the polish tin he carried it to the outside wheelie-bin and tipped the stub in. There were flecks of ash left behind so Tom brushed them away, and wished he could brush Kenny away as easily.

Tom took his lunchbox home. Evie was eating silently on a seat in the garden.

'Thought I'd have mine at home with you.' He put his box beside her and sat down. The sun, though warm, wasn't really quite warm enough to sit outside but that was Evie all over. If she wanted to eat outside she would, even in the depths of winter.

'Bit cold for you.'

Evie nodded.

'Happy?'

Evie nodded again, shielding her eyes against the sun to watch a robin pecking at crumbs.

'Grand little chap. Nice to have time to watch him.'

Evie smiled.

'Been working this morning?'

Evie gave him the thumbs up.

'Good. Nearly finished the Nativity?'

'Yes.'

Rewarded at last with an answer Tom said, 'Good. Good.'

'I've got an idea for the next one.'

'Excellent. You could have an exhibition.'

'No, not an exhibition.'

'Why not? It could trigger off this embroidery class Sheila's keen on.' Remembering Sheila brought Kenny to mind. Tom, impatient with himself, stood up and headed towards the house. He put the kettle on, made them a coffee each and went back to Evie.

'Is it your sugar day? It had better be because I've put it in without asking.'

Evie gave him one of her infrequent smiles.

'Kenny's been round to see me.'

Evie began to shake. Her coffee spilt out of her mug and scalded her hand.

'Don't worry, now. You're not to get worried. Here, let me take your mug. There, there. Now, now.' He put an arm round her shoulders. 'I wish I'd never said.'

'You won't, will you, Tom? You won't.'

'No. You've got my promise on that.'

'I can't bear it starting all over again.'

'It won't. I made a promise.'

Tom kissed the side of her head, smoothed her hair back from her face and kissed her cheek. 'You and me's all right, Evie, believe me.' He sank his teeth into a piece of Evie's flapjack. It was so hard he thought for a nasty minute he'd broken a tooth.

When Tom returned to church after his lunch Peter was in the vestry. 'Ah! Tom!'

'Good afternoon to you, Rector. Had a good holiday? Nice to see you back. Never quite the same without you in the Rectory.'

'Yes, I have. Thank you.'

Tom looked at him and decided he'd got some of his old energy back. 'Nothing happened since you went. Downright dull it's been.'

'Not dull enough. I smelt cigar smoke in here when I walked in. You don't smoke, do you, Tom?'

'Must have been someone in while I was at lunch. Went home to eat it with Evie.'

Peter looked hard at him and Tom had difficulty keeping his gaze steady. 'Mmmmmm. Because, you know, we cannot afford to have a fire started by someone smoking. If it was proved we wouldn't get a penny on the insurance – these old timbers would go up like kindling. If you catch someone smoking turn them out.'

'I would, immediately, you can bank on that.'

'Good. This funeral on Thursday. Everything in order?'

'Willie's run through it with me, and I'm all set. Grave dug already.'

'Good. I'll get off home for some lunch then.' Peter got to his feet and, towering over Tom, he looked down at him. Those intense blue eyes of his shook Tom a little; he thought they could see right inside him. God help him if they could. 'You seem to be doing a good job, Tom. I'm glad you applied, I think we're going to get on well together. You've already got yourself organised and that's excellent. Evie well?'

'Yes, thanks.' Peter went out of the vestry, crossed himself as he passed in front of the altar and left Tom to get back to his polishing. Somehow the swish of Peter's cassock as he strode down the aisle tugged at Tom's conscience. All he longed for was to be truthful like Peter was with him, and he couldn't, not to save his life he couldn't.

Chapter 12

Ever since Don had thrown out the contents of his kitchen the whole village had been on red alert, waiting to see what would happen next. The story being told at coffee mornings and in that convenient corner by the tinned soups in the Store and by the crowd of waiting mothers at the school gate was that Grandmama and Don had been into Culworth DIY and ordered a complete new kitchen. They found this hard to believe as Don and Vera had always been so very short of money. Maybe, someone slyly suggested, Grandmama had lent him the wherewithal for his services in a completely different direction. After the initial burst of laughter at the idea, they scoffed at such fantasy.

The other matter occupying their idle tongues was where was Don eating? No kitchen, no cooker, no food. They'd speculated on an arrangement between Grandmama and Don, but dismissed that because someone volunteered they'd twice seen him coming out of Willie and Sylvia's. One or two brave souls had dallied with the idea of asking Jimbo outright but at the last they'd got cold feet. It was

Vera who, in shock at the sight of her kitchen in pieces outside the front door, finally asked him the million-dollar question one afternoon when the rubbish had still not been moved and people were growing tetchy about it. She'd cadged a lift with the man who delivered groceries to the nursing home and to the Store and gone straight in, wedging the door open for him so he could get in and out more easily.

She found Jimbo standing by the till, idly casting an eye over his empire. 'Seeing, Mr Charter-Plackett, that you know most of what goes on in this village due to the fact you love listening to gossip,' Jimbo pulled a face at this remark and tried to look innocent of the charge, 'no good pretending you don't because you do, can you tell me what's going on?'

Eyes round with innocence Jimbo took off his boater and smoothed a hand over his bald head. 'About what?'

Vera gave him a nudge. 'About my kitchen being out in the road. I've been to look. It's true, it's just like they've said. So? I understand your mother is to blame.'

'Blame? I wouldn't say that. Not blame, she's aided and abetted, yes, I agree.'

'Well, then, what are they up to?'

Jimbo bent towards her and spoke in a low voice. 'Don't know if I should be telling you this, but he's ordered a new kitchen. Coming at the weekend and Barry Jones, and the electrician and the plumber from the Big House, are spending the weekend fitting it. Under Mother's supervision, so you know it will be done right.'

Vera was aghast. She drew in a couple of deep breaths while she studied over what he'd said and finally came out

153

with 'Ah! But where did he get the money? That's what I want to know.'

Jimbo shrugged his shoulders. 'Got to go. Customer.' And he fled to attend to his business leaving Vera none the wiser.

All his life Don had been virulent about people who bought on credit. Go to hell sure as maybe will all them what borrow money. A sure and certain path to damnation is borrowing. So although he'd appeared to be doing some strange things since she'd left him, borrowing money almost certainly wouldn't be one of them, because Don had always had a very healthy respect for hell. A terrible suspicion began to dawn on her. Maybe all these years when she'd been scrimping and saving he'd been saving too. Maybe he earned an awful lot more at work then he'd ever let on. She cast her mind back and thought about always getting a proper payslip from the nursing home telling her how much she'd earned, how much the thieving government had taken from her in tax and things, so she knew for certain how much she'd have in her pay packet. But had she ever seen one of Don's slips? No! She had no more idea how much he earned even after all these years than she had had when they married, and what's more she'd never thought to question him. Come to that, had she ever seen a bank statement? There'd never been one come through the post, that she knew for certain. In a flash she knew Don wouldn't trust a bank anyway. So just what had he been keeping from her? How much, and where was it? The lowlife, the stinking rotten lowlife.

Vera stood in the middle of the Store so carried away with her thought processes that she didn't realise she was in everyone's way. Someone bumped into her and apologised. She moved her bag to the other hand and felt the hardness of the cottage key as it banged against her leg. The message it gave travelled from her leg up to her head. She looked up at the lovely old clock Jimbo had on the wall behind the till. The beautiful shapely brass hands were saying half past four. Don 'ud be another half an hour before he got home. The key was in her bag as her leg had just witnessed, that huge key more fit for a castle than a cottage. Here was her golden opportunity to find out. Vera marched home, heart beating fast, too fast, but she didn't care: she had to find out before he got back.

She glanced quickly up and down Church Lane: the only living creatures in sight were Jimmy's geese waiting outside the Rectory. Vera swiftly put the key in the lock, turned it and disappeared inside. The sight which met her eyes horrified her. Every inch of space was taken up with the contents of her kitchen shelves. Only one chair was free, and that was placed directly in front of the telly. She smiled grimly to herself. Typical. Under the mattress was the usual place for people of Don's kind to hide things. She climbed the tiny twisting stairs; on every step some item was laid which Don should have put away in the bedroom but which had never got further than the stairs.

The bed was unmade and it looked as though the sheets had not been changed since she'd last slept in it. She wrinkled her nose with distaste, but pressed on with her quest.

Lifting up one side of the feather mattress she splayed her fingers and patted as far as she could under it, spreading her arms as wide as possible, but found nothing. She went round to his side of the bed, the one nearest the window, and did the same. Her fingers closed on a fat envelope. Inside were loads and loads of banknotes. Vera pulled them out. They were all fifty-pound notes. Neatly bundled with pages torn from an exercise book and fastened with sticky tape. Feverishly she made a hasty calculation. Over seven thousand pounds! Sweat rushed from every pore. The shock of it! So where had he kept all this lot when she lived at home? Certainly not in the bed. She'd have noticed. But it didn't matter. What mattered was the deception. Making her use all the money she'd earned to keep them and contributing as little as he could, so he could save. But she couldn't understand how *much* he'd managed to save. What really hurt was the thought that she could have had the new kitchen years ago.

The throb-throb of his motorcycle engine sounded outside. He was back from work. Vera raced down the stairs, picked up the first thing which came to hand, which by chance was the very cast-iron pan she'd hit him with the day she left, and charged outside.

Don, his back to her innocently unaware of his fate, was calmly immobilising his bike and still wearing his crash helmet, so he didn't hear her breathing heavily behind him. Despite her anger she knew it would be pointless hitting him whilst he still wore his helmet, so she bided her time.

Don, having read outside a bank somewhere that helmets should be removed before entering the premises, always took his off before going in the house. His leathers creaked as he turned. If she hadn't been so furious with him she'd have burst out laughing at the expression on his face when he saw her standing there, the pan held in both hands, raised ready for attack.

'Vera!'

'You thieving little runt! I've found yer money! That nice little hoard you thought you'd keep for yourself. All that money and me living in poverty! Where've you been keeping it? Eh? Tell me that!'

'I haven't been keeping it! Let me tell yer! Just listen!'

But she wouldn't. She aimed a great swipe at him and, with memories of the last time she'd hit him with that same pan, Don dropped his helmet and started to run with Vera in pursuit. Jimmy's geese, still grouped around the Rectory door in the hope that the children would be coming out to feed them, began honking loudly and followed in a stream behind the two of them, half flying half running in pursuit. Neither Don nor Vera was as fit as they would have liked and Don, hampered by the weight and the restriction of his motorcycle leathers, lumbered awkwardly past Jimmy's cottage and round the Green, with Vera shrieking the worst words she knew as she chased him. Fortunately she'd never learned really bad ones, so when the the children came out of the Rectory and Jimbo's four poured out of their house and the early birds at the Royal Oak came out to see the fun they didn't need to cover their ears. By the time they reached the Store every customer was out cheering in Stocks Row to see them go by.

'Go on, Vera. Give him it!'

'Run, Don! Run!'

'Now, Vera! Give it up! The poor chap!'

'What's he done?'

Running and shouting at the same time meant Vera was

panting heavily as they passed the school, and by the time they reached their cottage again she was completely out of breath.

'The money! You rotten dog! The money! You thieving, lying hound!' She lunged at him yet again with the pan but he had just enough breath left to dodge out of her way. 'All that money!!' They both looked at the open cottage door, at each other, shouted, 'The money!' in unison and tried to squeeze through the door together. The geese, still in a state of extreme excitement, were pecking at Don's legs as they tried to join the crush at the door so Don paused to kick at them and consequently Vera won. As she clambered up the stairs, on her hands and knees, too exhausted to walk upright, she made up her mind that half that money at least belonged to her.

Don almost had a heart-attack when he saw all the notes laid out on the bed. At the top of his voice he shouted, 'You daft beggar! Leaving the house unlocked and all this money about! If you'd just stop to listen.' He gasped for breath and sank on to the eiderdown, his head down, heaving great gulps of air into his lungs. Vera collapsed into the Lloyd Loom chair that had been so dear to his mother's heart and began to laugh. Quietly at first and then more and more hysterically until tears began running down her face and she sobbed. Sobbed for her lost years, for her yearning for a better life, for being married to a man who loved her so little.

'You've got the wrong end of the stick, Vera. I meant to tell yer.'

'Shut up! Shut up!'

'If you'd just calm —'

They heard a voice downstairs. 'Hello! Hello! It's Peter from the Rectory. Is everything all right?'

Don hastily pushed the money under the mattress and called out, 'Coming down, won't be a minute.'

When he reached the bottom of the stairs Don said, 'Vera's been a bit upset.'

'I guessed. Is she feeling better now?'

'She will in a bit. It's a misunderstanding, and she doesn't want to hear.'

'I see. Would she like a lift home?'

'That's all right, I'll take her.'

Peter raised his eyebrows.

'Well, perhaps not.'

'I'll take her. Tell her come to the Rectory and knock when she wants to go and I'll drive her.'

'Thanks.' Don looked up at him, hesitated a moment wondering whether to confide his troubles to him and decided this wasn't the time.

'You've blotted your copybook, I think, Don.'

'Yes. That's right.'

'Tell Vera I'll take her as soon as she's ready. I'm working at home the rest of the day.'

Peter glanced round the little living room, looked long and hard at Don and left. Don sat down on the empty chair in front of the TV and switched on. Damn me! if it wasn't one of those home-improvement programmes. He switched it off and flung the remote control into the farthest corner. It clattered to the floor behind the Be-Ro recipe books stacked on top of his mother's green enamel casserole dishes and it took Don a whole week to find it.

He couldn't remember feeling so low. The exhilaration

of smashing the kitchen to smithereens had long since passed and now Vera was so wild with him she'd probably never speak to him again. He'd been in a mess for some time but this beat all. If only she'd listen to what he had to say.

He heard her footsteps coming down the stairs. She arrived at the bottom and he turned to speak. For a brief moment his heart swelled with a loving thought. 'The Rector'ull take you home, he says. Will yer let me explain? Please.'

Without addressing another word to him Vera left and crossed the road to the Rectory. Caroline answered her knock, swiftly closing the door behind her because of Topsy.

'Come in, Vera. Peter's on the phone, he shouldn't be long now. There's tea in the pot. Would you care for a cup?'

Vera nodded.

'We're in the kitchen.'

Alex and Beth were still finishing their meal. Alex shouted, 'Hello, Mrs Wright! You didn't catch Mr Wright then?'

Caroline hushed him, but Vera didn't seem to notice his question. Caroline sat her in the rocking chair beside the Aga, and handed her a cup of tea.

'Sugar?'

Vera shook her head.

The children found her silence unnerving, and soon asked to be excused. Caroline sat at the table finishing her pudding. Feeling the need to express her sympathy she said, 'I'm sorry you're having such trouble.'

Vera looked at her, then at the table which, despite the

ravages of a meal almost done, still looked inviting and wished, oh, how she wished. 'All I ask for is some consideration from him, but what do I get? An almighty kick in the teeth. You're so lucky. So very lucky. We only have to see the Rector look at you and we know how much he loves yer. Don't ever do anything to lose that, because you'll regret it as long as you live.' Vera blushed for having been so familiar, and longed to go. 'Will the Rector be long?'

'That sounds like him now.'

'Has he finished his meal?'

'Yes.'

Vera stood up ready to leave.

They drove all the way to Penny Fawcett in silence. Peter looked at her occasionally but her face was so set in misery he couldn't bring himself to disturb her.

He pulled up outside the nursing home, opened the car door for her, and as she got out she said, 'Rector, I think I've reached an all-time low today. I was so excited when they told me Don was having the kitchen done. I thought, at last he's taking some notice of what I want. At long last. But after what I've discovered today . . . I know just how little he thinks of me. Zilch. Nothing. Zero. Nought.'

'Look, Vera, I don't know, obviously, what caused that furore just now but whatever it is, if you feel the need to talk to someone about it, the Rectory door is only locked to keep Sheila's cat Topsy in, not you out. You only need to knock and either I or Caroline will listen, and we'll help you all we can.' He took her hand in his as he said this and made the sign of the cross on her forehead. 'God bless you.'

'Thank you, Rector. Thank you. I'm grateful for that.'

A week later in the post came a communication from a bank informing her that she needed to call at their Culworth Branch with some documents they specified to sign papers for the opening of an account in the joint names of Donald Isambard Wright and Vera Renee Wright. She had to read it twice before realisation began to dawn. Never having received a letter from a bank before, it took some understanding. Had he put all the money into the bank and she had a share of it then? He couldn't. He wouldn't, wouldn't Don. Or had he? How could she find out? She puzzled over this all morning till finally she became so confused someone asked her if she wasn't well. 'Oh! I am. It's to do with money. I've got to get to the bank today, it says so. I'll work extra tonight to make up.'

So she trundled to Culworth on the lunch-time bus with the letter in her bag, wearing her newest jacket and skirt. She didn't have to see the manager, someone else, a nice young girl who didn't look old enough to be working, let alone managing customer's accounts dealt with it. She showed them her birth certificate and a letter from the council addressed to her at the nursing home, signed the papers, nodded that the address was correct, and then asked, 'Excuse me, is it all right for me to ask how much is in the account? My husband set it up, you see, and forgot to tell me.'

'Seven thousand five hundred pounds.'

Vera never let her face slip, not an inch, not even one of those new-fangled millimetres. 'And if I want to take money out?'

'By cheque, or by a cash card with a pin number, but that will take a while to set up.'

'You mean one of those machines in the wall?'

Sitting on the Penny Fawcett afternoon bus Vera was forced to the conclusion that Don was a far nicer man than she had thought. Still, time would tell, a leopard doesn't completely change its spots, not all at once anyway. She'd bide her time, but she would send him a little note to thank him for what he'd done. When the bus pulled up outside the Store, out of habit she rose to get off then remembered she was going on to Penny Fawcett. Her mistake triggered off the thought that however kindly she might come to think about Don she wasn't giving up her job and going back to live in the cottage. He'd have to come to her at the flat. She thought about his dyed hair and giggled. Who'd have thought it?

Chapter 13

Muriel was at Orchard House to welcome Ron and Sheila back from the hospital. Vera's cousin Dottie had cleaned the house and changed the beds and generally titivated everything for their return. Ralph and Muriel had been to the Store to get in some supplies for them, Caroline and Sylvia between them had baked cakes and made a trifle to help tide them over the first couple of days, and Jimbo had sent round a bottle of Sheila's favourite sherry. Several of the villagers had arrived with flowers and, much to Muriel's despair, she'd had them to arrange. The thought of Sheila's skill with flowers had inhibited her and she'd made a poor job of filling the various vases.

Still, as she stood appraising the sitting room just before they arrived she decided that, yes, it did look welcoming, and the small table set with the necessities for morning coffee looked very attractive.

She heard a toot and saw Gilbert's car slide gently to a stop outside. Sheila walked in as though she'd just been out for a stroll, but Ron moved awkwardly and his face was white with pain.

'Oh, Sir Ronald, do sit down, you look to be in such pain!'

He grunted, which she took to be a yes, and gently lowered himself into the nearest armchair. Muriel took his stick from him and propped it against the wall.

'There, Sheila, where are you going to sit?'

Sheila gave a great sigh. 'It is so lovely being home. I thought at one time I wouldn't want to come here ever again but I do. I thought we'd have to sell up and go somewhere else, but how could I?' She beamed at Gilbert who was coming in with their belongings. 'I couldn't leave my dear Louise and her lovely Gilbert, could I?'

Gilbert grinned at her and said, 'Now, now, Mother-in-law, less of the flattery. Where shall I put these?'

'I mean every word. You're the best son-in-law anyone could hope to have, isn't he, Ron?'

Ron nodded. 'He is. The best. Thanks for this morning, Gilbert.'

'The least I can do. Louise will be round tonight, she's leaving me in charge while she comes. Just sorry the baby's too poorly to be left.'

'Upstairs, Gilbert, please.'

He went to do as Sheila asked, leaving a silence behind him.

Muriel filled it by asking if they'd like coffee.

Sheila groaned. 'Would I like coffee! I certainly would. That stuff at the hospital tasted like lavatory cleaner.'

'But they've looked after you quite splendidly, haven't they?'

'Oh, yes. The medical attention is first-rate. Couldn't be bettered if we'd paid a thousand pounds a day, but the food . . .' She looked round the room and noticed the flowers. 'Where have all these flowers come from?'

'The roses are from Nick and Ros Barnes, the Michael-mas daisies and chrysanthemums from Dicky, Bel and Georgie. Tom and Evie sent this wonderful pot plant with a little note and –'

'How are they? Tom and Evie?'

Gilbert came down and said he'd have to get back to work, and anything they needed they only had to ring, and on no account was Ron to cut the lawn, he, Gilbert, would do it at the weekend. Ron moaned at the prospect, and Gilbert left in a flurry of laughter.

Sheila smiled. 'Such a lovely boy, Gilbert. I don't know where we would have been without him these last weeks. So Tom and poor Evie?'

'Very well, so far as I know.'

'It must have been a shock for them, that happening to us after such a lovely evening.'

'I'm sure it was. Tom took it very much to heart.'

'That nice superintendent is absolutely foxed as to why we got beaten up. It wasn't as if it was a burglary and we'd interrupted them. They beat us up full stop.'

'It must have been dreadful.'

Sheila quietly began to cry. Ron gestured to her in sympathy but couldn't face heaving himself out of the chair, and Muriel went into the kitchen to make the coffee. There was nothing she could find to say. It must have been terrifying and then coming back had inevitably revived all the horror.

Muriel carried the coffee pot in. Sheila was wiping her eyes. 'I'm sorry about crying, it's not like me.'

'Don't be sorry, it's only to be expected. You've had a dreadful time and then you come home and have it to face all over again.' As Muriel poured out the coffee she said, 'There's post in the kitchen, I'll get it for you, that is if you want to bother with it.'

'Oh yes, I love getting post. Yes, I'll open it.'

Muriel finished serving the coffee and went into the kitchen to pick up the letters. The topmost one was addressed to Orchid House. Oh dear! That relief postman was getting himself all confused. Orchid House. Orchard House. Orchid House! Why? Surely not. It couldn't be, could it? Had the attackers got themselves confused just like the postman? It was dark, and with no street lighting . . . Why ever hadn't she thought of it before?

Muriel rushed back into the sitting room. 'Sheila! This letter is addressed to Tom and Evie at Orchid House. Don't you see? Orchard House. Orchid House. That was the mistake! In the dark. They meant to hurt Tom and Evie, not you. It wasn't you at all!'

'Let me see.'

Ron struggled to his feet. 'Of course! It was *them*, not us.'

Sheila scoffed at them both. 'Don't be ridiculous. What have poor Evie and Tom done to deserve it any more than us?'

Muriel felt very silly. 'Of course, it's just as impossible, isn't it? I'm sorry, I really must stop jumping to conclusions. Who'd want to batter a harmless verger?'

Sheila, her mind working furiously, suddenly began to find very good reasons for supporting Muriel's theory. 'Ah! But he hasn't always been a verger, has he? Let's face it, we none of us knew what he'd been up to before he became verger. All that supposed wheeling and dealing. Import, export. That covers a multitude of sins, or it could.'

Ron sat down again. He battled with the pain for a moment and then said, 'Well, I feel too ill to bother. At least we're alive and we know it's not happened because of something we've done, so let the police get on with it.'

'No,' Sheila protested,' we can't let the matter drop. Can we, Muriel?'

'I feel very silly actually for even thinking it. Ralph won't want me to get involved, so I for one am not going to say any more. I'll take the letter to Tom's and not say a word. In fact, I'll pop it through the letterbox and I won't knock, because I feel too embarrassed.'

'Well, if you won't take it further, I will.'

'But we don't know, do we, what they could possibly have done to deserve it? You have to be very careful.'

'Poor Evie. Makes you wonder what she's had to put up with all these years. All that terrible silence must mean something. Perhaps she daren't speak because she's afraid of giving secrets away. That'll be it. He's silenced her.'

'But Tom's not like that.' Then Muriel remembered how she'd told Ralph she didn't like Tom wearing those orange overalls, and how he'd pooh-poohed it. Maybe Tom really was a malevolent creature planning to take over the world, or at least their part of it and Ralph was wrong.

The doorbell rang in the midst of all these suppositions and when Muriel answered it there stood Ralph.

Him having been uppermost in her thoughts at that moment Muriel was startled to find him on the doorstep. 'Oh! It's Ralph!'

He looked surprised at her greeting. 'Yes, this is your

husband here. I live with you across the Green, you know, next door but one to the Rectory.'

Muriel laughed. 'Don't be silly, Ralph!'

'Can I come in?'

She stepped back and opened the door wider. 'Of course. Sheila and Ron are in the sitting room.'

Sheila winced. If only she'd called it the drawing room, in front of Sir Ralph too. 'Come in, Sir Ralph, please do. Here we are, all cosy in our lovely drawing room again.'

Ralph bent to kiss her cheek. 'Welcome home, Sheila, and you too, Ron.' He shook hands with Ron. 'Lovely to have you back all in one piece. I must say you're looking remarkably well considering what you've been through.'

Sheila smiled her hostess smile saying, 'Lovely to see you too. Can we offer you coffee?'

'Thank you, no. Muriel and I are out to lunch today and we must be leaving shortly, but I felt I must come to say welcome back.'

'That's so thoughtful of you. Do you know, Sir Ralph? Muriel has come up with an answer as to why we were attacked.'

Ralph raised his eyebrows at Muriel. 'Have you?'

'No, I haven't not really, dear.'

'You have, Muriel, hasn't she, Ron?'

'Well, I'm not convinced . . .'

'It should have been Tom and Evie who got beaten up not us. In the dark they confused Orchard House for Orchid House. Why did they change the name to Orchid House? Just to cause this kind of confusion, do you think?'

Ralph shook his head. 'No. Tom specialises in growing orchids. I've seen them. He's quite an expert.'

'Oh, that's what the fancy greenhouse is then? I wondered what it was for.'

'That's right.'

'Still, it means we were on the receiving end of whatever was intended for them.'

'Now, Sheila, you do not know that. You only surmise. Please be careful, you know what rumours are like in this village. A seed becomes a monstrous tree in the course of a day.'

'But don't you think the police should know?'

'Possibly they have already thought that out for themselves.'

'Well, Sir Ralph, if that is true why haven't they done something about it?'

'They may have and drawn a blank like they have about you and Ron.'

Ron, too weary to tolerate Sheila's persistent questioning, said, 'Look, let's leave it for now. I'm quite sure the police can manage perfectly well without our assistance. I'll have more coffee, if I may.'

Muriel poured it for him and then said, 'I'll wash up before I go.'

Sheila shook her head. 'No need. That Dottie Foskett is coming back to make the lunch. She's at Louise's at the moment. We're going to share her for a while till I feel better, which won't be long if I've anything to do with it. How our Louise puts up with Dottie I'll never know. Louise says she's conscientious and punctual and never asks to go early. But the gossip! Louise says sometimes she's had to send Gilbert out of the room so he won't be embarrassed. Such an innocent is Gilbert. However, she did tell . . .'

In case Ralph got treated to a sample of Dottie's gossip

Muriel decided to leave. 'You have my number, Ralph and I will be only too pleased to help, any time, don't hesitate. I'll pop in tomorrow just in case.'

'Thank you, Muriel, very much. Everyone's been so kind.'

Muriel popped the letter for Orchid House through the letterbox and as they crossed the Green she said, 'You know, I'm sure I'm right.'

Ralph tucked her hand into the crook of his arm and held it there. 'You well could be, but don't say anything. Like Ron said, the police know what they're doing. That Proctor chap has more than his fair share of brains. He'll sort it out.'

'It's the orange overalls. I did say, didn't I?'

Ralph stopped by the pond and watched the geese with their broods of young ones preening themselves by the water's edge. 'I love your imagination, Muriel. It gives me great pleasure, so childlike, not childish, childlike, but you've got it wrong.' He finished what he had to say with an emphatic 'So please say no more about it.'

'I'm not used to you laying down the law to me.'

'I know you're not, but I am, just this once. Your thoughts transmitted to anyone else will grow in their minds and before we know it it will turn into a witch hunt, and we shall be rolled back three centuries in a single decisive moment. So for everyone's good, forget it, my dear.'

'Like when they stoned the Baxter sisters' house.'

Ralph nodded. 'Exactly. I can't quite find the right words to describe it, but whatever it is, something gets called up from way back in time and makes them erupt into quite violent action. Very alarming really when it happens.

Lunch, I think.' He looked at his watch. 'Ten minutes and we've to be off.'

'Oh, Ralph, I'll never be ready in time!'

Sheila had plenty of visitors that first morning, which quite exhausted Ron and he had to retire to bed after lunch completely worn out. Dottie stayed long enough to make the lunch and clear away and then set off on her bike again for Little Derehams and Louise's, but not before Sheila had tested her new theory out on her.

'It was Lady Templeton who twigged what had happened, she was very convinced.'

'Well, she should know what's she's about, her a Lady.'

Sheila nodded. 'Yes, you can rely on her.'

'But what's he been up to?'

'Ahhhh! That's it, isn't it?'

'Yes.' Dottie shifted her weight to her other leg and lifted the corner of Sheila's nets to peep outside. 'Does the police know? 'Cos they're just about to knock on the door.'

'What?' Sheila straightened herself up, patted her hair and regretted not having repaired her lipstick since eating her lunch.

They heard the doorbell ring.

'That's them. Shall I let them in?'

'Of course.'

Dottie hovered in the hall listening to them talking. The upshot of the conversation with the police was that they would prefer it if Sheila and Ron, in the circumstances, had a police officer on duty at the house at all times, only as a precaution, of course.

'Dear heavens! Whatever for!'

'We'd prefer to move you to another house. Is there anywhere local like Penny Fawcett or . . .'

'My married daughter lives in Little Derehams but their cottage is full. They've two babies, you see, we'd get no peace and Ron isn't at all well. We don't want to go a long way away because Ron's still having treatment.'

'In that case we'll do as I first said and you can have a police officer here at all times.'

Panic set in and Sheila began to tremble. 'I'm not at all well myself and now you've frightened me. I don't know if I can cope with anything more.'

'There's no need to worry, it's just a precaution.'

'But I am worrying. Why on earth do you think we need someone here? Are they going to come back?'

'As I said, it's just in case.'

'What have Tom and Evie done?'

'Tom and Evie?'

'Yes. You've got to come clean about this. It was them not us they were after, wasn't it?'

Superintendent Proctor got to his feet. 'The less you know the better.'

He left behind a charming woman officer, who looked too fragile to prevent a manikin attacking them never mind a gang. 'Are you sure she's . . . capable?'

'Judo black belt.'

'Oh, I see.'

'She'll give you the run-down on what to do. Take care, Lady Bissett. My regards to Sir Ronald.'

'For how long do you think?'

'Few days.'

That night Ron had a very restless sleep. He'd got worked up about having a police officer in the house, about his injuries, and damning to hell whoever'd kicked him because the internal bruising was taking so long to go away, his pain-killers were ineffective and altogether he wished himself anywhere but where he was. 'Sheila! Could I ask you for a cup of tea?'

Sheila struggled awake. 'What? What?'

'A cup of tea. I'm having such a bad night, you've no idea.'

'Oh, I have! You keep grunting and shuffling about.'

'I can't help it, love. I'm sorry. I'm just so uncomfortable.'

She flung back the duvet and found her slippers by shushing her bare feet about the carpet till she located them. 'Right. I'll have one myself. Don't go to sleep, will you? I won't be long. On second thoughts, I'll put my bedside light on, it'll keep you awake.'

'Fat chance I have of falling asleep.'

Sheila wended her way downstairs, filled the kettle, got out the small tray with the Portmeirion pattern on it, and laid it elegantly. If a job's worth doing, she thought. While she waited for the kettle she went into the sitting room and stood by the window looking out. It was so good to be home. So very good. She loved the view from her window. The stocks, the pond, the old oak tree . . . at the height of the summer the tree somewhat obscured her view of the church but she didn't mind because it was so beautiful. She smiled to herself about the old legend, if the oak tree dies so too will the village. A likely story. Take more than a dead tree to finish this village off.

The deep silence of the middle of the night was broken

by the sound of a car. Who on earth could that be at this time? Surely not the – Oh, God! The car was coming round Stocks Row past the pub. And no headlights. Dawn was just beginning but it still wasn't light enough to drive without . . . They were stopping! Outside Tom and Evie's! Oh! Not another beating up. Sheila froze. But they wouldn't stop right outside, would they, if they were up to no good? The driver got out. By craning her neck she could see him open up the boot, then the sound of a door, then . . . surely not! It was. Tom and Evie! He had his arm round Evie's waist and a case in the other hand. Another man appeared out of the car and then the case Tom was carrying was put in the boot. Evie seemed close to collapse and was shaking her head in refusal. It appeared to take all Tom's efforts to persuade her to get in to the car. He shook his head at one of the men as though despairing and then they all got into the car and drove away. Poor Evie! Poor Tom! Had they been kidnapped? No, they went easily enough in the end and the men weren't forcing them in. She was sure Tom would have put up a fight, even if it was only for Evie's sake. But perhaps they had guns and he'd no alternative! They were in a hurry because the car engine had never even been switched off. They were expected, because the case was already packed. Such haste. And what for?

Ron's tea! She made the tea and rushed as fast as she could to tell Ron. Half-way up the stairs she remembered the policewoman. Some good having her in the house, lying there fast asleep and all this happening. Sheila put the tray on her bedside table saying to Ron 'Let it brew. I won't be a minute.' She scurried along the landing to the police-woman's bedroom.

'Claire! Claire! Are you awake?' Tapping on the door brought no response so Sheila opened the door slightly and called again.

'Yes?'

'Tom and Evie have been taken away in a car. Do you think they've been kidnapped?'

Claire sat up with a start. 'Have they? Are you sure?'

'I saw them being driven away.'

'God help us!' She fished under her pillow for her telephone and dialled a number, waving Sheila away as soon as she made contact. Quite put out Sheila closed the door thinking, I expect she didn't want me to hear her getting a dressing-down for being asleep when she should have been on the *qui vive*. Still, she couldn't keep awake twenty-four hours a day, could she? They should have sent someone else to relieve her. No, they shouldn't, thought Sheila, I don't want the entire police force in residence when not even one is necessary.

Ron had sat himself up in bed and was waiting patiently for his tea. 'It took a long time. Did you forget to switch the kettle on?'

'No, I didn't. Here, get hold of it tight, we don't want tea all over the bed. You know what a long way even a drop can go.' She gingerly climbed back into bed, remembering how the slightest wrong twist or turn could cause her pain. 'No, it's Tom and Evie, they've been taken away. In a car.'

'Sheila!'

'It's true, I saw them.'

'God! What next? Bang goes the quiet-English-village-where-nothing-happens theory.' He sipped his tea. 'Maybe the policewoman is a good idea after all.'

'Fat lot of good she is fast asleep.'

'Well, at least she's reassuring.'

'I suppose so. Make sure the duvet's pulled well up, we don't want her embarrassed, she might come in with a message.'

Each one of Sheila and Ron's visitors the next day went away with a dramatised version of the great escape of the Nichollses.

'I saw them with my own eyes. Believe me, they were hustled into the car, Evie's feet barely touching the ground. You should have seen! Terrified she was! Weeping heart-broken. What I should like to know is who were they and why were they removing Tom from the scene? Tell me that. Of course the police will tell me nothing. We might as well not have this Claire Thingummy here, complete waste of time she is. The only thing she's useful for is answering the door and saving me getting up out of the chair. Strict instructions we have, *don't answer the door*. In fact after the last time Ron answered it I don't think I want to answer it ever again. Well, would you?'

That second night when they guessed Claire would be asleep, Ron quietly opened the front door and went for a stroll. A very careful, guarded stroll, one foot placed slowly in front of the other, one hand clutching the side where the worst of the kicking had been, breathing in the fresh air in deep gulps, appreciating it all the more after the clinical smells of the hospital and enjoying the peace of the midnight hour. Thank God for it, thought Ron, I'd go mad if I didn't get out, and that damn bossy Claire wouldn't hear of it, but he needed it for sanity's sake.

It was Sheila's idea to wait until everyone had gone to bed and truth to tell he was glad he'd waited, because he was forced to walk so slowly he felt an idiot; an old fellow in his dotage, no less and – My God! Just by his shoulder he thought he caught a glimpse of the net curtain at Tom and Evie's sitting-room window moving just slightly. No lights, but the curtain had certainly moved. So it was all a tale about them being kidnapped. Honestly, why did Sheila have to exaggerate everything so? He passed their other window and was creeping round the corner down Royal Oak Road when he felt a hand on his shoulder.

It clamped down, gripped him fiercely and a voice whispered, 'What are you doing out?'

His heart went completely out of control, thudding so erratically he was convinced his chest would explode. When he found his voice he said, 'Taking the air. Who are you?'

'Police. Shushhhhh! Home, if you please.'

Disgruntled at having been found out like a small schoolboy misbehaving, Ron grunted, 'All right, all right. But why can't I take a walk?'

'Because. Here, let me help you.'

'I can't hurry. It's the bruising, you know.'

The two of them turned round and started back home to Orchard House. Squatting in the front of the Royal Oak under the window of the lounge he spotted a shadowy figure and he could just make out someone else standing behind Jimmy's fence in the shade of his chicken house. My God, the place was full of police. Wait till he told Sheila.

Chapter 14

Kenny and Terry had not been home all that night having, unbeknown to each other, each found himself a woman. Terry, the barmaid from the Jug and Bottle, and Kenny, someone he'd picked up in a Chinese restaurant in Culworth. Consequently it was something like twenty-four hours before both their cars were parked once more in the drive of number six Hipkin Gardens. By curious chance Terry arrived home within a moment of Kenny.

Terry didn't bother to lock his car it being, as he well knew, quite valueless and anyone wanting to steal it was welcome to it. 'Where've you been?'

Kenny replied, 'Ask no questions get told no lies. Got yer key?'

Terry put his hand on the front door to steady himself while he put the key in the lock only to find that the door swung open of its own accord. 'That's funny. You must have left the door open yesterday.'

'I never did.'

'Oh, God! Damn and blast it! We've been burgled!'

Kenny pushed Terry aside and marched in. It was difficult to find a place to put your feet for all the carpet downstairs had been heaved up and every stick of furniture pulled out of its place. Shouting expletives his mother would not have known the meaning of, Kenny rushed from sitting room to kitchen, from stairs to bedroom to bathroom then back downstairs and up to his bedroom again. He stood in the doorway confused as to why nothing appeared to have been stolen yet . . . Kenny looked round the crash site that had been his bedroom: everything had been overturned including the bed. His clothes, his beautiful, fashionable new clothes which he'd left hanging neatly in the wardrobe, were heaped on the floor, every drawer emptied, every picture off the walls. They'd done a thorough job. A cold sweat broke out on his forehead, ran down his neck, trickled on to his shirt collar and some of it poured down his spine. This wasn't petty robbery this was . . .

He could hear Terry howling in the kitchen about some discovery he'd made then his footsteps racing up the stairs to view his bedroom. It was the same all over the house. Their possessions thrown about in a cruelly systematic search.

Kenny scrambled down the stairs and slumped down in his big leather armchair to think. Think what? Who? Why? What for?

Terry asked in anguished tones why their house had been picked on.

Kenny looked wryly at him.

Terry exploded with an idea. 'Ring the police!'

'For God's sake, Terry! Sorry, Mr Plod, but our house has been done over and we can't think why. Oh, yes!

They'd love that, wouldn't they? They'd be laughing all the way from the station.'

'Who's done it then?'

'Use yer brains, Terry. Who do you think? Them what have toes that we've trodden on.'

'What d'yer mean? Who did it to us?'

Kenny looked scornfully at his brother and wondered how he'd managed to be burdened with such a fool. 'Turkish Delight?'

Terry paled at the thought. 'Oh, God! It'll be 'im, you're right.'

'We'd better stay low for a while. He's given us a warning, that's what this is all about. If he'd found our money . . .' He gestured at the mess. 'This is 'im telling us he knows. This is only for starters is this warning.'

Terry laughed, but there was a tremor in his voice when he replied, 'You and me! Come on, us compared to them! You've got ideas above your station you 'ave. You and me a threat to 'im? That's a laugh! Why should Turkish Delight bother with us? We're small fry in comparison.' He sat down in the more meagre chair allocated to him by Kenny.

''Cos he's heard about our activities up in town and he's not having us trespassing. Safest thing we can do is get the money and make a fast exit for a while.'

Terry sat up abruptly. 'You mean leave Turnham Malpas? Go somewhere new? Leave everything behind?'

Kenny mocked him. 'Yes! Next time we might be at home when they come.' He blanched at the thought of their narrow escape. 'I'm not into violence and that's what it's going to be if we aggravate old Turkish Delight any more. Violence with a capital V.'

'Just when we're building up a good business. Blast it. I'm never going to make it big, am I?'

'We will, one way or another. We've been too cocky trying this. We've watched enough serials on telly about drug-dealers being buried in concrete overcoats to know when to do a bunk.' Kenny shuddered. 'I'm going to church. Right. Won't be long. The money's not safe there anyway with Tom gone. Willie's not so ... amenable.'

Terry, scared though he was, sneered at the word 'amenable'. 'You mean you 'aven't got a hold over him.'

Kenny gestured at the chaos around his feet. 'That's right. Tidy up, OK? Shan't be long. I want to leave it spick and span. Don't want Sir Ralph upset with us.'

'Won't matter if he is, we shan't be here.'

'Just do as I say. See yer.' He left then came back in again. 'While I'm gone pack a couple of bags for us, and put my new clothes in mine and don't forget your toothbrush, if you can find it that is. And don't forget to rescue the white stuff from under the shed.'

Willie was devoting his time to a thorough cleaning of the memorial chapel. He'd just got used to his freedom and here he was back again doing the verger's job. Poor Tom. Still it was enjoyable, made yer feel needed, and the money would be useful for their holidays. Who'd have thought it, him, Willie Biggs, swanning off to outlandish places like Minorca? He only did it for Sylvia's sake, or pretended he did. Let's face it, he thought, as he wrung out his cloth in the bucket, I enjoy it as much as she does. The hot sun, the new sights, the company, the hotel. Yer came back renewed. He got up from his knees and settled himself on a chair facing the altar to ease his cramped legs for a moment, to his left the huge carved memorial screen shielding him from the main part of the church, in front of him the altar where the Rector said his prayers each day.

Times had changed and not half. He looked at the names on the brass memorial tablet beside the altar, and tried to imagine what the village must have been like all those years ago when things like beatings for no reason at all simply didn't happen. A cart track into Culworth, no TV, scarcely even a telephone. A motor car, he supposed, up at the Big House. No washing-machines. No videos. Nor this new-fangled Internet they all talked about.

As he sat there thinking, the opening of the church door barely touched his consciousness. He belonged to the history of the village. Two of his uncles on the memorial plaque and there'd been Biggses living in his cottage since . . . well, heaven knew how long, certainly a hundred years but in the long life of the village that was a mere moment. Domesday Book they'd been mentioned in. He'd seen it in a book. And them Roman ruins up at the Big House before . . . What was that?

A strange noise he couldn't relate to anything. It didn't sound like visitors: they usually whispered loudly and crept noisily about. He cautiously stood up and moved towards the screen. Finding a hole through which he could see into the main body of the church, Willie put his eye to it. By turning first right then left he had a view of most of the church. The only bit he couldn't see was the font right at the back. His scalp prickled and he felt as though his hair was standing on end for, as he looked towards the Templeton tomb, he saw someone rise up from the narrow end of it. They'd actually come from inside it. A ghost, was it? A ghost like he'd always said! He'd been right, it was haunted. Had he gone completely mad? Then the world righted itself and he saw it was Kenny Jones standing there. Grave robbing! Whatever next?

Willie leaped out of the memorial chapel like a man possessed, his desert boots making no sound as he pounded down the aisle. 'Kenny Jones! What you up to? Eh? Tell me that!'

Kenny looked up, startled out of his mind: dusty and dishevelled, in his hand a Tesco's carrier-bag.

'What's that you've got there, you thieving runt, you? Grave robbing! Whatever next!' As he reached Kenny, Willie met Kenny's fist head on. It smacked him straight between the eyes and he fell on the stone floor unconscious, blood pouring from his nose. Breathing heavily, Kenny carefully replaced the marble end panel of the tomb, dusted himself off and headed for home, his car and anonymity.

Willie regained consciousness very slowly. First he couldn't think where he was, till he felt the chill of the stone floor penetrating his sweater. Then he realised his face felt peculiar and when he tenderly tested it with his fingers he found blood everywhere and he remembered. Kenny Jones! Kenny Jones had hit him. Willie sat up, his head throbbing. Curiously everything appeared to be in order yet he could have sworn ... Yes, he was right, Kenny had been interfering with the tomb. He pulled himself up by the tomb using the foot of the marble knight laid atop of it. He could tell just by looking that the end panel had been moved. Robbing a grave. How could he? Surely it was a criminal offence.

Willie struggled up the aisle determined to get to the Rectory. He locked the main door so no one could interfere with his evidence, and with a handkerchief pressed to his face as his nose was still dripping he hammered on the Rectory door.

Peter knew instantly who it was as Willie always knocked in that way even if what he had to say was something quite innocuous.

Peter gasped when he opened the door. 'Heavens! Willie! What on earth has happened? Come in.'

Willie's voice was thick and unrecognisable. 'No, I won't, thank you, sir. It's Kenny Jones what's done it. Hit me he did. I caught him grave robbing.'

'Grave robbing? Kenny Jones? I don't believe it! Whose grave?'

'The Templeton tomb in the church. Come and see for yourself. Come on.'

'Shall we wash your face first and inspect the damage? It looks incredibly painful.'

'No. We need the police. Come and see, I caught him red-handed.'

Peter locked the Rectory door behind them and followed Willie into the church. 'But what did he steal?'

'I don't know, but he had a plastic carrier-bag in his hand with something in it and he was dusty.'

'I can't see Kenny being keen on opening up a tomb, can you?'

Willie took the handkerchief from his face and said 'Look, there you are.' He pointed to the panel that had been replaced. 'It was open when I saw him and then he socked me one and when I came round he'd gone and the panel was back in place. I tell you he deserves all he gets. Will you phone the police or shall I?'

Peter inspected the panel, observed it wasn't quite, just not quite, fitted back correctly and he looked at the fine particles of dust on the floor. 'Better not touch anything.' Peter straightened up and dusted his hands together. 'It does seem extremely odd. What on earth is he thinking of? I'll phone the police.'

'Muriel told me he'd started coming into church, but being Muriel, kindly like, she thought it was to pray. Fat chance. It was something to do with this 'ere tomb. It gave me a fright I can tell yer.'

In the bar of the Royal Oak that night the attack on Willie was the sole topic of conversation. The man himself had returned from Casualty with Sylvia at eight o'clock and insisted on a meal in the dining room and then a drink afterwards.

By then his face was black and blue, and the strips of plaster they'd used to hold the lacerations together while they healed, created an interesting criss-cross pattern on it. There was also considerable swelling, one eye being closed and the other just a slit.

Sylvia patted his arm. 'You're not well enough to go out, Willie. You look a real sight.'

'That Kenny Jones isn't keeping me away from my ale. 'Elp to dull the pain it will. Come on. You need feeding too as well as me.'

'All right, then, but it's madness. Here, take my arm, because I'm blessed if you can see a thing.'

A cheer went up as they entered.

'Come on, Willie, let's see the damage.'

'My, that Kenny can punch.'

'You'll be a fortnight before you're right.'

'Break yer nose, did he?'

'They've phoned Mike Tyson to let him know you're available!' This last was greeted with hilarious laughter.

'Must have given you a shock, Willie, 'im dressed all in white stepping out of a tomb! You've always said it was haunted.'

Willie laughed off the teasing as best he could. He wasn't feeling quite so full of life as he had been, and the pain felt to be getting worse. Truth to tell, it was bravado which had got him into the bar, and he didn't know if it would carry him through the rest of the evening.

Two people got up to go, saying as they shrugged on their jackets, 'We'll go play spot the policeman.' This witticism was greeted with another outburst of mirth.

A chap sitting at the bar shouted, 'No wonder the rates keep going up. It's to pay for that lot hanging about doing nothing all night.'

'They wouldn't do it if they didn't think it was necessary.'

'But just what are they expecting to see? That's what I would like to know.'

'But just think, that Kenny opening up a tomb.' The speaker shuddered. 'What on earth must it be like after two hundred years.'

'Is it that long since it was opened up then?'

'Says so on the side. Eighteen hundred and one.'

'But robbing a grave! How low can you sink?'

The conversation broke up after that, and Willie was allowed to go for his meal and eat it in peace.

When he and Sylvia had finished they returned to the bar to find Don Wright and Barry Jones seated at the table where they usually sat. 'Evening, Don! Barry! Mind if we join you?'

Don moved along the settle to give Sylvia more space. 'Here. Sit yourselves down.'

Barry looked embarrassed. 'I'm dead sorry about your . . .' He gestured towards Willie's face. 'I don't know what got into him.'

Willie, beginning to find it painful to speak, said, 'He might be your brother but you're as different as cheese from chalk, so don't worry yer 'ead about it. No' your fault.'

'At least let me get you a drink.' Barry got up. 'What will it be?'

Sylvia smiled up at him. 'Gin and tonic for me and a glass of Dicky's home brew for Willie, please.'

Barry strode away to get the drinks and Sylvia said, 'Different, aren't they, him and their Kenny and Terry? Barry has all the vigour and they . . . well . . .'

Don agreed. 'He's working that hard for me. Says he won't take any payment for it but he will.'

'Nearly done?'

'Kitchen's finished and the plumber's tiling the bathroom. White it is, snow white from top to bottom. Even got a shower over the bath, and it's not one where the water dribbles out, it comes out in a rush. I can't wait to 'ave a go. Smashing. Wait till Vera sees it. Thrilled she'll be.'

Privately sceptical that Don might ever get under that

shower with any enthusiasm Sylvia decided to speak up on another matter. 'We're all getting a bit fed up of looking at that mountain of rubbish outside your door. Time it was moved.'

Barry came back with the drinks. 'Here we are then.' He handed out the glasses then raised his to Willie. 'Thanks for being so nice to me about our Kenny.'

'That's all right.' Willie sipped his ale with relish. 'Sylvia's right about that rubbish, Don. What are you going to do about it? The pile gets bigger every day. Spoiling the village it is.'

Barry wiped the froth from his top lip. 'I've an idea about that. Harvest Festival next week, before we know where we are it'll be Bonfire Night. So . . . I think all your stuff would make a good basis for the fire. I'll ask Mr Fitch if we can use the van to carry it up to the field. If we cover it with plastic sheeting anchored down, it'ud be all right.'

Willie laughed as best he could. 'One time you'd have used it and not asked old Fitch. Things have changed.'

'Been decent to me, has Mr Fitch just lately. In fact, he's been decent to everyone just lately. Barry grinned.' So I've decided to behave myself. Given us all a rise, and he's much more nice now. As head gardener my father-in-law can't put a foot wrong if he tries. Got a rise and an extra week's holiday. When they meet it's Greenwood this and Greenwood that. All very friendly. And as for Jeremy! Well! Buddies, they are. Buddies.'

Surprised at the prospect of Mr Fitch being buddies with anyone at all Sylvia asked, 'How is Jeremy, then? We haven't seen him since he was in hospital.'

'If you did you wouldn't know it was him. He's lost four stones.'

'Four stones!' Sylvia couldn't visualise Jeremy four stones lighter.

'Still more to lose but he's looking so much better. Started swimming now.'

'Swimming!' Sylvia couldn't visualise that either. 'Jeremy swimming? The mind boggles.'

Barry laughed. 'Not a pretty sight, but he's doing it every day. To get back to our Kenny, I'm blinking sorry about what he's done. Heaven alone knows what he's up to. Mother's heartbroken. Losing her job over him, Dad without a job too and then what Kenny's done today, it's nearly finished her.'

'Tell her it's not her fault. Heaven alone knows she's tried to bring the three of you up well.'

'She has indeed.' Barry shook his head.

Sylvia decided to ask Barry about the hedge while he was in such a reflective mood. 'Barry, if ever you hear any news about the hedge could you let me know? You being up there every day I thought perhaps you might, you know . . .' Sylvia cupped her hand around her ear and pretended to listen. 'Dr Harris is determined to stop him pulling it up and I'd like to help.'

Barry winked. 'I shall be on the blower as soon as I hear. The Rector's had no effect on him at all. The news is old Fitch will have it done before the winter sets in.'

Sylvia's eyes opened wide. 'No! He's definitely going ahead with it, then?'

Barry nodded. 'Don't know exactly when. When I do I'll let you know.'

'Thanks. They do say that Lady Templeton is all ready to throw herself in front of the digger.'

Barry laughed. 'No-o-o-o! She's always so ladylike I can't quite believe it. She means business then.'

Sylvia nodded vigorously. 'Oh, yes! we all do. It amazes me that he can be so much nicer to all of you and yet takes us all on yet again about the hedge. I know I go on about it but I can't help feeling that there's more to it than just the hedge. They say he's after widening Pipe and Nook Lane at the same time, and there must be a reason behind that. Why else should he give away a long strip of land like that?'

'I reckon he'th got the counthil in hith pocket.' This from Willie who was finding speaking increasingly difficult.

'For what, though?' Barry asked.

'Houtheth?'

'What? Oh! *Houses.*' Barry laughed. 'On Rector's Meadow! He'd never get planning consent.'

Willie pretended to tap the side of his nose. 'Oh, no? He'd get blood out of a thtone he would. Money talkth. I'm off home.'

'Good night, Willie. Hope you feel better tomorrow. Sylvia, soon as I hear a whisper I'll be in touch.'

'Thanks.'

By eleven thirty not a single human being was about, Jimmy's geese were sleeping, the occasional owl swept across the village over towards the motorway embankments searching for mice, not a light shone, the only disturbance being that caused by the wind ruffling the leaves of the old oak and the roses and honeysuckle growing around the cottage doors. The moon came out from behind the clouds and briefly illuminated the village, making the white walls of the cottages appear almost fluorescent, but then flirtatiously it disappeared behind the clouds again. Still waiting behind Jimmy's chicken house, and in the shelter of Misses Senior's garden and over the wall in Tom and Evie's were the policemen, and in the early hours silently and swiftly, just like the owls, they struck, captured their quarry and stole them away.

Chapter 15

Vera not visiting the Royal Oak as frequently as she had when she lived in the village kept up to date with Turnham Malpas news by questioning anyone and everyone who called at the nursing home and might know any gossip. This morning she was keeping an eye out for Jimmy whom she knew was booked to take a patient on a shopping trip into Culworth. As the bonnet of his red Sierra came into view round the rhododendrons she dashed to the front door.

'Good morning, Jimmy! How's things at 'ome?'

'Still call it home, do yer? Well, now, there's a chap called Don going to take a fortnight off to do some decorating,' said Jimmy. 'You won't know your house when you see it.'

'I don't want to see it.' Vera turned away, then turned back to ask, 'The kitchen? Is it good?'

'Good! What a question. Barry's done a wonderful job, lovely new cooker, smashing cupboards like something out of a magazine, I tell yer. And the bathroom! Well!'

'He's done the bathroom as well?'

'Vera! You didn't have what could rightly be called a

bathroom before, did yer? But you have now. Snow white from floor to ceiling. All gleaming and a shower an' all. Yer should go see it.'

Vera shook her head. 'Not likely.' She hesitated and then said, 'He'll expect me to go back there and I won't. First chance we've had to make real money renting out that cottage while we live 'ere, and I'm not going to give in. In any case I don't know if I want him back.'

Jimmy saw his fare coming tottering out of the front door of the home and made ready to depart. Before he opened the taxi door he said, '*He* wants *you* back. I understand he's putting all the furniture on the bonfire. Complete clean sweep he's 'aving.'

'What?'

Jimmy grinned at her, and having stowed the old gentleman safely in the front seat he swept out of the gates still grinning.

On her first afternoon off after this conversation with Jimmy she caught the lunch-time bus into Turnham Malpas to see for herself. Confident that Don would be at work she marched round Stocks Row and slotted her key in the lock. There was an old car parked outside and she thought, What a cheek, someone parking their car right outside our house. But at least it was clean and polished even if it was old. It'll be one of the weekenders, just like 'em.

The cottage was quiet. She ignored the living room still stacked high with the stuff out of the kitchen, and went through into the back and stood there amazed. Their Rhett would have said gobsmacked and she was. The sunlight was coming in through the window and illuminating, that was the only word for it, illuminating the kitchen, the cupboards a kind of pale oak colour, she knew there was a fashionable word for it but she couldn't think of it at the moment, the knobs so elegant, and there under the shiny draining board a brand new washer. The cooker! Well! It was way beyond anything she had ever dreamed of.

Vera opened a drawer and let it slide smoothly closed, she did it again then tried a cupboard door, and then the new blind over the window and the one on the back door. A kitchen for the future and not half. Give her her due, Grandmama Charter-Plackett had made a good job of the kitchen, for nothing was more certain than that it hadn't been Don alone who'd organised this.

Back in the living room she opened the door at the bottom of the stairs and began climbing. The tiny bathroom had been transformed. Somehow they'd fitted in a basin as well as a toilet and bath. The whole effect was of a glimmering, shimmering paradise. Her mind was in such turmoil at the changes Don had wrought that she didn't become aware of the swish-swish of his decorating brush as he painted their bedroom walls until she'd completely studied every last inch of the bathroom. Standing in the bedroom doorway she gasped. Without looking at her at all he said, 'This is all for you.'

'How did you know it was me?'

'Saw you looking at my car.'

'Your car?'

'My car.'

'Since when?'

'Saturday. They brought it today.'

'But where did you get the money from to buy a car? There won't be a penny left.'

'I've kept telling you how valuable that motorbike and sidecar were, but you wouldn't have it. A classic I kept saying. Well, I got eight thousand for it.'

Vera had to clutch the door frame to keep herself upright. She was speechless.

'Polished it up and that, put a new clutch in and that, had the seats restored and that's what I got so I could well afford the car. Will you have a ride in *that*?'

'I might be tempted. I like the kitchen. So where *did* you get the money from, Don?'

Don climbed down from the ladder and stood his emulsion brush on the lid of the clover pink paint he was putting on and sat down on the old bedroom chair. 'Remember the old allotment me dad had in the war?'

'That one you always talked about resurrecting after he died, but never did? What happened then? Did they strike oil?'

Don grinned at her joke. 'No, not oil, but the allotment association got an offer from a builder wanting it for posh houses. Grand spot, looking out over Havers Lake. I used to fish there when he took me up to the allotment when I was a boy.'

'So . . .'

Don paused to reflect on the happy times he'd had fishing by the lake. 'So they had a vote and I never thought they'd all agree, thought there'd be someone who'd put a spanner in the works preferring to escape her indoors and 'ave a quiet smoke and a game of cards in their huts, but they did and we got paid out. Twelve and a half thousand pounds I got, and I've spent five of it on the kitchen and the bathroom.'

'Well, I never. So Dad turned up trumps at last.'

Don answered, 'Yes, he did.'

'Thanks again for putting it in a joint account. I haven't taken anything out.'

'I know.'

'It was nice to be trusted.'

'That's all right. Only fair.'

Vera inspected the painting. 'Nice colour. It'll look good.'

'Hope so. Time for a cup of tea?'

She was tempted to have a go at making tea in that wonderful kitchen but feared she might take a liking to it. 'No. Thanks. I'll be going.'

'OK.'

'Jimmy says all the rubbish outside is going on the bonfire on Guy Fawkes night. Make a great blaze. I shall be glad to be there to see it all go up in smoke.'

'And the furniture too.' Don gazed innocently about the room, half a smile on his face. 'It'll let better unfurnished.'

Vera took umbrage. 'I don't know where you think you're going to live.'

Don felt the ground giving way beneath his feet. 'I had thought . . .'

'You'll have to wait and see, won't you?'

Very quietly Don said, 'There's not much more I can do to make amends, Vera. I've missed you that much.'

Vera felt a small sliver of interest. 'You'd have to let that dye grow out. I liked yer better with iron grey hair not that funny black. Anyway we'll see. Bye.'

Her heart fit to burst with delight, Vera made her way to the bus stop calling in at the Store first to get something nice for her and Rhett for their tea. She mustn't appear too eager, well, just a bit perhaps, because he had worked hard. The decision did appear to be hers, though. Rent for the cottage, she'd ask Jimbo.

Linda was on duty in her post office as usual. 'Hello, Linda. Bet you were glad it wasn't your house got trashed. Them Hipkin Garden houses all look the same – they might have made a mistake.'

'You should have seen it! What a mess. Nothing damaged really, just everything thrown about. You don't miss much though, do you, even though you live out in the wilds?'

Vera scoffed at Linda's remark. 'Can't call Penny Fawcett out in the wilds, now, can you?'

'No regular bus service, no church, no school, no shop. Come on, Vera!'

She had to laugh. 'You're right! It is. But I love it.'

Slyly Linda enquired if she'd be coming back to Turnham Malpas now Don had got the cottage to rights.

'Mind your own business, Linda Crimble. You're worse than Jimbo for gossip and that's saying something. Is he in?'

'Find out for yourself.'

'Thanks, I will.'

Rhett and Vera had finished their evening meal and were washing up when there was a knock at the door.

'Not another crisis! Go answer it, Rhett.'

She half listened to the conversation and suddenly recognised Don's voice. It couldn't be! Not Don. Vera caught a quick reflection of herself in the mirror by the kitchen door and wished she'd had lipstick on and her hair fresh combed. Too late now.

Rhett came back. 'It's Grandad. I couldn't say he weren't to come in, could I?'

'Of course not. I'll just finish tidying away and then I'll be in. See if he wants a cup of tea or something.'

Back came Rhett. 'He doesn't. He's sitting by the window gawping at the garden.'

Vera snapped at him, 'Don't make him sound as if he's in his dotage, 'cos he isn't.'

'I know that. I only told you what he was doing.'

'You off out tonight?'

'Why?'

'Are you?'

'I could be.'

'Well, buzz off then. Sharp.'

Rhett smirked at her. 'I see, courting are you?'

She aimed a hasty swing at him with the wet tea-towel and he ducked and laughed. Vera did wonder how near the mark he might be with his joking.

'Hello, Don. Nice surprise.'

In his hand Don had a bunch, no, a bouquet of flowers. Beautifully wrapped in Cellophane like Jimbo always did the special flowers. Carnations and lilies and roses. They'd cost a packet.

''Ere, these are for you.'

Tears brimmed in Vera's eyes. He hadn't given her flowers since their Brenda was born. 'Thank you, very much. I'll put them in water and arrange them properly later.' Vera got out her plastic bucket, filled it with water and put them in it. Lovely they were. Lovely. Things had changed.

Back in the sitting room she said, 'Would you like to look round?'

'I would.' So she took him round, showing him the bathroom and separate toilet, the lovely bedroom with the huge window looking out over the garden, the bright kitchen with its view of the drive, Rhett's bedroom and the big airy storage cupboards and wardrobes she had.

'We get a good view from up here. These rooms were part of the servants' quarters and the nurseries, you see. Lucky, aren't we, Rhett and me?'

Don looked at her properly for the first time. 'It's done you good coming 'ere.'

Vera almost blushed at his close scrutiny. 'Yes, it has. I love it. It's the furniture and that, and the lovely big rooms, elegant like, and that lovely kitchen. Should really be for the matron but she's got four kids and it wouldn't do.'

'I fancy going to the pub —'

Quickly Vera interrupted him, 'Not the Royal Oak.'

Don was disappointed because he wanted to show her off, but he agreed and suggested trying the Jug and Bottle.

'Not the same standard but it'll do. I'll get changed. Put the telly on if yer want.'

What was she doing getting changed to go to the Jug and Bottle for a drink? Anything would do in there so long as yer weren't stark naked. She wished she hadn't thought that. It made her remember a time long ago . . . Fifteen she was. In the hay barn at Nightingales' Farm after helping with the harvest . . . her and Don. It hadn't been the clumsy fumbling of two virgin adolescents, for the gift of glorious passion had been theirs that night and their Brenda had been the result of all that tenderness and joy. Her father had

200

threatened to kill Don, till her mother pointed out that if he did Don couldn't never make an honest woman of their Vera. Sixteen with a baby. How did she cope? Those were the days.

She'd stand out like a sore thumb she would in this outfit in that dump, but stand out she would. That was how she wanted to be tonight, standing out from the crowd. Don looked good too. That new sports suit and that tie! She wondered who'd persuaded him to buy that tie, or was it that the spark he'd had years ago was returning?

When they got back, Don didn't go up to the flat again, he said goodnight to her at the front door. 'Give us a kiss to be going on with.'

'A kiss. Huh!'

'Go on, Vera. You know yer dying for one.'

Indignantly Vera denied she was. 'There's a long way to go before I want a kiss from you. You've ignored me for years and now all of a sudden you want a kiss. Come off it.'

'Don't I even get full marks for trying?'

'No. You're not having your way with me as easy as that. I'm not saying I'm not impressed, but . . .'

'Yes?'

'Good night, Don.'

'With my cottage done up I might find there's more fish in the sea than you. A well-modernised cottage could be tempting for a woman.'

Furious at the prospect Vera said, between clenched teeth, 'Well! Who is there who'd be tempted by you?'

Don smiled one of his rare smiles. 'Dottie Foskett?'

He could be right. She'd better be a bit more flexible. 'Go on then. One kiss. Here on my cheek.' She proffered her cheek but his knuckle under her chin turned her face so he could kiss her mouth.

Vera went all trembly and fled inside.

That week, with help from one of the weekenders recruited by Grandmama Charter-Plackett, Don had the living-room furniture outside by the front door ready for Barry and the estate van.

Now that the bedroom furniture was back in place and she'd had the chance to inspect it more closely, Grandmama was struck with an idea. 'You know this bedroom furniture, Don?'

'Yes.'

Well, I think it's far too good for the bonfire. The three-piece suite and that old sideboard thing are only fit for burning, but I think those wardrobes might be Georgian, and that chest of drawers and the bed-head. They all match. Let's ask Sir Ralph, see what he thinks.'

'I'm not having Sir Ralph poking about in my old furniture. Heavens above! He wouldn't want to.'

'Not even if he thinks it's worth a lot?'

'What d'yer mean? Fifty pounds like?'

Grandmama shook her head. 'If I'm right it could be worth a whole lot more than fifty pounds.'

'It's been in that bedroom for years. Never moved till I started decorating. How the blazes we'd get it out I've no idea – couldn't go down that twisty staircase and through the door.'

'There's ways like taking windows out. After all they didn't build the house round it, did they? It must have got in somehow.'

'No, yer right.'

The prospect of more money to dangle in front of Vera rather excited him and he strode off post-haste over the road to speak to Ralph.

'It's Grandmama Charter-Plackett's idea, sir, that my . . . our bedroom furniture might fetch a rare penny or two, so before it goes on the bonfire she wondered if you'd care to have a look, you being in the way of antique furniture.'

'Why not? I don't profess to be an expert by any manner of means but, yes, I'll have a look.'

'The bedroom's newly decorated or otherwise I wouldn't ask.'

Ralph looked at Don with new eyes. 'Pleased to see the effort you've been making. I'd be glad to have a look, see your alterations too. Could Muriel come?'

'Of course. If she wants. I'm off to the DIY in about an hour, if you'd like to come over before then . . .'

'I'll get Muriel, she's tidying the garden at the moment. We won't be long.'

Don went home to wait. He occupied himself making a list for his shopping expedition. Sunny yellow for the small bedroom, he thought. White paintwork, make it look bigger. Nice new curtains with a touch of the yellow in them. Those magazines Grandmama had lent him came in useful for ideas. He'd better measure for the curtains and the curtain rail before he set off. Now everything was out of the sitting room he could make a start on that too.

There was a tap on the front door. It opened and Muriel put her head round. 'It's us! Can we come in?'

'Of course. This way.'

When Ralph saw the bedroom furniture he was amazed.

'My word, Don! You've got a treasure trove here. How do you come to have such wonderful stuff?'

'My grandma used to say it all came from the Big House, but I find that hard to believe. Your Big House, that is. She said her grandmother had it given to her as a wedding present. Why, I've no idea because she wasn't in service there. When I asked why her grandmother had been given it, my grandma just tapped the side of her nose.'

Ralph opened drawers, looked at the dovetailing, inspected the door hinges, peered at the bed-head, ran his finger along the mouldings. 'Oh, yes. They'd fetch a pretty penny in an auction house.'

'They are Georgian then?'

'I'm fairly sure they are. But do you want to sell them when they've been in the family such a long time?'

'Yes.'

'What does Vera say?'

'She doesn't care. Hates 'em cos she can't . . . couldn't . . . move the wardrobes to clean. How do I go about it then?'

'If you'll permit me I'll contact the auction house in Culworth and get someone to come out and take a look.'

'I want them out of the way, yer see.'

Muriel, dismissing from her mind the idea that the furniture seemed familiar to her, asked to be allowed to view his alterations. When they'd admired everything Ralph said as they left, 'And Vera. What about her?'

'I'm thinking she's right. I started all this for her to make her come back, but she's that stubborn.'

'She has got a point. A good tenant in here paying rent, you'd have a little nest egg by the time Vera retires.'

'Shall I give in then and go live at the nursing home?'

'Why not? You've got wheels, so it's no problem.'

'Will she have me? That's the other question.'

Muriel, who'd been listening sympathetically to their conversation, said, 'I'm sure she will. Play your cards right and offer to do as she suggests. Take her on holiday, treat her well. She'll come round.'

'She's only just back from Torquay.'

'What does that matter? Ralph and I are always going away. It does you good. Even if it's only two or three days. Come along, Ralph, Don wants to get on. It's beautiful what you've done, an absolute transformation. It's nice to see someone achieving something worthwhile after all we've gone through these last few weeks. No news of Kenny and Terry?'

'Not that I know of. No news of Tom either. Pity that. I liked Tom and poor Evie. Strange woman.'

'Indeed. But happy in her own quiet way. Bye-bye, Don. Thank you for the tour of your home!'

Pointing at the contents of Don's house still out in the road Ralph's parting shot was 'You'll be getting all this stuff out here moved, will you? Makes the village look unsightly.'

'Tomorrow. Make a grand bonfire, won't it, and shall I be glad to see the back of it all!'

'Good. Good. Got to keep up standards.'

As Ralph and Muriel opened their own front door Muriel said, 'How odd him having such wonderful stuff. Do you suppose it's true?'

'True?'

'About it coming from your old home?'

Ralph locked the door behind him, something they'd all started doing since the trashing of Kenny's house had made them nervous, and then said, 'Muriel! I have a sneaking suspicion it might have been given for services rendered to the master at the Big House, or one of his sons perhaps.'

Muriel's eyebrows shot up. 'Ralph! You don't mean . . .'

'I do. Why else is it there? Don's great-great-grand-mother being given that kind of furniture as a wedding present, she was being bought off, don't you think? The price for her silence? The Wrights have been poor for generations, they certainly would not have been able to afford such good stuff, ever.'

'Well, well!'

'That's the only reason I can think of for it being in that cottage. Far too grand for it.'

'Oh, Yes! Even I can tell that. You don't want to buy it, do you, seeing as perhaps it was once yours, so to speak?'

'No, I do not. Reminders of my ancestors' immoral misdeeds I do not need! But thank you, my dear, for being prepared to take it on.'

Muriel was silent for a moment and then she said speculatively, 'You know the antique washstand we have on the landing, and you don't like the colour of the marble top, you don't think it might belong . . . ?'

Ralph's eyes widened as he contemplated Muriel's idea. 'You could be right. Surely not . . .'

They both rushed up the stairs and Ralph turned on the landing light so he could see more easily.

Muriel snatched at the flowers and the runner she kept on it. 'There, we can see better.'

'My dear! I do believe you're right. When we were

looking at Don's stuff I thought it was familiar. It belongs, doesn't it? It's part of Don's suite.'

'Look, the moulding's the same and the handles on the drawers.'

'Well, well! I'm sure we're right. It is identical.'

'Maybe there just wasn't room for it in that bedroom and it had to go back to the Big House.'

Ralph smoothed his hand over the marble top. 'Can you imagine the gossip when it all arrived at that cottage of Don's? I've never liked this colour. Too red somehow. It seems a shame for it to be separated from everything else.'

Muriel sighed. 'It must have been so lonely all these years wondering where everything that belonged to it had gone.'

'Oh, Muriel! My dear. Of course. When the chap comes from the auction house I'll show him this first then Don's suite and see what he has to say.'

Muriel slipped her hand into the crook of his arm. 'Let's do that. It's only right it should be together with the rest, where it belongs. I think Don's going to be amazed at the price he'll get for it. I don't think he's any idea how valuable it is.'

Chapter 16

Peter heard Sylvia answer the knock at the Rectory door and guessed it was the one he'd been expecting: Tom Nicholls. He had to admit he wasn't exactly relishing this meeting, but at least an explanation of all the weird and incredible happenings in the village just lately would be more than welcome.

Sylvia tapped at the door and ushered Tom in. Peter shook his hand, and pulled out a chair for him.

Tom cleared his throat and said abruptly, 'I haven't brought Evie back, not yet, not till I get things straightened out with you, Rector.'

'I'm glad you've come. The village has been seething with rumours ever since you left so mysteriously and since then with the police popping out from behind every wall. We'd no idea where you'd gone, you see. Look, if it's a long story . . .'

'Which it is.'

'Then we'll have coffee and sandwiches, if you don't

mind. Would that be all right with you? I haven't had lunch yet and I breakfasted what seems like years ago.'

Tom nodded his thanks.

'I'll ask Sylvia to make two lots and then we can settle down.' Peter closed the study door behind him and sought out Sylvia in the kitchen. 'Before you go for lunch, Sylvia, could you make another set of sandwiches? I think Tom's going to be a long time and I'm starving.'

'Back, is he? I hope it's not permanent, we've suffered enough because of him.'

'I am reserving judgement until I've heard the full story.'

She looked up at him and seeing the honesty of those eyes of his, she retracted her statement. 'You're right, of course. But the story had better be good.'

'We'll see. Coffee as well, please, and a slice each of . . .'

Laughing, Sylvia flapped her hands at him. 'Get on with you! I'll bring it in.'

'Thanks.'

Tom didn't begin his tale until the sandwiches were in front of him. He poured sugar into his cup as though he needed every ounce of support he could get, had a good drink and began. 'I'm sorry there's been all this trouble. I never intended it to be so. We thought we'd escaped into paradise when we came here, but it didn't work out that way, did it? You see, the root of all our problems is that I've been a police officer since I was eighteen. Loved the job, I did. Truly felt I was making a real contribution to the world. Evie and me, we married at twenty, but unlike you and the doctor we weren't able to have children. Evie had several miscarriages, just couldn't carry, and they couldn't find out why. Broke her heart it did, but such is life. We can't order these things, can we?'

Peter shook his head.

'Started as a constable and then I moved up to sergeant and then got a chance to go into plain clothes, Detective Sergeant Nicholls. That was a proud day I can tell you. London was a rum place to work in. There was a taste of every criminal activity under the sun there. Somehow one fateful day when they were short-handed I went out on a job with the drugs squad. That was the first day of the rest of my life. Like an idiot I enjoyed the adrenalin rush, the sheer bloody thrill of it all. The surge of power it gave yer when it came off and you'd made an arrest and put another pig of a dealer behind bars. There were the bad days, days when you failed and they got away to ruin dozens more lives, when you sank so low in spirits you nearly gave up.'

'More coffee?'

Tom held out his cup. 'Yes, please. This was when Evie began being ill. She'd had another miscarriage, five months she was so we'd just begun to feel hopeful, but she'd lost it yet again. I was up to my neck in the squad, coming home at all hours and her never knowing if I would come home at all. I didn't see the signs, thought it was losing the baby that was the trouble, which it was, but it was anxiety over me that compounded the problem.' He paused a moment, shook his head as he remembered how it had all been.

'Anyway, came home about two o'clock one morning and she'd cut all the curtains up, and was laid eyes wide open staring into space in the middle of a heap of shreds. Lopped them off just below the curtain hooks she had and set about cutting them up. So I had to insist she got help. It nearly finished me, the pain, oh dear! The pain.' Tom swallowed hard. 'She wasn't communicating at all so you never knew what she was feeling. Like a dummy she was. So docile. So terribly, terribly sad.'

'I'm so sorry, Tom. I'd no idea.'

'I asked them to take me off the drug squad, which to give them their due they did. Eventually Evie came home and her mother came to stay with us to give her a hand, keep her company like, and she'd begun to accept that children would be out of the question. She seemed so much better that daft Tom here decides he can take the risk and get doing what he loved best, undercover work. This time I worked at getting accepted into a gang on the fringe of the big stuff. It was like being an actor but being yourself all at the same time. Two lives lived in the one body. Living a life which was against all your better instincts with the objective of pulling in the gang and getting them off the streets.'

'You don't seem like a man who could do this.'

'Like I said, two people in one body. Funny existence. Sometimes when you woke up you couldn't remember what you were, him or me. I'd be days away from home, unable to communicate with Evie, except an officer at the station would phone her from time to time to say I was still in the land of the living.'

'Poor Evie.'

'Indeed. Yes. Poor Evie. Then things began to get too hot. I was very close, very involved, well accepted, but I had this sixth sense that someone was becoming suspicious of me. Nothing positive, nothing I could put my finger on, just a feeling. But I stuck to it, knowing how close we were to getting to the big boss. Then the balloon went up. We got it all together one night, and we arrested the big boss just leaving for an important dinner in the City, Rolls-Royce, dinner jacket, chauffeur, the works. What a triumph. They arrested me too to keep my cover, but you're not safe in prison, you know. If you want to get beaten up that's the place to go. Some prisons, the prisoners rule not the screws, believe me. I feigned an epileptic fit and they rushed me to the prison hospital, then took me to an outside hospital for treatment, they said, but that was the excuse. In fact they whisked me and Evie away to a secret address.'

'Tom!'

'We kept having to move. New identity, new names. It wasn't easy. Evie had another breakdown, more serious than the first. The only plus was that we'd got our man and broken up the ring. Millions of pounds they were making from selling drugs. Coming in from all over the world. If you saw the lives torn apart like I've seen them . . . you'd understand the triumph of getting the beggars behind bars. You'd sacrifice anything, anything at all.'

Something about the despair in Tom's voice prompted Peter to ask, 'To look genuine, to blend in kind of, you didn't have to take drugs too, did you?'

'No, no, I made them think I did, I'd seen enough to know how to behave. The one plus about Evie being in hospital for a second time was that while she was there they taught her to do embroidery and it saved her life, literally. You should see her work! You'll be amazed, such talent, it's unbelievable. She's going to have an exhibition when we get back, Sheila Bissett says she'll organise it – well, she said she would but maybe by now she mightn't be so keen.'

'I didn't know that. She's never said anything about it. So how did you come to be here?'

'Well, we were watched and guarded in the safe houses, I dyed my hair, shaved my moustache, Evie had always had short hair so she grew it long, and spent hours and hours and hours and hours embroidering without speaking, never going out because she was too afraid. However, prisoners are not prisoners for ever and I started getting twitchy about things. Thought I was being followed, you know the sort of thing.'

'Well, no, I don't.'

'Of course not, sorry. Well, I didn't think Evie could take any more. She'd come close a few times to suicide and as it was all my fault I decided we'd strike out, independent like, and give our minders, the police like, the slip. We couldn't be worse off than we were. Eventually we found here, I bought Mrs Beauchamp's house, lock, stock and barrel, and we moved in. But . . .'

Tom looked up with a rueful smile on his face.

'Yes?'

'Who should I meet? Kenny Jones. By a million to one chance, I'd met him briefly while I was in prison. I didn't know him from Adam, but for some reason he'd remembered me. So, round about the time I got the verger's job he went into the drugs scene to make his fortune, quick, and made me let him use the Templeton tomb to hide his money because he knew if anyone got on to him the first place they'd look would be his own house. He's been going into town at weekends selling drugs, so he's done well out of it.'

Peter was horrified. 'Kenny? Selling drugs! Kenny Jones!

And using the church to hide his drugs money? Dirty money? Tom, how could you? In God's house!'

Tom couldn't look Peter in the face, he was just too ashamed. Head down he said, in a quiet voice, 'He had a hold over me, you see, said he'd blow the gaffe if I objected, so for Evie's sake I kept quiet hoping that one day I'd sort it out . . . It made me feel really bad and I longed to tell you but I couldn't. I couldn't bear for Evie to be ill again. I've been so happy here and so has Evie. The thought of moving again, well, I couldn't even begin to think about it.'

Peter was speechless.

'Kenny, finding I was becoming awkward 'cos my conscience was troubling me, decided to put it around in the right quarter that I was living here and who I was. After Ron and Sheila got beaten up in mistake for us, the police whistled us away during the night and then kept watch.'

'So where did they take you?'

'To a safe house.'

'And Sheila thought you'd been arrested!'

'Over-active imagination! But she's been so kind to Evie. However, during one night they came back again to get us but the police were waiting and arrested them.'

'So that was why they were hiding everywhere. And Kenny and Terry? Where are they?'

'No idea. They've disappeared off the face of the earth. But they'll be found eventually. On the other hand, though, they might be under a couple of feet of concrete.'

Peter shuddered. 'Do you mean that?'

'Oh, yes. You don't start trading on Turkish Delight's patch without suffering the consequences.'

'And you? What about you?'

'Well, I'm prepared to take the risk of staying here in comparative ease until the lot I've put away are let out, and these henchmen who've just been arrested will be in for some time, believe me, including their bosses. Ten years at least. What I really want is to ask for my old job back.'

Peter shook his head. 'I shall have to think very seriously about that, Tom. You betrayed my trust. I know there were mitigating circumstances, but I'm afraid . . .' he shook his head again . . . 'you co-operated in the hiding of tainted money on church premises. That really was very wrong.' To change the subject and give himself a breathing space to make up his mind Peter asked, 'Are you here to stay now?'

'We shall be very shortly, the sooner the better. Next week, I think. Evie's pining for home.'

'Leave me a contact number or an address, whichever. The village feel you've brought great danger to them all, so there could be a lot of opposition to your return. They can't stop you living in your own house, of course, but as for the other . . .'

Tom looked Peter straight in the face and pleaded, 'For Evie's sake, if nothing else, I'd love to stay and get on with my job. She's been better here than she's been for years. This village is so healing, you see. Me getting the job as verger just seemed to put the seal on our safety, to say nothing of her happiness. But, of course, that's up to you.'

Peter stood up and reached out to shake hands. 'Thank you for being so candid about things. I shall do my very best for you.'

Tom shook hands. 'Thanks for listening and thanks for the lunch.'

'My pleasure.'

'There's my phone number. I'm going to collect a few things from the house then I'll be away.' Peter went to see him to the door and they shook hands again.

'I shall quite understand if you can't work the miracle. I know there'll be a lot of opposition and perhaps I've no right to be asking after all that's happened.'

'What would you like best to happen?'

'Me and Evie back here, which we shall be shortly, her having an embroidery exhibition and me as verger again. That would be the very best that could happen. Right where we can feel safe again and welcomed, for a while anyway.'

'I'll do my best.' Peter watched him stride away over the Green to his house. What a man. What a predicament! Could he see any way in which he could give Tom his job back? No, he could not. There was no way he would allow him a position of trust within the church ever again. It quite simply was not to be. Tom had broken the trust he had in him in every way: lying about his past, understandable in the circumstances but not excusable, and letting Kenny get the upper hand. Peter cringed at the thought of money tainted by filthy greed and agony and very possibly murder being hidden in his church.

A week to the day after speaking to Peter, Tom and Evie came home. Willie had locked up the church hall after Scouts and had just turned into Church Lane when he saw their car turn right from the Culworth Road into Stocks Row.

Willie hesitated outside his cottage, his hand poised to lift the latch and go in to his Horlicks and bed. But something of Peter's compassion filled his heart and he decided to follow them round Stocks Row and give them a word of welcome.

Evie was unlocking their front door while Tom was lifting a heavy box from the back of his car.

'Tom! Evie! Welcome home!'

Evie gave a little shriek and dropped the door key. Tom put the box down again and turned to speak, his face alight with appreciation. 'Why, Willie! Thank you! We've come late because we wanted to get settled in, in peace, kind of.'

'Well, I for one am damn' glad to see you back. This verger business is for a much younger man than me and I'll be glad for you to take the reins over again.'

Tom shook his head. 'I don't know about that, Willie. We're back but I'm not sure I shall have my job back.'

'Why ever not?'

Evie said softly, 'I can't find the key in the dark.'

Willie pulled his torch out of his pocket. 'Here, let me look. I always carry a torch when I'm locking up, just in case.'

He bent down to shine the torch around Evie's feet. To his surprise she was wearing calf-high fur-lined boots, which seemed a little excessive at the height of an Indian summer, but he made no comment. 'Here it is! Look!' He picked it up out of the honeysuckle, dusted it off and presented it to her with a bow and a grin. Evie gave him a shy smile, thanked him, slotted the key in the lock, turned it and went in.

To Tom's relief Willie offered to help unload. 'Thanks, that'll be great. This one's heavy. I'll take it, if you could bring this, and this with the shopping in.' Between them they emptied the car, and Tom asked Willie to have a drink before he left. 'Least I can do.'

'Thanks, I will.'

Leaving Evie to wander about the cottage and acclimatise herself, Tom dug in the Sainsbury's carrier-bags and brought out a four-pack of Guinness.

'You couldn't put a good word in for me, could you, Willie?'

'I could always try but it's not up to me.'

'They can't stop me living in my own house.'

Willie nodded in agreement. 'They can't, but they can turn very funny in this village. They take umbrage and nothing stops 'em . . . Well, the Rector can but he's about the only one. He's stepped in more than once when things have got nasty.'

'Nasty? I can't believe it. You all seem so kind.'

'Oh, we are, but just now and again . . . Like when they made an effigy of Mr Fitch, and when the Baxter sisters got their house stoned for kidnapping Flick Charter-Plackett, and Dicky and Bel got attacked because –'

'Good heavens. For Evie's sake I don't want . . . Oh, there you are, love. All right?'

Evie stood in the sitting-room doorway, her face alight with joy. 'Oh, Tom! Willie! It's lovely to be back home!'

Tom, so full of delight at her pleasure, agreed with her, his voice breaking as he answered, 'You're right, it is. Lovely!'

At that moment Willie made up his mind that, for the sake of gentle Evie and her very obvious joy at being back where she felt secure, he would do all he could to make certain they stayed and Tom was verger again.

It might be an uphill task. He enlisted Sylvia's help. 'The most positive thing we can do,' she said, 'is have that exhibition of Evie's embroidery. I know Sheila Bissett exaggerates but she really was impressed with how beautifully Evie embroiders, and she's bursting to have an exhibition for her. That way they'd all see what a clever person she is, and she and Tom would have to be there and meet everyone and people couldn't be rude to their faces, could they? What do you think? In aid of charity, and with cups of coffee and gâteau. How about it? One Saturday morning? The exhibition in the small meeting room and the refreshments in the big hall.'

Willie nodded. 'It wouldn't take long to organise – it's not like a village show or something, is it? I'll get the diary out tomorrow and check the first free Saturday.'

Stirring her Horlicks to rid it of the last bits which hadn't quite mixed in Sylvia said, 'But we shall only succeed if we do a lot of quiet propaganda – you know, when we meet people and that. A word here and a word there.' A thought struck her. 'What does the Rector think?'

'He had a word with me yesterday, saying he hoped when they got back there wouldn't be any trouble. I just hope he gives Tom his job back, I can't keep up with it all any more.'

Sylvia patted his hand where it lay on the blanket. Putting her empty beaker on her bedside table she snuggled down saying, 'If there's one thing I've learned in life it's to live every minute to the full. We're neither of us getting any younger, you know. We never know when we might get called to higher service, do we?'

Willie was appalled. 'Called to higher service! I'm not about to pop my clogs, you know, far from it.'

'I wasn't meaning it like that, I meant we should do all the things we want to do and see all the things we want to see before it's all too late. Dying with regret must be –'

'Just shut up, Sylvia, I don't like talk like that.' Willie slapped his beaker down and looked into those grey eyes he so loved. 'Sorry for that, but you mustn't. We've years yet together enjoying ourselves and you've not to think we haven't. You know, I saw tonight how much Tom loves Evie and seeing her pleasure at being as she called it "back home" I thought, they're just like my Sylvia and me, in love with each other, and it made me decide to do my best for 'em. And I do love you, and every minute is precious and perfect and . . .'

'Willie, you're sounding quite poetic.'

'That's how it gets yer.' Willie settled down in bed and took Sylvia's hand in his. 'She's a strange woman is Evie, but you can't 'elp but like her. There's an innocence about 'er that's rare nowadays. Childlike, almost, and yet all that talent. She had her fur boots on. In this weather her feet must have been near casseroled!'

'Never mind her boots, did you get a chance to see her embroidery?'

'I carried a box of sewing stuff into her workroom for her. Stunning it is. Stunning. Wait till they all see it. Just wait.'

When the posters advertising the exhibition appeared in the window of the Store and on the church noticeboard there was a great deal of comment, not much of it favourable. The

Charter-Plackett children did a leaflet drop all around the village too, so when the villagers found it on their doormats there it was staring them right in the eye: the Nichollses were back and intending to stay.

Despite their opposition to Tom and Evie returning, curiosity finally drove them to visit the exhibition, their excuse being that after all it was in a good cause: all them refugees, and the money given to someone who was going out there with medical supplies for the poor beggars, that made the difference; you weren't just handing out money to some vast faceless organisation, this way the person concerned was accountable.

The exhibition opened at ten. Sitting at the entrance taking the money was Sheila Bissett, a broad smile on her face.

'Thank you, that'll be four pounds, please, for the two of you.'

'*Two pounds*! For a few pictures on a wall.'

'It's in a good cause. You'll be amazed, it's worth every penny.'

'I should hope so.'

'Oh, yes. It was me discovered her talent. We've got plans for classes. Sign up when you come out, I've got the list here.'

'They're intending to stay then?'

'Of course.'

'I'm surprised you're so keen after what happened to you and Ron.'

Sheila stifled a shudder. 'They'll all be behind bars for years to come, and I for one am not going to let what happened affect me.'

'Well, I reckon you're brave. I really do. You're an example to us all. We'll let you know if we think it worth it.' The ticket buyer leaned over the table and whispered, 'Are Evie and Tom here?'

Sheila nodded. She wasn't feeling nearly so brave as she made out, because this was the first time she'd taken part in village life since . . . well, anyway she was here but it had been a real effort to come out and sit taking the money. But, as Ron said, you couldn't spend the rest of your life frightened of your own shadow, and he for one, now he was feeling so much better, was going to put it all behind him. So Sheila agreed with him for once, not because she was brave but because she couldn't bear the thought of allowing herself to be stuck in the house too nervous to go out.

Sylvia was wielding the coffee-pots and Willie was fidgeting about in the exhibition room, nervous that his lighting arrangements might not be showing Evie's work off to its best advantage. My, but they were splendid were these pictures: they lit the heart up with their beauty. Willie couldn't imagine how one small quiet person could have such skill, such an eye for colour, such splendour in their very soul. He listened to the exclamations of delight from the villagers and convinced himself that Tom and Evie would be here to stay and he wouldn't have to be verger any more. Relief covered him like a rash and he realised he was grinning like a Cheshire cat.

Caroline was serving gâteau and putting in a discreet good word for Tom and Evie as she did so. 'Two more coffees, Sylvia, please. Chocolate, lemon or almond?

Lemon, that's Harriet's contribution. It looks lovely, doesn't it, so tempting? What do you think then? Isn't Evie clever?'

'She most certainly is. Not a word for the cat, yet all that going on inside her head. So beautiful!'

'Such an asset to the village, aren't they, the pair of them?'

'Oh, yes! Such an asset.'

Sylvia winked at Caroline and they both smothered their laughter. To have such a success on their hands was more than they could ever have hoped for. The door opened and Peter came in, his eyes searching for Caroline immediately. Having found her he smiled and her heart went instantly into overdrive; for one blinding moment she couldn't see a thing except his eyes and the whole of his face glowing with love for her. He raised a hand in greeting and she almost choked with love for him. I'd forgotten how handsome he is! And he's mine! All mine! All that love is mine!

'Dr Harris! A slice of the chocolate for Willie, please. Dr Harris?'

All mine! I'd forgotten how much I love him. And there he is. All splendid and wonderful. She smiled back, but he'd turned to answer Sheila and the chance to show that her feelings for him had sprung back to life was lost.

'I'll cut it, shall I?'

Caroline was trembling with shock, her beloved Peter was there, still loving her, still supporting her after all he'd been through. Well, this was the end of making him jump through hoops, because . . .

Sylvia said, 'Shall I serve Willie?'

Caroline looked down at the cake slice in her hand. 'Oh, right, which would you like, Willie? The chocolate's very popular.'

She cut him his slice then excused herself, saying her hands were sticky and she'd wash them in the kitchen. Standing at the sink letting the cold water rush over her hands and wrists, Caroline hoped Peter wouldn't come after her. She needed time to catch up with her feelings. Three months since Hugo had left, and now at last she'd become wholly herself once more. To think she'd even considered going away with Hugo, he who was a shell of a man compared to Peter. She must have been out of her mind. She'd be indebted to Peter for ever for not asking for more than she was able to give.

'Mummy! Alex is wanting another piece of cake. I've told him he can't. He'll be sick.'

Caroline dried her hands, took her bag out of the cupboard where she'd put it for safe-keeping and handed a pound coin to Alex, who straight away rushed off, and offered another to Beth.

Beth patted her stomach. 'I don't think I can, Mummy, thank you. He will, you know, he'll be sick, he's so greedy. Sylvie's wanting you, she's says she's rushed off her feet.'

'I'll be there in a minute tell her.'

'Your voice is funny, are you all right?'

Caroline bent down and kissed her cheek. 'Oh! I'm absolutely fine. Daddy's here somewhere.'

'Is he? I'll go find him.'

Caroline wished *she* could go find him and take shelter within his love as she had no doubt Beth would do, but for now she had to take time to realign herself. The relief of finding her life had value again was overwhelming her and –

'There you are, my dear! Are you all right? Sylvia's anxious in case you're not well so I've come to . . .' Muriel studied Caroline's face and could not interpret the look she saw there.

'Muriel! Couldn't be better! Just needed to wash my hands, they were sticky, you know.' She fled back into the hall to help Sylvia reduce the length of the queue. Muriel stared after her, still puzzled by Caroline's expression, but then Muriel didn't know that Caroline, not five minutes ago, had fallen in love.

Sheila had ten names on her embroidery class list, added her own and felt she'd had a very worthwhile morning. 'Evie! Evie! Come here! Look! Eleven names! Isn't that wonderful?'

Evie came across to her, a glass of water in her hand. Without speaking she picked up the list and studied it.

'Isn't it encouraging? I'm so excited. I have a little place in my hall where a picture would just fit, I was going to ask you to do one for me, but if I come to your class I could do it myself, couldn't I?' Sheila looked up at her, eagerly awaiting her reply. But she saw a tear begin to roll down Evie's cheek.

'Now, Evie, come along, we've had a lovely morning, everyone full of admiration. There's nothing to cry about.' She fished in her bag and brought out a clean tissue. 'Here, use this.'

At a loss to know how to tackle the situation Sheila looked around for help, and to her relief Tom came. He put an arm around Evie's shoulders and hugged her. 'Now, come on. It's all been great, hasn't it? You said so yourself.'

Evie dabbed her face with Sheila's tissue and pulled herself together. In that strange deep voice of hers Evie said,

'It has and it's all thanks to Sheila. It'll help me if you come to the class.'

'Oh, I will, I'm on the list.'

'Then I shall do it, immediately, seeing as it's October. I've never done anything like it before but we can always give it a try.'

Tom took his arm away from Evie's shoulders and beamed at Sheila. 'I told her it would be all right and it has been. All we need now is for the Rector to persuade the others to let me have my job back. Then everything in the garden will be lovely. The meeting's on Tuesday night so we should know then, I hope.'

Chapter 17

Muriel put down the receiver and held on to the chair for a moment to steady her nerves. Well, she'd said she would do it and now was the time to stand up and be counted, but she was trembling so much she'd have to sit down. Why did she make these pronouncements in the heat of the moment then so deeply regret them? But she had said she would, and if she was ever going to hold up her head again, she'd have to do it. Stand there and *do it*. Surely there must be another way, but there wasn't, was there? She'd tried, Peter had tried, Jimbo had tried, but Mr Fitch had remained adamant.

Ralph! Where was Ralph?

'Ralph! That was Barry on the phone.' Dear God! Help me. 'Ralph! Oh, there you are!'

Ralph looked gravely at her. 'It's D-Day, is it? I never thought for one minute he'd go ahead with it. I really didn't. As the weeks slipped by I was sure he'd changed his mind. Damn him! Damn him!'

Muriel nodded. 'First light tomorrow morning they're moving in. Oh, Ralph! Am I brave enough?'

'None braver.'

'Shall you have one last try?'

Ralph shook his head.

'No, you're right, it would only make him more determined.'

Ralph stared into space for a moment then said, 'Sit down again, here's your list of people to ring. I have to go into Culworth, on business. I shan't be in for lunch.'

Muriel looked up at him and anxiously enquired if he really needed to go.

'I do, yes, I do. Don't worry I shall be back, hopefully by the middle of the afternoon. Things to do, you know.' His lips tightly pressed together and his eyes intensely preoccupied, Ralph stared into the distance.

'I shall need you tomorrow for moral support.'

'And you shall have it, all you need.' He bent to kiss her, squeezed her shoulders, picked up his car keys and disappeared through the back door calling, 'Bye, my dear. Good luck with your phoning.'

She wished he hadn't gone, she wished he'd stayed and braced her for what was to come. It was an odd thing for Ralph to do. He'd said nothing yesterday about having to go into Culworth. Still, she was clever enough to organise things without anyone's help, it would be tomorrow when she needed . . . The telephone began to ring and when she answered it was Caroline, consumed with enthusiasm. 'You've heard from Barry? Good. So, we have lift-off. I'm about to start on my list of calls. I'll ring you back when I've completed them and tell you what support we can expect. Muriel? Are you there?'

'I am. We've got to be brave, haven't we?'

'Of course. I can't wait to get at it. He has got to be stopped.'

'Oh, I know. I know. Right, here we go. Come round with your list, instead of phoning. We'll have coffee and compare notes and plan our strategy.'

Muriel was encouraged by the enthusiasm of her supporters. They all promised to get neighbours and friends to come too if they could, and by the time she'd gone through her list Muriel was beginning to feel more confident. If it came to it, with a *crowd* lying down in front of the diggers she wouldn't be quite so obvious, would she? The newspapers! Of course! She'd ring and get them to come. A big splash in the local paper would do nothing but good. If she kept the thought of that little wren with his bright brown twinkling eyes in her mind she'd be all right.

Muriel didn't sleep that night, of course. Mad, scary scenes of confrontation and police and being arrested raced through her mind. Of course she might be arrested, that would be a distinct possibility, causing a breach of the peace. What would her dear mother have said? Frankly she would have been appalled. 'No real lady would do such a thing,' she would have said. Well, Mother wasn't here so Muriel could do as she wanted, within limits.

Ralph rose first before it was light and went downstairs to make breakfast for her.

'No, Ralph! Let me do it.'

'It's the least I can do. Put warm sturdy clothes on and bring a brave heart with you. Come down when you're ready.'

'I don't think I can eat anything.'

'Oh! You must.'

He stood over her while she ate a bowl of cereal and drank a cup of tea.

'Here's your banana.'

Muriel shook her head. 'No, Ralph, I really can't manage that at this time in the morning. Thank you all the same.'

'Put it in the pocket of your Barbour then, for later when there's a lull.'

'Very well. The most terrible thought has struck me. Will Mr Fitch be there, do you think?'

'He goes abroad such a lot, he most probably won't be.'

'I can't bear the thought of him seeing me behaving ridiculously.'

'Is that how you see it?'

'Yes.'

Ralph took hold of her hand and put it to his cheek. 'You have too much innate dignity, Muriel, ever to be accused of behaving ridiculously. Now, where are your placards?'

'At the Rectory.'

'Then off you —' He was interrupted by a knock at the door. 'That's probably Caroline, I'll go.'

Muriel discovered it was a bright, very crisp autumn morning when she went outside. Going through her gate at the end of her back garden and out into Pipe and Nook felt symbolic: a moment of change, a moment when Muriel went from being a quiet, shy, back-room support type of person to becoming a front runner, a stand-up-and-be-counted person. She braced her shoulders, smiled at Caroline and marched sturdily towards the entrance to the field. It wasn't directly opposite her house but below it on the way out of the village. The entrance was blocked by a huge old farm gate, with a chain and padlock on it.

Caroline propped the placards against the hedge and she and Muriel stood in front of the gate. They'd only been there a moment or two when their supporters began arriving in twos and threes. There was Sheila and Ron, Tom and Evie, Anne Parkin, Mrs Jones, two of the weekenders in what they considered to be appropriate country wear, Liz Neal, and trailing on behind were the two Misses Senior, their woolly hats suited to the chill morning air. A chorus of 'Good morning' ensued, and there was an inspection of the placards with praise for their apt wording, a rubbing of hands to ward off the chill and above all an air of anticipation and excitement.

After a lull came more supporters, eager for the fray, Linda Crimble with her little Lewis on a trike, Georgie Fields, Jimmy Glover and Willie and quite a few of Mrs Jones' neighbours from down Shepherds Hill. Arthur Prior, Ralph's cousin, came as promised escorted by his bevy of granddaughters. What they hadn't expected was the arrival of some members of the local Environmental Studies group from Culworth.

Their leader called out cheerfully, 'Morning, all! Never fear now we're here!' Under their arms they carried placards at whose inflammatory slogans Muriel quaked.

'I didn't know anyone else knew.'

'Ha! Ha! Nothing much goes on in the environment that we don't get to hear of, and we rather felt this was a situation which required not just the foot soldiers but the cavalry too.' Looking down the lane he asked, 'So where are the –' he spotted the look of distaste on Muriel's face and changed it to – 'beggars?'

Muriel said firmly, 'I want it absolutely understood that this is our village and our protest, and it will be conducted with dignity and restraint.'

'Dignity and restraint! These greedy landlords don't know the meaning of the words. They'll ride roughshod over you and anyone else who gets in the way, four-legged or two.' He nodded his head towards Rector's Meadow. 'Got this lined up for housing, and it's not on.' He took off his glove and exposed a hand the size of a gorilla's. 'Gareth Edwards.'

Muriel's hand disappeared inside his and was gripped painfully. 'Muriel Templeton.'

'Well, Mrs Templeton . . .

Tom hissed, 'It's Lady Templeton, actually.'

Gareth bowed mockingly. 'Beg pardon, milady.'

'That's quite all right, you weren't to know.' As she spoke the rumble of heavy machinery was heard in the distance. 'Housing? We didn't know that.'

Gareth winked at her. 'We have a mole in the planning department. Not much goes on we don't know about.'

The word 'housing' flew round the lips of the protestors and served to heighten their determination.

Muriel asked, 'Are you sure?'

'Positive. Old Fitch has them under his thumb.' Gareth pretended to count out banknotes with his fingers.

'I don't believe it! Mr Fitch!'

The rumble of the equipment grew louder and Caroline hastily shared out the placards and they made a double line of defiance across Pipe and Nook Lane.

Chin up, but with trembling knees, Muriel faced the

enemy. Great yellow giants they were, impressive and very threatening. Muriel felt her breastbone shuddering with the vibrations caused by their mighty engines. Surely they must stop. The driver of the foremost vehicle had enormous protective earphones on his head, there'd be no use shouting to him he would never hear, so she waved her arms above her head, palms towards him and the others joined her.

The digger tested her resolution for it ground to a halt only six feet from her. Muriel went round the side and gestured to him through the open window to take off his earphones. He did, but the noise of the engine made it almost impossible to shout loud enough for him to hear, so she pointed to what looked to her like an ignition key though she wasn't sure, for the cab appeared to be full of gadgets and levers.

'We're here because we don't want to have this hedge taken down. We're sorry to be interfering with your work but we feel so strongly about it that we are compelled to stand here and do what we are doing. Please, could I ask you to agree not to dig out a hedge which has been growing for something like three centuries that we know of?' She smiled up at him, this strong healthy young man, a product of an age she had little in common with, and didn't expect to get any sympathy from him at all.

'Now, little lady, we're going to be paid a lot of money to do this job, and I've got men to pay, and they've their children to feed, and a roof to keep over their heads. Do you really think I'm going to refuse to do it?'

'We can't let you. I'm sorry but there it is. You will have to run us over to get into that field, and I know you can't possibly work from this side because the lane is too narrow for you to manoeuvre.' She tried the sweet smile again, and for a moment thought she'd melted his heart.

From a shelf below his windscreen he picked up a mobile phone, pulled a piece of paper from his top pocket and began to dial the number written on it.

He said, 'Thank heavens for mobile phones.' He listened for a moment.

Caroline asked, 'Who are you ringing?'

'Mr Fitch. Hello, sir. Good morning to you. Blair here, we've arrived but half the village has turned out to stop us getting into the field.'

From where she stood on the road she could hear Mr Fitch going berserk. The digger driver held the phone away from his ear. It went dead and he switched it off. 'He's coming.'

Nonchalantly he climbed down from the digger and stood leaning against one of the enormous wheels lighting a cigarette. The protestors went into a tight circle muttering about their situation and should they this and should they that.

Muriel looked at Caroline with raised eyebrows. 'This is the last thing I wanted. He will think I've gone off my head.'

To encourage her Caroline gripped her elbow. 'No, it's him who's gone off his head. We've got to stand firm. How can they run us over? We just must not break ranks.'

Gareth was smirking. 'Good. Good.'

'Good?' Muriel said, 'Good?'

'Of course. There's been no abuse from that Blair, so that's a victory.'

'I don't see how.'

'If they're abusive then you're in trouble. He's being reasonable so that's a plus.'

'Oh, right, well, I expect you know more about these things than I do.' Quietly to Caroline she said, 'I do wish Mr Fitch had been away. I shall feel such a fool.'

'It's all for a very worthwhile cause. Why should you worry what you look like?' Caroline quite fancied having an opportunity to stand up to Mr Fitch. They'd all taken so much from him in the past.

Mr Fitch roared up the lane in his Land Rover, dust flying from his wheels. He'd leaped out almost before he'd braked, and charged up past the machines to confront them all. He stopped short when he saw Caroline and – surely not! – Muriel at the front of the group.

'Muriel! Go home at once. This isn't a suitable place for you to be at all. Go along, go home.' He waved a hand at her expecting her to capitulate immediately, but Muriel didn't. In fact the way he treated her, as though she was a child and ought to be in school, stiffened her spine.

'Had you not decided on this cruel and heartless action I would not need to be here at all. The fact that I am here is entirely your fault, Mr Fitch.'

'My fault?'

'Of course. I cannot stand by and allow you to ruin my countryside – no, our countryside, it belongs to us all.'

Caroline stepped in, fearing for Muriel. 'Mr Fitch! We beg you not to go forward with this plan. Someone has told us that you are intending *building* on Rector's Meadow. Surely that cannot be true?'

If Caroline had thought she would shame him into surrender by the disappointed tone in her voice, she was mistaken: he had a lot at stake. The only thing which troubled his conscience was Muriel being there, for he valued her principles enormously.

He stood on the step of the digger and raised his voice so they could all hear. 'Now see here, I'm not getting rid of the hedge as such –'

Gareth shouted him down 'What is digging it up by its roots but getting rid of it?'

'There'll still be a fence there, and Rector's Meadow will still exist.'

'Oh! Yes!' shouted Gareth. 'Who yer kidding? Birds and plants can't grow in a fence. Our heritage is at risk!' This statement proved a rallying cry and all Gareth's group waved their placards and shouted, 'Our heritage! We shall not be moved! Down with greedy landowners!'

Scathingly Mr Fitch said, 'Your heritage! You don't even live here!'

'No, but we're here to support our brothers . . . and sisters!' Gareth put an arm around Muriel's shoulders and squeezed them.

Muriel thought she would die. 'Mr Fitch, this is all most unseemly.'

'It is.' His shoulders drooped and Muriel thought, Victory!

Ron stepped forward to speak. 'In view of my experience in negotiations on behalf of the union could we perhaps retire for a discussion? I would willingly offer my expertise.'

'Hear, hear!' some of them shouted.

Mr Fitch glared at him, and momentarily Muriel saw disdain in his ice cold eyes. Speculatively he appraised the scene and appeared to come to a decision. 'Well, if you're so determined, far be it from me . . . these great machines can't turn round in this lane, though, and it's too far for them to reverse all the way down into the Culworth Road. We'll unlock the gate and they can turn round in the meadow and then when they're sorted we'll have that discussion, Ron. All right, Muriel?'

Out of the corner of her eye Muriel could see Caroline furiously shaking her head. But he was right, they couldn't turn round, they were far too big, so yes, she agreed, they'd better turn round in the field. For the moment half a victory seemed better than none. 'Very well. We agree, and then we'll talk.'

Gareth almost exploded. 'No. No. No. We can't allow it.' He thumped a big fist into the palm of his other hand and shouted, 'It's a trick. A dastardly scheming trick! Don't you see?'

Muriel calmly patted his arm and declared, 'Mr Fitch is doing his best to accommodate us, I'm sure he is a man of his word. We have got him to talk haven't we? and as you would say that is a plus.'

The driver had the key and they all stood back to allow him through. The huge gate swung open and the driver secured it with a stone. He climbed back into his cab, and in a moment their ears were filled again with the horrendous noise of his engine. The other two vehicles revved up and followed on into the field. Immediately, Muriel saw what was happening. He'd got the diggers into the field by the most reprehensible trick, but before she could do anything about it Mr Fitch had swung the gate shut and snapped the padlock closed. He was out in the lane, smiling to himself. Muriel who, though small, was about the same height as him, strode forward to stand in front of him. For the first time in her life she was shaking with temper. 'I am ashamed of you. Ashamed. You wish everyone to think of you as a gentleman, well, let me tell you here and now, you are not and never will be.'

He couldn't meet her eyes.

Gareth girded his group together and surrounded him. Muriel sensed an ugly feeling in the air, and when she saw Gareth beginning to shoulder Mr Fitch and shout abuse at him, she thought, There's going to be a lynching here. She wasn't quite sure what a lynching actually involved but the threat was there for all to see. She pushed her way into the mêlée surrounding Mr Fitch and shouted, 'This must stop. This instant. I will not have it! Do you hear me? Stop it.'

Ron, Arthur, Willie and Tom squeezed through to stand beside her, just in case. Caroline ran to get Ralph, but he was already there in the lane. Muriel went to climb over the gate and was in such a state of high dudgeon that she climbed over it without the smallest difficulty. Landing safely on the other side she beckoned the others to follow suit. 'Lie down front and back of them, then they can't move.'

In a trice the Senior sisters were over the gate and rushing to lie down with Muriel. They were closely followed by Caroline and all the others. Three vehicles: there were at least four people to every one of them and effectively they put paid to any movement. Muriel stared up at the sky, her heart beating faster than she thought possible. Never, never as long as she lived would she give Mr Fitch the benefit of the doubt again. He was a craven liar and trickster in her book, and she'd said to his face what Ralph had long declared . . . Where was Ralph? She could hear all the commotion going on, Gareth shouting a lot and, oh dear! that sounded like a police siren. So it had come then. She was about to be arrested. Did she care? No, the whole world had a right to know what a perfectly dreadful man Craddock Fitch was.

A flash from a camera almost blinded her. Oh, no. Now her picture would be plastered across the front of the paper. Muriel determinedly closed her eyes, and didn't care a damn that the dry spiky grass was pricking into her legs nor that there was a distinct feeling of dampness creeping into her bones. What was that compared to a wren losing its home and those dear shy violets being destroyed for ever? The sacrifice was well worth it.

In the ensuing struggle Muriel heard Ralph's voice, then, above all the chaos, Mr Fitch yelling '*What!*'

A stunned silence fell, so Muriel sat up to see what was happening.

Ralph, with a posse of men in suits standing behind him, was facing up to Mr Fitch. 'You *will* listen to what they have to say, Craddock. Right?'

'I shall not. They know what they have to say, and that is that I am at liberty to tear up this hedge, and neither you nor anyone else is going to stop me.'

A man whom Muriel assumed must be from Culworth Council stepped from behind Ralph. He cleared his throat, always a sure sign, thought Muriel, that someone is nervous. His voice at first was squeaky with panic and then as he went on it deepened. 'Mr Fitch, the council insist you must not take down this hedge. If you do you will be prosecuted and fined and will also have it to replant, every single metre of it.'

'That's not what you said when I gave —'

The man from the council held up his hand. 'I'm sorry, but under the Hedgerow Regulations of 1997 this ancient hedgerow cannot be removed.'

Mr Fitch, seething with temper, took the man aside. 'What are you talking about? You knew, I knew, I couldn't take it down but you agreed I could.'

The man from the council took Mr Fitch's hand from his arm and said, 'Well, now I've changed my mind.'

'Had it changed for you, you mean.' Mr Fitch, boiling and almost speechless with temper, turned to Ralph a fist raised, and Muriel, through the bars of the gate, could see that things were getting even uglier. She leaped to her feet, scaled the gate and was beside Ralph ready to defend him before Mr Fitch had sufficient control to speak.

'You supercilious sod, you.' He drew in a deep, shuddering breath. 'Been throwing your aristocratic weight about, have you, down at the council offices?'

'Be careful what you say, Craddock, the press and the police are here. I merely showed these council officials the error of their ways. Money, after all, you see, cannot buy absolutely everything.' The council officials had the grace to look embarrassed.

'Damn and blast you. You bloody interfering old has-been.'

Muriel said, 'Mr Fitch, please.' Her quiet protest brought a semblance of control to him. His fist was put at his side, his breathing slowed.

He turned to speak to the council officials, taking them

aside for a muttered conference. Muriel slipped her muddy hand into Ralph's and squeezed his fingers. She whispered, 'Thank you, dear.'

Mr Fitch's parting words were spoken with a finger stabbing at the three men from the council. 'You owe me! And don't you forget it.' He walked away down the lane to his Land Rover and they watched it reverse rapidly and erratically down the lane to where it joined the Culworth Road. A cheer went up. The Environmental Studies group, still in the meadow, danced a celebratory jig, shouting and laughing, slapping each other on the back. The rest of the Turnham Malpas supporters shook hands with each other and congratulated themselves on a victory well won. The council representatives went off to speak to the police and the press, and Blair unlocked the gate and asked for space to drive out.

Gareth came to Ralph, shook his hand and said, 'Thanks for that. We knew about the Hedgerow Regulations, and suspected he'd bribed someone.'

'Oh, he had, well and truly. They were very busy lining their pockets. Now I think it's time I took my dear brave wife home.'

'She's been a splendid fighter this morning, all credit due to her. I don't suppose you would consider joining our group, would you? You'd be a fantastic asset with your . . . connections?'

Ralph shook his head. 'No, thank you. It's not quite my thing. But I do wish you every success. Come, Muriel, my dear. 'He raised his voice and asked for silence.' Thank you to everyone who turned out this morning. I wish it had never been necessary, but I wasn't entirely sure that the council would come this morning so I had to let the protest go ahead just in case they didn't. We've won! We've saved this precious hedge! Thank you, everyone, thank you very much indeed. Splendid job you've done!'

They gathered round and shook his hand, thanking him for his intervention. 'Not at all, the least I could do.'

Caroline called out, 'Three cheers for Muriel!'

'And for you, Dr Harris,' Willie added.

Muriel had decided to go to bed early that night, because she was emotionally and physically exhausted: having summoned up so much of her resources there seemed to be nothing left of Muriel at all.

'My dear, why not get ready for bed and I will make us a drink and you can come downstairs to drink it before you finally expire? Sitting in front of the fire will be very calming.'

'They won't use that picture of me laid in front of the tractor, will they?'

Ralph smiled. 'I expect they most likely will.'

'I said unforgivable things to Mr Fitch, you know. But I meant them. They were true.'

'You told me.'

Muriel shook her head. 'It was such a dastardly trick after I had believed him. I must be a complete simpleton not to have realised what he was up to.' Muriel sighed. 'I'm going to get ready for bed like you suggest. I'll have Horlicks tonight, please, dear.'

She was half-way down the stairs, wearing her best dressing-gown and matching nightgown when the doorbell rang.

'Ralph! Who can that be at this time of night?'

When Ralph opened the door the very last person she ever expected to see was standing on the doorstep.

'Craddock! Good evening, do come in.'

Muriel half hesitated and debated about whether to turn tail and run back upstairs again, she couldn't face him not after what she'd said, but Mr Fitch caught sight of her and called, 'Please, Muriel, I need to see you.'

'But I'm . . .'

'That's of little consequence tonight. Please.'

Ralph courteously invited him to sit down, and after having seated Muriel in her favourite chair he sat down in his own winged chair and waited.

Mr Fitch fidgeted with his hands for a moment, head down. He crossed his legs, raised his head and said, 'I have come to offer you both the deepest of apologies. I behaved in a disgraceful manner this morning and I am deeply ashamed. You, Muriel, said I wasn't a gentleman and never would be . . .' Muriel cringed at his words. 'You were right, I'm not.' Mr Fitch held up his hand to silence Muriel, who appeared about to interrupt him. 'No, let me finish. I am thoroughly ashamed of myself. I always will try to bring the business world to Turnham Malpas and, of course, that's not right. It has no place here. Only loyalty and affection and understanding have a place. Those three qualities will achieve far more. How I could ever have contemplated building houses on Rector's Meadow I will never know. I've been for a walk right round it this afternoon, by myself so that I could think, and I had a revelation. Don't laugh, I did, even hard-boiled old Fitch can have his weaker moments!' He smiled wryly. 'I saw all of what it was you people talk about. I concede that I am merely a custodian of the land, for the land will still be here centuries after I am dust, therefore I must do my best by it, like so many men before me.'

Ralph nodded his agreement.

'Well, I understand that fully now. I apologise most sincerely to you, Ralph, for calling you what I did, I was seriously at fault and I have no excuse for it. I apologise to you, Muriel, for my behaviour, it was unseemly, as you said. Will you forgive me?'

Ralph stood up and went across to shake his hand. His voice was rough with emotion as he said, 'I accept your apology. Let's forget it, shall we?'

'No, not forget, but let's put it behind us, perhaps.'

Ralph nodded.

Mr Fitch got to his feet and went to Muriel. He took her hand from the arm of the chair where it was resting and put it to his lips. 'You are not only a lady by name but by nature too. Next time I face a moral dilemma I shall consult you. It will be your job to keep me on the straight and narrow.' He smiled down at her, and she smiled up at him.

'I'll say good night then.' Mr Fitch nodded his head at the two of them and let himself out.

Chapter 18

When he got back from the meeting about Tom that night, Peter found Caroline stretched out on the sofa with a bottle of wine and two glasses waiting on the coffee table, warming her bare feet at the fire.

'Hello, darling. I've made a start on it, I'm afraid. Long, exhausting day and I needed to relax.'

Peter leaned over the back of the sofa and kissed her several times. This was as far as they had got since he'd come back from Yorkshire. There were times when he felt he was too reserved and more eagerness on his part would bring them closer more quickly, but since her brush with cancer and the need for his reticence because of it, and then Hugo, he'd willingly fallen into the habit of acquiescing to Caroline leading their relationship.

'Good meeting? Did you get the result you wanted?' She handed him his glass of wine.

Peter looked grim. 'No, I did not. I've told them all that nothing short of one hundred per cent agreement will satisfy me, as I feel they should all bear the responsibility of Tom. I am the only one to object to him being verger again. I've taught them to have compassion and now it's backfired on me.'

Caroline wagged her finger at him. 'They could have a point.'

'They have not got a case. He cannot hold a position of responsibility within the church ever again.'

'Peter!'

'He has lied, he has withheld the truth, and he has connived, whatever his reasons for doing so, to assist a drug-pusher to hide his ill-gotten gains, and I'm sorry, but it's not on. He was an excellent verger, none better, but . . . I won't have him back.'

'Here, drink this. Put like that I'm sure you're right, but it doesn't stop him living in the village, does it?'

'No, it does not. He'll have to exist on his police pension.'

Peter, sitting in the armchair opposite her, sipped his wine with approval. 'Good choice this.' He took a moment to admire Caroline's beauty. It was the clean lines of her he loved. A tad too thin since her cancer but at the same time it had brought a greater beauty to her face: heightened her cheekbones and brought her jawline into a prominence which flattered. But best of all he loved her dark eyes: her deep compassion for people, her shining honesty were still there in them despite her troubles. She caught his glance and, for a brief moment, he thought he saw her love for him shining out too, but she quickly turned her face towards the fire and the impression was lost. His blood was drumming through his veins though, and to cover his emotions he took another drink of his wine. 'This is very good.'

'Poor Tom, he wouldn't have known which way to turn.'

Peter nodded his head in agreement. 'It must put you in a terrible dilemma when you know your wife's sanity depends on your actions. You know the trashing of Kenny's house, that wasn't anything to do with Tom. It was done as a threat to Kenny and Terry, for muscling in on Turkish Delight's patch in Culworth.'

Caroline burst out laughing, a rip-roaring joyous laugh he hadn't heard from her in months. It completely took over and she abandoned herself to it. The laughter became so infectious that Peter caught it and joined in.

Caroline hugged her side. 'Oh dear! I shall have to stop, I've got a stitch! I cannot believe I have heard you say that. I thought Big Harry and Mack the Knife and names like it only belonged in nineteen fifties Ealing comedies. Oh, God! I've got such a pain!' She rubbed her side. 'Is it really true what you said? Do they call them names like that still?'

'Of course – well, that's what Tom said anyway. Turkish Delight is very big in drugs.'

'What I can't understand is, if you know this then the police must know it, so why don't they arrest him?'

'They have.'

'Oh, right! And Kenny? And Terry?'

'Tom says they'll find the pair of them eventually, but possibly under a couple of feet of concrete.'

Caroline sobered up. 'Poor Mrs Jones. She has idolised those boys all their lives, I can't begin to imagine how she feels.' She stared into the fire for a few moments and then said, 'We have so much to be thankful for. Haven't we?' She took her eyes from watching the flames and looked at

Peter. He was holding his glass close to his lips, his eyes shut, enjoying the warmth of the fire and the peace after a long day.

For such a big man he had very slender fingers, strong but slender, it would be possible to describe them as elegant. She admired his face, half in light, half in shade. She tried to decide which half she admired, no, loved the most. There again that twin impression: his features strong but at the same time so gentle and just lately so vulnerable. She watched him take another sip of his wine, his eyes still closed. Caroline wished he'd open them because she wanted him to look at her. Wanted him to see that all her love for him had mysteriously, and unbidden, come flowing back on Saturday when he'd come through the door and looked for her. Wanted him to see her gratitude for his understanding and, above all, longed for him to witness her bodily need of him.

She poured herself another glass of wine. This was her third, she'd better stop otherwise she'd never get up the stairs to bed. She looked at her watch, half past ten, looked at Peter. Swiftly she got to her feet and gently removed Peter's glass from his hand for he'd obviously fallen asleep and the remains of the wine were threatening to spill on to his cassock.

The thought crossed her mind that perhaps Peter no longer wanted her physically as he had always done. She'd kept away from him all this time because one couldn't deceive Peter: he could always pick out pretence and that was exactly what her approach to him would have been. Complete pretence. Well, she was sincere now, right from the soles of her feet to the top of her head. Totally genuine.

He'd shown no signs since he'd come back of how he felt about her, except just now when he'd come in and kissed her with rather more urgency than for a long time.

Sometimes it might be better if they didn't expect so much of each other, that they simply came together because they wanted sex with someone, or because of outright lust for each other. Right now a dose of honest-to-goodness lust would fit the bill and they could leave the high and mighty motives of adoration and worship, devotion and loving-till-death-us-do-part for another time.

Caroline looked to see how much wine was left in the bottle. She was reaching out intending to top up her glass when Peter said, 'Is there anything left for me?'

Startled, having thought him asleep, Caroline looked up at him, her passionate thoughts plainly written on her face. His strangely phrased question didn't appear to relate to the wine, but just the same he was holding out his glass to her and she filled it for him.

Almost inaudibly Peter asked, 'Am I to have it all?'

Because at that moment she didn't want soul-searching between them only plain honest need, she shied away from answering him directly and instead showed him the empty bottle and simply nodded.

The challenge in his next question was unmistakable though. 'Are you sure?' This question was not begging a reply it was demanding one. Now he was gazing steadily at her and somehow it unnerved her. There could be no pretending he was talking about the wine. Now she had to say it and say it she did, eagerly. 'Yes, I am.'

Peter didn't look at her again or speak until every drop of his wine had gone. It seemed to Caroline it took him an age to drink it. At last he put down the empty glass on the table, and very slowly took out his cross from his belt, looped the chain over his head and placed it on the table beside the glass. She watched the fingers she had so admired a few moments ago begin unfastening the buckle on his belt. Having removed it he neatly arranged it in a circle around the cross and the wine glass. His clerical collar he laid down to make a smaller circle within the belt. He undid his cassock and dropped it on the floor beside the hearth.

Peter came to kneel in front of her. Lifting her bare feet, one in each hand, he kissed them in turn, savouring the way the heat from the fire had warmed her flesh. With the same heat burning the skin of his back through his shirt, and with his eyes on her face, he slowly began to unfasten the row of buttons that ran from hem to neck of her dress.

'Caro! You're stark naked underneath!'

'I was determined there would be nothing to prevent me having my wicked way with you tonight.'

'You wanton woman, you!'

Caroline was in the kitchen making breakfast when Peter came back from his morning run. He stood in the kitchen doorway breathing heavily, rubbing the sweat from his face with the hem of his running vest. 'I'm back!'

Beth moved her mouthful of Weetabix to one side and mumbled, 'We know, Daddy, we can hear, and we can smell all that sweat.'

Alex smacked his spoon down in his empty dish and said, 'Wait till I'm old enough to go running with you, Dad! I'll get home first.'

'I've no doubt you will! I shall be past my prime by then.'

Caroline looked up at him. 'Darling!'

'Yes?'

'Nothing. Just, darling.'

'I see. Be down in ten minutes.'

'Your dutiful wife will have your boiled eggs done to a turn.'

'Think I'll have scrambled this morning.'

'Scrambled? Why break the habit of a lifetime?'

Peter shrugged his shoulders, winked at her and disappeared upstairs.

Beth, having closely observed the exchange between them, said, 'Daddy's happy this morning.'

'Isn't he always?'

'No. Not lately.'

Caroline recognised a woman's intuition in Beth's comment. 'Well, he is and let's be thankful.'

'I don't like it when Daddy isn't happy.'

Alex cleared his mouth of marmalade and toast and said, 'I don't either.'

Acutely aware that the children had sensed all too well that the atmosphere between their parents had not been of the best these last months, Caroline remained silent. When she heard Peter walk into the bedroom overhead Caroline began to cook his scrambled eggs.

He returned to the kitchen dressed and shining new. Beth lifted her face for a kiss. 'That's nice, Daddy, I don't like you when you smell.'

'Honestly! Good honest sweat never did anyone any harm. Good morning, Alex.' Peter bent to kiss the top of his head.

'Morning, Daddy.'

Caroline turned from the Aga to place Peter's breakfast on the table. 'Off you go, the two of you, and let's have those teeth cleaned really well this morning for once. Please.'

Beth protested, 'I always do.'

Alex answered, 'You don't.'

'I do.'

'You only brush at the front.'

'I brush longer than you do.'

'You don't.'

The sound of their bickering trailed away up the stairs. Caroline went to stand behind Peter's chair. She placed her arms around his neck and with her cheek resting against his head she hugged him.

Peter put down his knife and fork and bent his head to kiss her wrists. 'My darling girl.'

'You haven't said Grace.'

'So I haven't. I'm topsy-turvy this morning.'

'So am I. That's what happiness does for you.'

Peter looked at the clock. 'You're going to be late for surgery.'

'I know. Give me a kiss before Sylvia comes.'

'I'm wishing it wasn't Sylvia's day.'

'So am I.'

'I'm wishing we had the house to ourselves for the day. Hang the parish for once.' Peter glanced at the clock, contemplating the possibility of holding back the hands. 'Much as I regret it, you really must go.'

Caroline grunted her agreement and bent to kiss him once more. 'You do realise I've fallen in love with you all over again?'

'I guessed as much last night.'

The front door clicked shut and they heard Sylvia calling out, 'Only me.'

While Sylvia hung her coat in the hall cupboard and put on her apron, Caroline kissed Peter yet again, said, 'Love you,' and went into the hall. 'Hello, Sylvia, I'm running late, I'm afraid. Can I leave everything to you?'

'Of course, it's what I'm here for. Nice morning.'

'Oh, it is. Wonderful! You'd never think it was almost the end of October, would you?' Caroline raced up the stairs and Sylvia went into the kitchen.

'Good morning, Rector.'

He looked up at her lost in thought, a forkful of scrambled egg half-way to his mouth. She saw that the terrible strain, which had been evident in his face for months now and which he'd striven so hard to disguise, had utterly vanished and been replaced with profound happiness. Sylvia rejoiced.

Peter, in his endeavours to swing the tide of opinion towards preventing Tom continuing as verger, wandered into the Store later that morning.

Jimbo looked up from the till as Peter's tall shadow fell across the counter.

'Why, good morning, Peter, what can I do for you?'

'Have you a minute? To spare for a chat?'

'In five minutes Bel will be here and then I shall. Is it important?'

Peter nodded. 'I'll pour myself a coffee, may I, while I wait?'

'Of course, help yourself.'

The five minutes stretched to ten and then in bustled Bel. She was barely recognisable nowadays, having lost such a great deal of weight. Gone were the dresses constructed like tents, and the heavy flip-flops she'd always worn at work. Now she wore flip-flops which no longer needed to be built like barges to accommodate her large fat feet, and instead of the tent-like dresses a slim skirt and a sweatshirt with Turnham Malpas Stores emblazoned across the front.

'Right, Bel, on the till for a while, if you please, shelf-stacking as and when.'

'Sorry I'm late, someone was sick just as I was leaving.' She smiled that captivating smile of hers, which lit up the whole of her face and instantly Jimbo saw no need to point out how her being late angered him. He ruefully acknowledged that had it been Linda he would have been bound to say something to aggravate her.

'I see. The Rector needs a word with me. Bring your coffee through, Peter.' He poured one for himself, black no sugar, his one stringent discipline in his fight against the flab.

Jimbo took him into his office, put his straw boater on top of a filing cabinet, pulled out a chair for Peter, then settled himself on a stool. After taking a sip of his coffee Jimbo said, 'I guess I know what this is about.'

'You do?'

'It's Tom, isn't it?'

'It is.'

'You know, usually, Peter, I see eye to eye with you on everything. We've been through a lot together in one way or another, you and I, but on this I shall not be moved.'

'You won't?'

'No.' Jimbo drained his cup. 'That's not hot enough, the

damn machine must be on the blink again. What's yours like?'

'Fine, thanks. I really would like you on my side in this. We must have a verger whose word we can trust, and I can't trust Tom any more.'

'That's as may be. But I shan't change my mind. So your well-known persuasive powers will not work this time, I'm afraid.'

'But, Jimbo . . .'

'But, Peter . . . Is that all?'

'I haven't finished yet.'

'But I have.'

'Please, Jimbo, listen.'

'He won't.' This was from Harriet, who had stopped in the doorway on her way to the kitchens. 'I've tried, and what's more he's doing his best to persuade everyone else to insist on Tom being reinstated as verger.'

Peter stood up as she came in, as did Jimbo who offered her the stool. 'No, thanks, Jimbo, I'm too busy to sit down. All I can say is, Peter, I'm very disappointed in my spouse, as you must be. He's a stuffed shirt and a moral blot on the landscape.'

Peter would have laughed if the matter hadn't been so serious. 'People respect your opinions, you know, Jimbo, and it would be tremendously helpful to me if we were both on the same side. It's very important that the post of verger is filled by the right person, and Tom is not the right person as well you know. Willie admits he is beyond the job now, but even so one doesn't employ dishonest vergers just because there is no one else.'

Jimbo huffed and puffed for a moment and then said

'What about the Church and Christian forgiveness? Isn't that what it's supposed to be all about?'

Faced with that kind of challenge Peter was silent. Then he broke his silence by saying, 'To be honest I hadn't looked at it from that point of view.' He paused again. 'However, I still feel the same. I cannot trust him any more.'

Jimbo shook his head. 'Then I'm sorry, we're still on opposite sides.'

Harriet sighed. 'Well, I'm on Peter's side. I'm sorry but I am.'

Peter pressed his argument. 'The fact remains that he knew what Kenny and Terry were up to and never split. Morally he was in the wrong and he knows it. He's hiding behind Evie's skirts begging for his job back but –'

'Peter!' Jimbo turned to pick up his boater, intending to leave. He made a move towards the door then turned back to say 'OK, OK. We'll both have another think about it. Must press on.' He tossed his boater into the air, caught it on his head, adjusted the angle and left Peter and Harriet looking at each other.

'I'm so sorry, Peter. He has a lot on his mind at the moment, you know, but really that's no excuse.'

'The trouble is, on the face of it he's right. Maybe I should bend over backwards to accommodate Tom, but I do not want him back, despite Jimbo's attitude.' Peter twisted his paper cup round and round in his hands too miserable to look at Harriet.

She sighed. 'It's not only him, it's Ralph, Arthur Prior, Neville Neal, and loads of people not on the council.'

'Those not on the council don't matter. I didn't realise Ralph still didn't agree with me?'

'He doesn't want to stir up trouble, you know how protective he is about the village, so he's willing to go along with it if that will preserve the peace, but at bottom he does want him as verger and, of course, Muriel is appalled at Tom's deceit but goes along with Ralph. She does consider him so brave to have done what he has.'

'I see.'

'Must love you and leave you. I'll work on Jimbo tonight, OK?'

'Thank you.'

Peter went off to call at Orchid House. It was Evie who answered the door. A strange Evie with a nervous tic that made her whole body shudder every few seconds. Her hair, with its striking resemblance to a bird's nest, and the curious outfit she was wearing reminded Peter of a bag lady he knew in his previous parish. Evie looked at him with blank staring eyes. 'Good morning, Evie. I've called to see Tom, is he in?'

Evie nodded, opened the door wider and let him in. She left Peter standing in the hall and disappeared through the door into the garden. Tom came in without Evie.

'Tom, Evie doesn't seem well this morning.'

'No, she isn't. Have you come to say I haven't got my job back?' Peter didn't answer him straight away so Tom continued, 'Make no mistake about it, if I haven't then so be it, I shan't lay blame at anyone's door because I can understand why.'

'To be frank none of the council agree with me at the moment.'

'I see.'

'It's the deceit, Tom, that's what I don't like. A position

of trust and you didn't come clean, and you should have done. You should have confided in me at the very least.'

'I know that now, but you see the state Evie's in? I did it to avoid this very thing happening. The signs are there again, and I can't bear it. She's argued herself into thinking that if I get the job back that means we're safe here. She loves it here, you see, and now she's going to have the embroidery class, well . . .' Tom's eyes filled up with tears.

Peter nodded. 'Curiously enough, it isn't the threat of someone else getting beaten up, it's not being truthful that's my stumbling block.'

Tom nodded. 'Living two lives for so long, the odd bit of not being truthful is kind of what I'm used to, if you see what I mean.'

'Give my regards to Evie and send her round to see Caroline any time. She's excellent at talking to people, being a doctor you know.'

Tom opened the front door saying, 'Thank you for that, be seeing you.'

'Indeed. God bless you, Tom.'

'And you.'

Next he called on Ralph, whom he found sitting in the big armchair which had so impressed the missing Kenny.

'Take a seat, Peter. Coffee? Muriel's not in but I am, despite what she believes, quite capable of making coffee. Please allow me to?'

'Thank you, no.'

'In that case let's get down to business.'

'I will. I was under the impression you agreed with me that we couldn't possibly have Tom back as verger. But I understand that's not so.'

'I don't think we shall find a better man for the job. He's efficient, meticulous, punctual, hard-working. In this day and age where would we find someone as good?'

'As Muriel isn't here we can speak quite frankly just between these four walls.' Peter looked at Ralph to assess his state of mind; he appeared amenable so he plunged on. 'You weren't here when Muriel had her breakdown. It was heartbreaking to see her so defeated, so withdrawn, sitting there in the hospital, dreadfully isolated and quite literally unable to speak. If you had seen her you would have been devastated. *Anything* that you could have done to protect her or to make her better you would have done, believe me, and I mean *anything*. Well, Tom cares as much for Evie as you do for Muriel, and that's why he acted as he did, because he desperately needed to demonstrate to her that they could put down their roots. Despite *all that*, I can't stomach his return.'

Ralph sat looking at his hands. He studied the backs and then turned them over and looked at the palms.

After the silence had lasted more than a minute Peter said, 'Well?'

Ralph looked up at him. 'One needs to remember that the ordinary fellow in the street has emotions just as powerful as one's own; his reasons cannot be ignored. But I do understand what you mean. When all is said and done it goes against the grain, doesn't it? The damned fellow even lied to Muriel one day. Told her she couldn't go in the church to polish the brass because he'd been spraying for spiders so she waited outside for ten minutes or more. Of course, it was really because Kenny was in there doing whatever he was doing with my family tomb. So he was downright lying to protect Kenny, that I can't forgive. You're right, of course, as usual, I see that now.'

Peter stood up.'Thank you for that. Evie is ill again, so to salve my conscience I just hope we can find Tom a job here in the village. Thanks again, Ralph. I've still got Jimbo, Arthur and Neville to persuade, though.'

Ralph grunted, 'Leave them to me, I'll persuade 'em. They'll all agree by the time I've finished with them, believe me.' He smiled rather grimly at Peter, who smiled thankfully back.

Ralph got up to see Peter to the door. 'Thank you for making me see sense. You've a gift for it, you know, though some would call it emotional blackmail.'

Peter grinned down at him. 'Me? Emotional blackmail! Never!'

They shook hands and Peter went home still feeling very uncomfortable at what might be the outcome of his objections, but determined to stick to his guns.

Chapter 19

The rubbish outside Don and Vera's cottage was finally removed by Barry and some of the labourers from the estate. Don swept up, viewed the plant that had been flattened by it, straightened a couple of them up and heeled them back into the earth again then went inside to prepare himself.

First he stripped and used the newly installed power-shower, the pride of his life, then he shaved. He'd already had his hair cut very short so that only the tips were black and the rest was growing iron grey, like Vera preferred. At the thought of Vera his insides quivered. He'd staked his all on her having him back. What more could a chap do but make a complete fresh start? The bedroom furniture had gone to the auction rooms along with Ralph's washstand, all the old rotten stuff was up at the Big House awaiting 5 November, he'd sold his motorbike, and what greater sacrifice could a woman ask than for a fellow to sell his BSA Gold Star motorcycle, which he'd ridden with such joy for more than thirty years?

He tied his third new tie since he'd renovated himself, inspected the state of his shirt collar. Ah! He'd forgotten those new stiffeners to keep the points straight. There, that was better. Right then, he'd be off. A bit of sly questioning of Rhett had established that this was Vera's Saturday off and there was no way he, Don Wright, was going to miss her.

He roared up the driveway of the nursing home at exactly nine o'clock. He saw through one of the big windows that the old dears who were mobile were breakfasting. Don rang the bell. The door was opened by a bright young thing wearing a cheerful golden yellow tabard over her white uniform.

'Good morning!'

'Good morning to you, young lady. I'm calling to see Mrs Wright.'

'Oh, Vera! Come right in. Do you know the way?'

'Yes, thank you, right to the top and turn left.'

She nodded.

Rhett answered his knock, gave his grandad a huge wink, admired the chocolates he was carrying and shouted over his shoulder, 'Gran! You've a gentleman caller.'

Don heard Vera calling out, 'Don't be daft! Is it yer grandad?'

'Come in, Grandad. We're just going to have some breakfast, want some?'

'Won't say no.'

Vera appeared. Don searched for a word to describe how Vera looked this morning but he didn't know the one he needed. If he had known it he'd have described Vera as vibrant. From the top of her well-groomed hair down to the naughty-looking gold slippers she was wearing she looked, well, great.

'Rhett's invited me to breakfast. Here, these are for you.' He held out the box and she took them from him.

'Thanks! My favourites. Rhett, set another place.'

They exchanged small-talk while they ate, a meal Don enjoyed for the kitchen was welcoming and the gay little posy of flowers Vera had placed on the breakfast table suited his mood.

Rhett pushed his chair away and stood up. 'I've a day's work to do. Will you be all right without me?'

Vera said, 'I didn't know you were working today.'

'Well, I am. They asked me yesterday.'

'Who?'

'The Bissetts. Neither of them are well enough to garden yet and they're worried about winter coming on and the garden needing tidying so I said I would. Then, on the proceeds, I'm going into Culworth with Michelle to the cinema and a meal.'

'Oh, all right, then. Take care of that girl, you know what I mean?'

'Gran! She's only fifteen.'

'Exactly!'

Rhett blushed bright red. Shortage of girls his age limited his choice. As for hanky-panky as his gran called it, he respected her too much for that. Besides, her step-dad Barry Jones was a man to be reckoned with and he didn't fancy getting at odds with him.

Rhett gave his grandad the thumbs up as he passed behind his grandma's chair. 'Will you be here when I get back, Grandad?'

'Don't know, do I?'

Vera didn't say whether he was welcome or not. Faced with this new Don whom she could scarcely recognise she was nonplussed. Chocolates? Flowers? Car! He must really mean business.

'Is it your day off?'

'You know it is, you old devil.'

Don laughed. 'Long time since you called me that.'

'Long time since you paid me any attention.'

Don lavishly spread butter on his last piece of toast. 'You know, Vera, I'd no idea how tired I was. All those night shifts. Tired right through to my bones I was. Dragging myself about. In winter I hardly knew what daylight was. I seemed never to see the blue sky, or hear the birds singing, it was just as if I was deaf and blind. Since I've been just doing days 'cos of them cutting back, and not working twenty-four hours I've caught up on sleep. Given me a whole new outlook. It's no excuse, I know, but for what it's worth there it is. The house, when I see it now, all shining and new, it's still the same house, you know, where I was born and where I want to die. I'd got in such a groove I thought if we changed it it wouldn't be the same, but it is and I don't mind. In fact I wish I'd done it years ago.'

Vera nudged his elbow. 'Get on with yer, yer daft thing.'

'But we couldn't have afforded to do what I've done now, then.' He winked at her, folded his last remaining slice of toast in half and pushed it into his mouth. When he'd finished munching it, and had rinsed his mouth with another drink of his tea, he patted his pocket. 'In here I've got a surprise for yer.'

Vera didn't show much delight, better not look too keen too soon. 'Oh!'

'A weekend away. Your choice.' He dragged a well-thumbed holiday brochure from his jacket pocket. 'You decide when and where and I'll fall in with it.'

'I've always fancied London.'

'London!'

'Yes, a good musical on the Saturday night and a chance to see some of the places you only read about.' Vera smothered her excitement as best she could. New horizons opened up in an instant. Strolling down Piccadilly past Fortnum and Mason's, peering through the railings at Buckingham Palace, eating in a restaurant in Leicester Square, climbing up to the Whispering Gallery at St Paul's Cathedral where the Princess had married, bless her. All the brightness, all the thrill of the place, all the lively noise of it was so vividly in her mind, she could almost be there already. Suddenly she realised Don was speaking. 'What did you say?'

Now he had to repeat those difficult words as if it hadn't been hard enough to utter them the first time round. 'I was saying, I'm more than willing to come and live here. I did all those improvements to get you to come back to the cottage, but I've realised you won't, so I'll have to come here and we'll rent out like you said. It's the most sensible thing to do.'

'I see.'

Don reached across the table and let the tips of his fingers touch her hand. 'That's if you'll have me, which is what I want, if you will, that is.'

Vera filed his request at the back of her mind and dealt with more immediate matters. 'It seems to me you must be living in an empty house.'

'I am, almost. I couldn't bear to put all that old kitchen stuff in those nice drawers and cupboards so I'm afraid I went two or three times to the tip the other day and got rid of it all. Most of it belonged to my mother, God rest her soul.' Amen to that, thought Vera. 'So apart from one chair and the telly, Rhett's bed and that built-in cupboard in his room, and a new kettle, yes, it is an empty house.'

'So what about yer meals?'

'Willie and Sylvia are very good. Jimmy asks me round and Mrs Charter-Plackett.'

'I'd heard but I didn't believe it. What's she like as a cook then?'

'Brilliant.'

Stirrings of jealousy manifested themselves in Vera's insides. 'So about this holiday, if we book it and I don't go, Grandmama Charter-Plackett could have my ticket, could she?'

Don spluttered his disgust. 'Look, she's grand and we get on very well, and it's her's inspired me to press on, and she has good ideas about colours and what's right, but I have to be on my best behaviour all the time and it gets wearing.'

'Oh, I see. I count as nothing then. You can burp or fold yer toast up in front of me and bung it in, but not in front of her, oh, no!'

'Could you enjoy eating meals with her day in day out? I've got to put a stop to it.'

'Dear, dear, you are in a fix.' She stood up and began to clear the table. 'Well, I don't know what you propose to do all day, but I'm not wasting my Saturday off.'

'Where did you intend going?'

She'd no idea and had to come up with an answer quickly. Vera plumped for the bus into Culworth.

'Don't bother. I'll drive you in and we'll go rowing on the lake and we'll have a look at the shops and have some lunch out. How about that?'

'Sounds interesting.'

'And while we're there we'll book this weekend away.' He pushed the brochure back in his pocket.

They got back about half past five having achieved the major objective of booking the weekend away. It was to be in two weeks' time, in London as Vera had requested. Don had been a courteous escort, which had gone a long way to persuading Vera that she might, just might, have him back seeing as she was getting all her own way, and above all they had enjoyed each other's company, which they hadn't done for years.

She'd forgotten that Don could row with such smoothness that the boat glided easily through the water, and the weather was so beautiful, sunny and warm with just a slight breeze. The trees had the first of their autumn colours and she lay back enjoying herself.

'I'll have a rest, we'll tie up under that willow there, while I get my breath back. I'm not the man I was.'

Vera studied him as he skilfully drew the boat under the tree and tied the painter around one of its stout trunks. He was right, he wasn't the man he was when he was seventeen but . . . 'Shall we sit in the boat or get out?'

'Sit in it. That bank looks too wet and slippery to stand on.' He lay back and spread his arms out so he was gripping the sides of the boat.

'I'd forgotten you could row.'

'Either you're a natural or you're not.'

Vera looked out over the lake and pondered again about having him back. 'I'm not having you falling into your bad ways again.'

'Bad ways? What do you mean?'

'Like being idle, and not washing enough. Sitting in front of

267

the telly for hours not speaking. Refusing to get dressed up when we go out, that is if we go out. Not being nice to me.'

'It's all self, isn't it, Vera? I've slaved to put things right these last weeks and still it isn't enough.'

'After thirty years and more of not putting yourself out you owe me something.'

'I'm only human. You're perfect, are you?'

Vera almost answered yes. She couldn't think of a single fault. 'So what are my faults, you tell me.'

Neither could Don. He caught her eye and magically they both burst out laughing. The boat rocked dangerously and Vera had to cling on. They hadn't laughed together like that in years. Somehow it cleared the air between them. Don looked at his watch.

'The time! They'll be charging us extra.'

'So?'

Don looked at her. 'So! What the hell?' They lounged there mostly in silence with Vera giving him covert looks to help her decide about him. From time to time they studied each other without speaking, finding this fresh development in their relationship both pleasing and satisfying.

'We'll have a coffee in that little coffee shop by the boathouse.' Don untied the boat and rowed them back. Now when he caught her eye she smiled, and all he'd done was row a boat that had cost him five pounds. When he thought of the money he'd spent already on the house . . .

But the coffee shop was dingy and unkempt, and whereas at one time it would have sufficed for Don, he turned his nose up at it today. 'This won't do, come on, let's go.'

They drove into the centre of Culworth and parked in the multi-storey. He took her arm and guided her through the sweet wrappers blowing about, round the cigarette butts scattered by a hundred feet, and the urine-soaked stairs, all things he would never have noticed before, out into the sun. 'The George! What about it?'

'The George? I'm not dressed well enough for there! What about the Belfry Café?'

'No, the George it is.'

They'd stayed so long drinking coffee that they had lunch there too. She was surprised by how well he conducted himself in the restaurant, there was a new finesse about him which, she decided, had come from dining with Grandmama Charter-Plackett. While Don paid the bill Vera went out to watch the swans go by, so Don begged bread from the waiter and took it out to her, and together they fed the water fowl, and laughed at the cygnets and Don took her arm and squeezed her hand. There were moments when Vera felt the old Don was back but mostly it was the new Don and she began to feel better disposed to his return. They went out to look at the shops and returned to have afternoon tea at the George too. When they got back to the nursing home Vera said, 'That's cost a packet that has.'

'As you would say. So?'

'You're right, why not?' Vera went to look out of the window, not trusting herself to look at him while she spoke. 'I've talked to Jimbo about renting out the cottage and he says no rent book. You have an agreement, a lease he called it, and you keep renewing it if they're satisfactory. That means you can get them out quick, if need be.'

'I see.' Don began to feel hopeful.

'So how about it?'

Don stood behind her, put his arms around her waist, and

locked his fingers so there was no escape. 'I'd like that very much.' He gave her a squeeze as he said it.

Vera chuckled. 'Then go get your stuff.'

'Yer mean it then? Yer serious? It's what I would like more than anything.' He looked round the room. 'I like this place, there's a feel about it, we could be happy here.'

'I mean it.'

Tentatively, not wanting to push his luck, Don asked, 'I'll go get me bits and pieces then, shall I?'

Vera squeezed around in his arms and, clutched stomach to stomach to the new slimline Don, she said, 'Fresh start. Eh?'

'Fresh start. Car. Money in our pockets, a nest-egg building up. A weekend in London. A brand new wife. What more can a man ask for?'

'Brand new wife?'

'Well, you are. You're different from the old Vera.' He whispered in her ear, 'And them gold slippers is real sexy.'

Vera pushed him away. 'Get off! I'll sort out some drawer space and that till you get back.' But she was laughing and he laughed too.

Vera, left to herself, didn't sort out anything at all. She stood quite quietly by the window looking out over the garden, wondering if she'd done the right thing. This might well be something she'd regret, but having learned out of desperation how to be strong, then maybe from now on she'd be an equal partner. Come to think about it, that was how it should be. She twiddled her engagement ring with its minuscule diamond, round and round, and thought about being sixteen and having to marry him willy-nilly. No, she'd done the right thing. Rhett would be leaving home soon and she'd be on her own and that was no joke. Now she'd have Don and she'd have to keep reminding herself how hard won her triumph had been.

Into her mind came a picture of him laughing with her in the boat when neither of them could think of a single fault of hers. Vera moved across to the mirror and winked at Don's brand new wife. 'Go for it, girl,' she said out loud. 'Go for it.'

Don drove home elated, a new man in every way. The birds sang louder, the sky was bluer, the country lanes more beautiful than he had ever seen them. He had the sun roof open and he put his clenched fist through it and punched the sky. What a day! Briefly, just for a moment, he did wonder whether he would not have had such an expensive day if he'd played his cards more circumspectly; perhaps there'd been no need for the lunch and then the tea because it seemed to him that while he was rowing her on the lake she'd had her change of heart . . . No, he was being mean and miserly again. Scrooge! He mentally cursed himself for so quickly returning to his old ways and shut the door on them with a bang.

When he went into the cottage he found a note from Mrs Charter-Plackett on the mat asking him to an evening meal. So he knocked and told her, and to his embarrassment she embraced him on the doorstep. 'I'm so pleased, Don, so very pleased. I shall miss you. We've had a good time, haven't we, doing up your cottage?'

'We have and many thanks, Missus, for helping, and the meals and that.'

'You're most welcome, it was a pleasure. Now, go on, hurry or Vera might change her mind!'

Chapter 20

'Willie Biggs, will you ever grow up? You're the same every Bonfire Night.'

Willie grinned at Sylvia and rubbed his hands together. 'Why not? It's a bit of harmless fun and a chance for once to get something for free from old Fitch.'

They were slipping through the little gate at the back of the churchyard, which had been made many years ago to accommodate the family at the Big House when they came to church. No one was supposed to use it now but Willie had never bothered about such dictums. Bother old Fitch and his rules. Why walk all that way round when . . . Behind him he heard footsteps. Someone else taking a rise out of Mr Fitch? It was Sheila and Ron.

Willie whispered, 'What you doing 'ere?'

'Same as you, taking a short-cut.' Sheila had a torch, which she shone in Willie's face. His red wool hat and matching fingerless mittens combined with the excited grin on his face gave a distinct impression of a little boy up to no good.

Sylvia said good evening and how were they both, and Ron replied they'd never been better and were looking forward to a good night.

Together they ambled across the field towards the crowds. There was no mistaking the direction they had to take for the whole area in front of Turnham House was floodlit. Smack in the middle of the field waiting to be lit was the highest, widest, biggest bonfire they'd ever seen. To one side was the refreshment marquee, close by the smaller beer tent, and on a platform made of pallets was the Scout band, playing as though their lives depended on it. Everywhere fairy-lights were strung, providing a magical touch to the whole scene.

'Well, I never! Half that stuff on the bonfire is Don and Vera's. Look at the size of the marquee, by Jove, he's really gone to town this year.' Willie rubbed his hands again in joyful expectation.

In the shadows in front of the huge kitchen-garden wall was all the paraphernalia of a massive fireworks display.

'This is his big apology to us.' said Sheila. 'That's what this is.'

Sylvia, nonplussed, enquired, 'Apology? What about?'

'Mr Fitch, feeling guilty about Jeremy Mayer. Could have killed him, you know. Very close brush with death Jeremy had, when they had that row. And guilty about the hedge. We got him there though, didn't we? Eh? Nipped his little scheme in the bud good and proper. His language! It was disgusting! Like Lady Templeton said, he'll never be a gentleman, but if this is him not being a gentleman then I'm all for it! Perhaps this time he'll have learned his lesson.'

'What lesson's that?'

'That you can't beat this village into submission, We've been here far too long for some newcomer to get the better of *us*. United we stand! Oh, yes.' She punched the air and laughed, and the others had to join in.

'They weren't the only ones to have a close brush with death, were they?' Sylvia took Sheila's arm and patted it sympathetically.

Sheila sobered and after a moment agreed with her. 'Still, we're all right now. Fit as fleas we are, Ron and me. Aren't we?'

Ron gripped her arm to lead her round a puddle and then said, 'We are indeed. I only hope Tom gets his job back, Evie's sore in need of assurance.'

Willie answered, 'Well, I think it's wonderful how you two have rallied round Tom and Evie. Real Christian forgiveness.'

Sheila was embarrassed at being awarded such lofty motives when all the time she was glad to have Evie as her friend, for truth to tell she hadn't got any real friends at all; acquaintances and associates but not real *friends*. For some reason she was the only person Evie felt free to speak to, well, not exactly free, but at least she did speak from time to time which made friendship easier.

They'd reached the edge of the crowd by now and all four of them gave themselves up to greeting everyone and waiting for Mr Fitch and Sir Ralph and Muriel and his guests to come out from the Big House to make speeches and light the bonfire.

There was always a big ceremony at this moment, Mr Fitch taking the opportunity to garner every ounce of publicity for himself and his good deeds. But the villagers

274

took care not to let him see their mirth because it wasn't courteous and, besides, they all knew which side their bread was buttered, regarding Mr Fitch. Sir Ralph's family had put the light to the bonfire for generations and now, with the sole survivor having returned to his roots, tradition had been revived, despite Mr Fitch's attempt some years ago to get a celebrity to do it. And yes! Here they came! A cheer went up as Mr Fitch mounted the platform with his specially invited guests.

Mr Fitch held up his hand for silence. 'Sir Ralph, Lady Templeton, ladies and gentlemen, children, it gives me great pleasure to be here this evening to participate in the celebrations. Before he goes up in smoke look closely at the guy on top of the bonfire. As you can see he bears a very strong resemblance to the real Guy Fawkes. In fact, he is the most splendid guy we've had in years.' A small cheer of agreement went up. 'Watch out when the flames reach his head, because it's been filled with dozens of jumping crackers! He was made by Evie Nicholls, the wife of our esteemed verger. Three cheers for Evie.'

A buzz of consternation flew round the crowd. 'Our esteemed verger'? But he wasn't, they hadn't agreed, or had they? Well, they hadn't up to yesterday.

Willie said under his breath to Sylvia, 'Not that I know of.'

'Me neither.'

They saw Ralph whisper in Mr Fitch's ear. After a moment of throat-clearing Mr Fitch said, 'Well, I thought it had all been decided but apparently it hasn't, so someone get their finger out and get it decided, for we can't do without them, can we?'

A ragged half-hearted cheer of approval went round the crowd, and then Mr Fitch continued his speech. 'All this,' he waved his arm encompassing the whole field as he did so, 'is due to the diligent application of one man, namely Jeremy Mayer. Where is he?' From the edge of the crowd a voice said, 'Here!'

'Step forward, old chap, with that dear wife of yours.' Now there really was a buzz of consternation, Dear wife? What was this? Something they'd missed and no mistake. 'Yes, I knew you'd be surprised! Jeremy and Venetia were married this morning, here in our church. One of the best-kept secrets this village has ever known. They didn't want any fuss, just a very quiet wedding. Well, then, step forward so we can congratulate you! Come on, up on to the platform!'

So Jeremy and Venetia climbed up and stood side by side waving. The cheer wasn't ragged now it was full-throated and they called for a speech. Venetia nudged Jeremy and he took a step forward. Though he couldn't yet be called slim, Jeremy had lost so much weight since his heart-attack that he was barely recognisable. While he spoke Venetia looked at him with pride and admiration, giving a very good imitation of an American political wife. More than a few sly remarks were made amongst the onlookers, on the lines of not before time, and what a change in him and in her, for she no longer advertised herself so blatantly, being dressed tastefully and with only half the makeup she normally wore, and her hair was not its usual outrageously dense black.

Jeremy got a cheer, but by now the crowd was wanting to see the bonfire lit because until then the refreshment marquee wouldn't be opened, nor the free beer tent. So Mr

Fitch, sensing the growing impatience of the crowd, signalled for silence.

'Now, ladies and gentlemen, the moment we've all been waiting for. Sir Ralph! May I ask you to do us the honour of lighting our bonfire?'

Ralph stepped forward, took the flaming torch from Barry Jones and went, as generations of his family had done, to light the Guy Fawkes bonfire. He walked round it lighting it at the various places pointed out to him by Barry and as the flames took hold a final roaring cheer went up.

Don and Vera, in the middle of the crowd, watched as their old life crackled and sparked its way to extinction. 'You know, Don, I have to admit I'm blinking glad all that old stuff has gone. Somehow it was never my home. It was always your mother's with all her old stuff in it.'

'She did give us a roof over our heads when we couldn't afford one of our own.'

'Oh! I know she did and we were grateful, but it was always her home not never ours. I once lost some money down the side of the sofa and when I dug about for it I came up with a pair of her old glasses, and that was years after she'd died. Turned my stomach it did.'

'You never said.'

'There's a lot I never said.'

'Such as?'

'Doesn't seem to matter now.' Vera tucked her hand in his and followed the flames up into the dark night sky. The floodlighting had been turned off as soon as the fire took hold, and the flames were leaping so high you had to tilt your head back to see their topmost points, and it made it seem as though the flames were lighting up the very stars. 'I wish we'd had more children.' Of a sudden the flames reached Guy Fawkes's head and, as Mr Fitch had said, it really was filled with jumping crackers. They darted and cracked all over the place and more than one landed amongst the crowd and they had to leap about to avoid them. 'I wish we'd made more of ourselves.' Slowly, very, very slowly, the fire began to collapse. Nearest to them was that old wooden chair from their bedroom, its four legs pointing uselessly now towards the sky. She'd had her alarm clock stood on it for more years than she cared to remember. 'We've lost a lot of years, you and me.' The wooden chair, its rush seat already gone, the varnish on it now severely blistered, became enveloped by the scorching flames and crumbled. 'Shan't have to lose any more. Got to make up for lost time.'

'Well, now,' said Don slyly, 'I thought that was just what we were doing.'

Next to go was that cheap wardrobe that had been their Rhett's and before that their Brenda's. What a hopeless failure she'd been. Married to a useless man, well, no more than a boy when they married, and he'd disappeared within three months, leaving her with Rhett. Where was she now? Lucky if they got a card at Christmas, and no address on it. So what did she care? Well, now it was up to Don and her to make the best of it. She turned to look at him and was surprised to see he looked almost handsome in the warm glowing light of the fire. Vera recalled his last comment, and kicked his ankle. 'You cheeky devil, you, I heard that.' But she had to laugh.

Don smirked. 'I've been thinking I might have a liking for a winter sun holiday. February, just when you're getting sick of the winter. Cheer us up. Could you get a week off?'

'I dare say.' Excitement bubbled, yes, bubbled up inside her.

'You choose the place.'

'I've a fancy for Tenerife.'

'Good idea. Tenerife it shall be. But a hotel, not self-catering, eh? It's the auction next Friday, we'll see how much we get for the bedroom suite. 'Spect it'll be only a few hundred pounds if that, but it'll go towards paying for the holiday.'

Vera turned to face him, feelings surging up inside her that she hadn't felt in years and so could scarcely recognise. 'I have to say it. Right at this moment, I love yer, Don. The feeling might not last for long so you'd do right to enjoy it while you can.'

If she didn't know better she might have thought she saw tears sparkling on the edges of Don's eyes.

Round the other side of the fire stood Evie and Tom. 'Never mind, love, never mind.' Tom pulled his old school scarf more closely round Evie's neck. 'It'll all sort itself out. I knew it couldn't be true, because no one had told me. I'm sure the Rector will sort it for us. He has a wonderful way of getting people to do as he sees fit, you wait and see. I've every confidence in him.'

Evie didn't answer. She just stood there, twitching, her eyes lit from the outside by the fire, but dead within.

Tom pointed out that the guy was finally burnt. 'You did

a good job there, Evie. Excellent. I don't know where you get all your ideas from, I really don't. Shall we go in the refreshment tent?'

She shook her head.

'Go on, love. A hot drink would fit the bill just right. How about it?'

'No, Tom. I just want to enjoy the fire. You go.'

'I tell you what, I'll go get something and bring it out to you.'

'If you want.'

'Don't move from here. Right?'

Evie nodded, watched him stride away and then turned back to watch the flames. All she had to do now was step forward, what, thirty paces? How quickly did you die in a fire? Would that be the best way? The quickest, cleanest way? Like cremation, except you were alive, like wives had to do in India years ago when their husbands died. Tom. Tom. He tried so hard to understand, but he couldn't. No one could, not this desolation so deep inside herself; this arid, shrivelled desert she carried around all the time. Perhaps that was the price she had to pay for having been given a talent. Maybe if she threw all her pictures, all her threads, all her fabrics, all her needles, on this fire, cleansed herself of all her skills, the desert within would flower instead and she'd find peace again.

She felt a touch on her arm. It was Sheila. Sheila, with her gutsy acceptance of what life threw at her. Sheila, who lacked charisma but was so warm-hearted. Sheila, who frequently made unforgivable gaffes but had an unexpected blundering insight. Sheila, who was the first friend she'd had in years and thus accepted her for what she was. Uncomplicated Sheila, who talked and filled her silences and made it so she didn't have to speak.

'Hello! There you are! I've been looking for you. I think it's been the best Bonfire Night we've had in years and you should see the refreshments! It's cost old Fitch a packet I can tell you. They're all in there stuffing their faces as if they were expecting a seven-year famine like in the Bible. I've come to get you, my Ron and your Tom are in the queue. Come on, let's join them.'

Evie half shook her head but changed it to a nod. Sheila put her hand in the crook of her arm and hustled her off before she wavered again. The marquee was packed. Long tables groaning with huge silver salvers piled high with all manner of savoury delights filled the length of the marquee. The queue wound its way around the other three sides, circling a few tables and chairs for those who couldn't stand and the drinks table serving soft drinks and tea and coffee. Jimbo had brought in serving staff from outside the village, but in charge was Barry Jones' wife Pat; they were all working with a will under her stern eye. Sheila squeezed Evie through the crowd and finally found Ron and Tom still nowhere near the head of the queue.

'Here we are! I've found her! We shall miss the fireworks at this rate. But what an evening. And we still haven't had the jacket potatoes and the children their toffee apples.'

'I love toffee apples.'

Sheila looked indulgently at Evie. 'Then you shall have one, even if I have to ask Mr Fitch himself.'

The delighted look on Evie's face was reward in itself.

Sheila couldn't cope with silence, and when she found

the four of them standing there with nothing being said she piped up with 'Isn't it wonderful how well Evie's classes are going? We've had to close the list now. Twelve's quite enough if we're going to get our share of Evie's attention. She and I have come up with the idea that when we've all got more . . . What was that word you used, Evie?'

'Proficient.'

'That's right, more proficient, we're going to start a project, all of us together. We don't know what yet, though, do we?'

Evie agreed. 'No, we don't.'

'But it'll be something inspired I've no doubt, knowing Evie. She's very talented your wife, you know, Tom, I'm just glad I discovered her. Ron and I got asked to eat with the posh people in the Big House but this is much more fun and you don't have to watch your manners quite so much, and you can be greedy without anyone noticing! Oh, look it's us next. Grab a plate, Evie, and help yourself. There's plenty to go at, so don't hold back. It's free. Go on. Go on.'

In the hall of the Big House Ralph and Muriel were talking to Arthur, Neville Neal and Jimbo. Balancing plates and drinks and making conversation always taxed Muriel, so she kept her concentration on eating rather than talk but her attention was caught by hearing Ralph say, 'So my accountancy firm has been bought out and it's now a massive concern and I'm not best pleased. One loses the personal touch, don't you know? Would you be too busy for me to come to the office to see you and we could have a discussion?'

Neville Neal's thin, almost emaciated face stayed expressionless. He swallowed the piece of quiche he had in his mouth without chewing it properly and he knew, just knew, he'd have severe indigestion before the night was out. 'Too busy? Why, of course not, Sir Ralph, not to see you. Delighted at any time. We at Neal, Parsons and Watts pride ourselves on our personal service. Any time. Any time.'

Ralph nodded. 'Good. I'll ring to make an appointment.'

'What a good idea. Look forward to seeing you. Very pleased. I'm sure we can be of service.'

Jimbo, listening to this, felt there were undertones to Ralph's proposals to which he was not privy. Then Ralph almost immediately turned to him. On the *qui vive* though he was, Ralph's comment to him caught Jimbo unawares. 'I've been elected to the committee of the county hunting, shooting and fishing lot, my title, I suppose, helps, you know, they think. They've become very dissatisfied with the caterers they've used up to now: changed hands and they're not up to par. Christmas Ball and such, you know. I expect perhaps you'd be too busy to quote.'

Jimbo almost shouted Bingo! out loud. He'd been after the contract for years. It meant, if he was successful, not just catering for the usual social functions but because people with the countryside at heart were often high-powered and they had weddings and twenty-first birthday parties and . . . 'I could quote, of course. Be delighted to. But I'm not a cheap option. If they want first-rate food and service they'll have to pay. But yes. Gladly. You can put our name forward.'

'Good. Good.'

Then Ralph offered to refill their glasses, which he did

with charm and élan and he included Muriel in their conversation for a moment then addressed Arthur Prior, his illegitimate cousin twice removed and not unlike himself in looks, and turned on the charm. 'I was having lunch at the Conservative Club in Culworth the other day, Arthur, and I overheard something which might be of interest to you.'

'Oh, what was that, Ralph?'

'You know the two fields on the east side of your farm between you and Wallop Down Wood?'

Arthur nodded. 'I do indeed.'

Ralph's face was full of innocence as he sipped his wine and paused solely for dramatic effect. 'They're for sale. Coming up for auction in Gloucester in February.'

Arthur's face lit up. 'For sale! I don't believe it. I've been after those two fields for years, but I've never found out who owned 'em. They've been neglected but with good husbandry they'd make rich pasture for my cows and no mistake.' He gave Ralph a friendly nudge with his elbow and said, 'Thanks for letting me know. Forewarned is forearmed, brilliant. That's made my day.'

'Not at all, Arthur, pleased to be of service.'

Arthur, positively hopping with delight, turned to Muriel and gave her a kiss. 'This husband of yours is worth his weight in gold.'

Muriel smiled and said, 'I know.'

Jimbo said he'd better wander off to find Harriet as he was neglecting her but Ralph called him back: 'This business of Tom . . .

All three of them said, 'Ahhhhh . . .'

'Excellent chap, but to be quite honest I've had a change of heart. I've decided that Peter is right. We can't condone deceit, nor dishonesty, nor the fact that he permitted polluted money to be kept on church premises. In this day and age we have to take a stand against the slackening of moral standards, and whilst it would be courageous and right to allow him to be verger after all that has happened, ultimately it quite simply cannot be.'

His statement was greeted with complete silence by the three of them.

'I mean it. We've got to reconsider our position. Seriously reconsider.'

They were in a cleft stick and they knew it. Not so much Arthur, who could buy the fields without reliance on Ralph – all he felt was gratitude for being told something he could well have missed – but both Jimbo and Neville sensed that their agreement to Tom not being reinstated was a necessary requirement for Neville to become his accountant and for Jimbo to get Ralph's support for the contract for the country-pursuits lot. If they refused they stood to lose and they knew it.

Ralph could almost measure the tension between the four of them: it quivered and quavered in the air as they pondered his request. Would they or wouldn't they? He wanted them to agree with him and hoped none of them would mention Evie, which would put his own determination not to reinstate Tom in jeopardy. He knew Jimbo would be the last to agree, if indeed he ever did, but Ralph guessed it would be Neville who would capitulate first and it was.

'I have great respect for your judgement, Sir Ralph, and if that's how you think it should be, then I for one won't stand in your way. I'll fall in with Peter's decision.' He flashed his self-satisfied smile at Ralph and then at Muriel, who almost felt he was inviting her to pat him on the head for being such a good boy.

Arthur, with nothing to lose, agreed. 'Why not? I'm sure Peter knows better than me how these things should go. I agree.'

Jimbo, angry at being outmanoeuvred and quite deliberately so, didn't answer for a moment. Ralph offered him more wine but Jimbo put his hand over his glass. 'No, thanks.' He glanced across the hall and saw Harriet, head back, laughing at some remark of Peter's and guessed what she would have to say if he told her he'd refused yet again to change his mind about Tom. 'Very well. Peter's got my vote. You can tell him straight away, if you like.'

'Good! Good! Now somehow between us we must find a job worthy of Tom which will keep him in Turnham Malpas. So please apply your not inconsiderable intelligence to solving the problem for him, and most especially for Evie. We must be seen to be compassionate which at bottom, of course, we really are.'

Ralph made a point of smiling at Jimbo, but Jimbo turned away, unhappy to realise that his relationship with Ralph would never be quite the same again, and angry with him for having taken advantage of his Achilles' heel so mercilessly. But Jimbo cheered up when he reached the conclusion that maybe Ralph might turn out to be proved right. How could anyone really know? As he reached Harriet's side she beamed at him and he winked at her and felt his good humour restored.

Muriel wasn't entirely sure she agreed with Peter about Tom but she had bowed to his superior understanding of the moral dilemma with which they were faced. Feeling forlorn she left the men to their conversation and wandered off outside. A jacket potato eaten by the bonfire suddenly had more appeal for her than socialising.

The potatoes were being distributed by the Scouts and it was Fergus Charter-Plackett who jokingly offered her one. 'There's a napkin too. Look, here.'

'Oh! yes, please. It's no fun eating one indoors. Thank you, Fergus, very much. I'm looking forward to the fireworks. Are you?'

Fergus was puzzled by her almost childlike appreciation of the fun of Bonfire Night. 'I am, Lady Templeton. Yes.'

Muriel wandered away tossing the scorching hot potato from hand to hand, grateful she had her gloves on. The crisp night air brightened her spirits and she decided to eat her potato away from the crowd, because one couldn't be discreet when eating them and she wanted to enjoy hers without regard to good manners.

She went to stand in the shadow of the refreshment marquee, from where she could observe the fire but not be seen. When she'd finished, she wiped her mouth with the napkin and was debating what to do with the potato skin, because she'd never liked them and had never eaten one in her life and wasn't going to start now, when she heard a rustling behind her. I'll ignore it, it'll be someone having a kiss and I don't want to know. But the rustling turned into a voice saying, 'Lady Templeton! Lady Templeton!' A man's voice which she thought she recognised but couldn't quite place.

Startled Muriel said, 'Yes? Who is it? Who's there? Well, make yourself known.' A close footfall and there he stood behind her. Muriel fumbled in her pocket for her torch and shone it straight in the face of the intruder.

She gasped out loud. 'Ohhhh! I don't believe it! Kenny Jones! I thought . . . we all thought you were . . . dead! You did give me a fright!' Her hand on her heart to stay its thudding she said, 'What are you doing creeping about like this?'

In a hoarse whisper Kenny said, 'I'm sorry to frighten you, Lady Templeton, but you being sympathetic like I thought you'd be the best to ask. I need a word with my mum.'

'Well, she's here. Go find her. She was heading for the . . . powder room the last time I saw her. Kenny, she'll be delighted to see you, she's been so worried.'

'Trouble is, I don't want no one else to see me, it's a bit difficult as you might say. But it is very urgent.' An anxious hand on her arm, he begged, 'Can you get her for me? But not a word to a living soul, mind. It's very important that, for no one to know I'm here. Promise?'

'I promise. Kenny! What have you been up to?' While Kenny framed a reply Muriel made up her mind to do as he asked. 'No, don't answer that. You wait there. I could be a while but I will get back to you. Take care, Kenny, the two of you have broken your mother's heart. Try not to hurt her any more. Good luck with whatever you do. I won't tell.' She patted his arm, twinkled her fingers at him and strolled away.

Muriel went round the front of the refreshment marquee and ventured in, thinking this would be the best place to try first, and there Mrs Jones was, in the midst of a laughing crowd from down Shepherds Hill, a plateful of food in her

288

hand, enjoying herself. How to get her out without too much fuss, that was the question. Well, she'd better be truthful and come right out with it, it was the only way. Some silly trumped-up excuse would sound ridiculous.

'Mrs Jones! I'm sorry to interrupt you but there's someone outside asking for you.'

'Asking for me? Who?'

'I don't know them at all,' she hoped she'd be forgiven for that white lie, 'but it's you they want.'

'Well, whoever it is, Lady Templeton, they'll have to wait till I've finished eating.'

'They can't. They're in a hurry.' Muriel became agitated, she really was no good at this cloak-and-dagger stuff. 'Really in a hurry.' Muriel tried winking at Mrs Jones but only managed to distort her face and look foolish.

Finally Muriel saw from her face that Mrs Jones had got the message.

'I see. Well, then. I'll come.' Her face a picture of studied nonchalance, Mrs Jones told her friends to keep an eye on her food, and she'd be back.

Outside the marquee Muriel whispered, 'It's your Kenny come to see you. Come with me.'

'Our Kenny? Oh, thank God! Where is he?'

'He's just round the back here. Call his name, he'll come.'

Muriel walked away with tears in her eyes.

Mrs Jones called out quietly, 'Kenny! It's Mum.'

When Kenny emerged from the shadows Mrs Jones wrapped her arms around him and hugged him close. 'Oh, love! Where have yer been? All these weeks, wondering. Our Terry, is he here?'

'No, he wouldn't come.'

'Why ever not?'

'Too scared.' He released himself from her grasp. He stood listening for a moment: the sound of laughter and happy voices could just be heard and then as he listened the band struck up again, and briefly he felt a deep sadness that he would no longer be part of this kind of life. 'They're having a good time, bully for them. Now, listen to me. In the morning Terry and me, we're going to Canada.'

'Canada!'

Kenny put his hand over her mouth. 'Shush! Out of the way. As soon as we get settled I'll let you know. Then in a while you and Dad can pretend to discover a long-lost cousin out there and you can come out to us.'

'To escape the police really, isn't it?'

'Well, them and other things. But we'll be safe there.'

'How will you find the money?'

'Money's no problem, believe me.'

'Oh, Kenny, what have you been up to?'

Kenny tapped the side of his nose. 'Don't ask. Give our love to Dad, and tell him not to worry.'

Clutching at straws she exclaimed, 'But you haven't got passports.'

'We have now.'

Her heart was fit to burst with joy that her Kenny had come specially to see her before he left. In the dark she wasn't able to see the expression on his face but she sensed he was different, and that he'd done something terrible and she wished she hadn't realised it.

Out of his pocket he took a wad of notes. 'I've counted it, it's to pay Sir Ralph the rent for the rest of the six months, and there's some extra for you and Dad. Sir Ralph had faith in me and I can't let him down. All the furniture is yours so take it, Dad'ull like that leather chair. But most important of all don't tell anyone where we are. You don't know a thing. Right?'

'Right. Take care, Kenny. Look after our Terry, he's not so sharp as you.'

'I will. I had to come, couldn't go without seeing yer. Got to go now.' They hugged and Mrs Jones so far forgot herself as to give him a big kiss. Kenny gruffly remarked as she was leaving him, 'Take care of yerself.' That was the nearest he got to endearments: and the nearest he got to Canada was New Zealand. After all, he knew his mother well and was absolutely certain he mustn't tell her the whole truth. Specially about ... He turned to walk away down through the trees towards his car, his heart more desolate than he had ever known. He'd made some bloody big mistakes in his life and recently done some dreadful things to save his skin, but somehow leaving Turnham Malpas for ever was the most painful of all.

Sylvia had been looking for Willie and in desperation had called in at the beer tent to see if he was still in there, though what state he'd be in, after all this time, she really didn't know. She couldn't go inside because she had the twins with her, having volunteered to look after them while the Rector and Dr Harris were in the hall having their refreshments with Mr Fitch.

They turned back towards the dying bonfire to continue their search. Hand in hand with the two of them Sylvia marched purposefully across the field. Alex and Beth were now getting very tired and if it hadn't been for the fireworks they would have gladly gone home.

Beth tugged at Sylvia's hand. 'I want my mummy.'

'So do I.'

The Scouts, having been resuscitated in the refreshment marquee, had reassembled and were playing an overture before the commencement of the display.

'Can we go find them?' Alex began to whine, and Sylvia decided she'd find Willie much quicker without two tired children in need of their mother.

'We'll go find them and I'll look for Willie by myself. He can't be far.'

Somewhat tentatively Sylvia stood in the doorway of the Big House hoping to catch Caroline's eye but the twins rushed in to look for her themselves. 'Mummy! We've lost Mr Biggs. Is he here?'

She took their hands and led them back towards Sylvia, standing in the doorway. 'No, darlings, he isn't. Thanks for looking after them, I do appreciate it. Can you really not find Willie?'

'Well, obviously it's not serious, he must be somewhere about, it's just that I haven't seen him for a while. They're both very tired, Dr Harris, they need to be in bed.'

Alex and Beth both protested loudly, stamping their feet and showing all the signs of going into serious tantrums. 'We're not going to bed! Not now. We want to see the fireworks.'

'Of course you shall. I'll get Daddy and we'll find a good place to stand. Hush now! Hush! That's enough.' Caroline put an arm round each of them and hugged them tightly to her.

Peter came across and together they all went out into the dark. The only light was provided by the vast pile of glowing embers, for the floodlights had been switched off again in preparation for the display.

Peter lifted the pair of them on to the stone wall surrounding the terrace and he and Caroline stood on the grass between them. Peter was wearing his heavy winter jacket and Caroline slipped a hand inside one of its deep pockets. In the hushed silence before the first rocket went up Peter took hold of her hand in his pocket and squeezed her fingers. Caroline looked up at him and smiled, 'Love you.' Peter looked down at her, his face radiant with the deep love he had for her, and then he kissed her smiling lips. They lingered over the kiss until Beth called out, 'Daddy! Stop kissing Mummy! I don't know what the parish will say and what's more she's going to miss the fireworks!'

Jimbo's firework displays had been considered truly wonderful but this . . . One moment the whole sky was heaving and tumbling with red light then turquoise, then yellow, then green, then a mass of multi-coloured swirling, then a sky-sized fountain of blues. They were all gasping with amazement. What a show! What a spectacle! Three cheers for Mr Fitch! Would this extravaganza never end? The finale was huge rocket after huge rocket firing off in all directions, higher and higher, filling the whole panoply of the heavens with myriad man-made stars. They cheered Mr Fitch at the end of the display spontaneously and gladly. What a night!

Reluctantly they made their way home; the entire village sated with good food, good companionship and Mr Fitch's brilliant final tribute. Tired children, weary parents wandered off, some to their cars, others on foot to find home and bed and sleep.

Ralph took a tray of tea with him when he went upstairs to bed. Muriel, having enjoyed every single moment of her evening to the full, was already sitting up in bed waiting for him.

'I don't think I have had a lovelier Bonfire Night in all my life. Wasn't it spectacular, Ralph?'

'It most certainly was. Don't pour yet, it's not ready. I'll do it when I've finished in the bathroom. You still haven't told me what you were doing when you disappeared.'

Cautiously Muriel replied, 'I've told you the truth. I got bored with the social chit-chat and went outside for a jacket potato and then I wandered about a bit.'

Ralph looked sceptically at her. 'My dear, you would never have done for the diplomatic service, you can't tell fibs to save your life.'

Muriel blushed. 'I know I can't, but I promised. I truly did promise not to say a word and I have a dreadful feeling that I did something quite wicked this evening because I should have told the police, which would have been very easy for they were about . . . but I didn't.'

'The police!'

'Yes.'

'My dear!'

'So it's best if I don't tell you, then you can't be blamed if it all comes out. But I helped a mother . . . and a son. Other than that my lips are sealed. Another bonfire been and gone. The years slip by so quickly, don't they?'

'I won't ask you again. I'm quite sure that whatever it was

294

you did, it was with the best of intentions. Yes, they do slip by when you're very happy.'

'And I am very happy. It's been such a year. Who would have thought that I, Muriel Templeton, would lie down to stop a digger tearing up my village's heart all because I met a wren? I was so terrified.'

'A wren! I do love your mind, Muriel. I'm glad I'm privy to your thoughts, it is such a delight.'

He was still standing by the bed and she looked up at him and smiled. 'I did, and we looked each other in the eye and I *knew* I had to save his homeland, for he was relying on me to do it on his behalf. Wasn't it exciting about Jeremy and Venetia getting married this morning? Such a surprise. I'm so glad. Peter never said a word, the naughty boy, I would have loved to have gone to it.'

'It's a pity Tom didn't realise that Peter knows how to keep a confidence. I felt acutely embarrassed when old Fitch made that blunder about him being verger, I doubted all over again about not supporting Tom.'

'Peter would have won the day anyway, dear, now, wouldn't he? He is so upright in his moral judgements, and I've become sure he's right. The only black spot for me is worrying about Evie. I do wish we could find him a job round here. It wouldn't even have to be in the village, just so long as he could travel to it from here. Then perhaps Evie might have a chance.'

'I have had a word with old Fitch and so has Peter. We think he may have found something suitable for him.'

'Oh, I'm so glad! Have you noticed Peter and Caroline are all right again?'

Ralph raised an eyebrow. 'No, I hadn't. How do you know?'

'Well, I just do. They are, you can feel it. I think that one of the big highlights this year was your birthday party. It went so well. We'll have another party next year to celebrate our tenth wedding anniversary.'

'Ten years! It seems an age.' Ralph groaned.

'Ralph!' Then Muriel looked at his face and saw he was teasing. 'As for this year we've still got Christmas to look forward to, and I do love Christmas.'